Charles E. Pascoe

A London Directory for American travellers

For 1874 - Containing the fullest information, in the best form for reference,

respecting all that is valuable in connection with a visit to London. With an

appendix

Charles E. Pascoe

A London Directory for American travellers
For 1874 - Containing the fullest information, in the best form for reference, respecting all
that is valuable in connection with a visit to London. With an appendix

ISBN/EAN: 9783337292614

Printed in Europe, USA, Canada, Australia, Japan

Cover: Foto ©Andreas Hilbeck / pixelio.de

More available books at **www.hansebooks.com**

A

LONDON DIRECTORY

FOR

AMERICAN TRAVELLERS

FOR 1874.

CONTAINING

THE FULLEST INFORMATION, IN THE BEST FORM FOR REFER-
ENCE, RESPECTING ALL THAT IS VALUABLE IN CON-
NECTION WITH A VISIT TO LONDON.

With an Appendix.

BY

CHARLES E. PASCOE.

BOSTON:
LEE AND SHEPARD, PUBLISHERS.

NEW YORK:
LEE, SHEPARD, AND DILLINGHAM.

1874.

CONTENTS.

———◆———

4 *CONTENTS.*

PREFACE.

It has often been matter of surprise to the Editor, in common, doubtless, with numbers of other persons, that the ordinary, every-day Guide-Book to London furnishes so little information on points really the first essentials to the enjoyment of any foreign trip, — the Where, How, and the When to do this or that thing in the proper way, and a thorough knowledge of which adds so materially to the personal comfort of every traveller. The purpose of this "London Directory for American Travellers" is to furnish a concise, reliable, handy, and cheap "Directory," rather than "Guide,", which will give the prominent place not to the ordinary Guide-Book information, but to such matters as these, — Fares, Arrivals and Departures of Trains, Hotels and their Expenses, Private Lodgings and their Cost; Diary of Forthcoming Events, Races, Fêtes, &c., during the summer months around London; the whereabouts of Operas, Theatres, Places of Amusement, their Specialties, and Prices of Admission; Couriers for the European Continent, Where and How to be obtained; Cab-fares, &c.; and last, not least, AN HONORABLE AND CAREFULLY-CONSIDERED GUIDE TO THE BEST AND MOST RELIABLE LONDON TRADESMEN, compiled by the Editor himself, without sacrifice of truthfulness or self-respect.

A residence of twelve years in London, and an intimate business-acquaintance with that city, a travelling experience of some years both in the United States and in Europe, and a recognized connection with the Boston Press and chief Periodicals of the United States for the last four years, will, the undersigned hopes, be evidence of his fitness for the task he has undertaken.

The Editor has compiled such a Directory for visitors to London; because, in his experience, it is the city of all others suggesting the most difficulties to Americans arriving in it for the first time; first, from its enormous size, and the multitude of its streets; and, next, from the density of its population. If a compass were pricked into the map of London at Charing Cross, and swept at a radius of twelve miles, so as to take in the rural suburbs, which are really, and to all intents and purposes, London, a population of more than four million souls would be lying within that radius. Add to this the fact, that, during the past ten years, 149,905 houses were built within the metropolis itself, and 635 miles additional length of streets placed in charge of its police, and what wonder if London does present to the stranger a "vast territory of brick and mortar," which to find one's way about in requires a more than ordinary degree of care, and foreknowledge of localities and points of interest.

It is intended to publish this Directory annually, carefully revised and corrected to the 1st of April of each year; and it is the Editor's hope and intention to make it as thorough in every respect as possible. Much of the information it contains will be obtained from official sources; and arrangements have been entered into for making the "Hotels," "Lodgings," "Diary of Forthcoming Events," and "Trade Directory" departments, prominent features of the book.

Owing to the limited time the Editor has had at his disposal, the correspondence with England that the publication of the book necessarily entailed, and the unfortunate delay that has sometimes arisen in obtaining the necessary information from London, it is feared that "The Directory" may be found lacking in much that would otherwise have appeared in its pages. For this the Editor has only to offer his present apology, and promise, that, in the future, every thing shall be done to make the "London Directory for American Travellers" as perfect and complete as possible.

BOSTON, Feb. 11, 1874.

All communications in reference to this Directory to be addressed, in the United States, to Charles E. Pascoe, care of the Publishers; and, in London, to the same, Grosvenor Hotel, Pimlico, S.W.

INTRODUCTION.

THERE are two questions, which, of course, enter very largely into the calculations of most persons contemplating a trip to London, — the question of expense, and that of the ocean passage, how best to get over it with the least possible amount of personal discomfort; and it would seem obviously improper to begin this little book without some sort of allusion to both. Now, there are degrees of expense. What to one man seems extravagance, to another means but a mere matter of every-day expenditure. A visitor to London will find that he can live there cheaper than in almost any other city, offering the like attractions, in the world. It only requires some knowledge of how to set about doing things, and to keep one's self as near as possible within the limits of paying out money only for necessaries, and not for luxuries. The tourist, in nine cases out of ten, will find that it is not the expense of lodging and eating, drinking and sight-seeing, that reduces the credit at the bank, but the constant laying-out of money for every little article of dress or fancy which he or she considers it would be advantageous to carry back to America. Of course, there are people with whom expense is a matter of no consideration whatever. They have an unlimited credit at their bankers', and can do just as they please, buy what they please, and go wherever they please, no matter what the cost; but this book is not written wholly for such persons. It is to be hoped that it may somewhere in its pages suggest to some of limited means a way by which they can effect an annual change in their summer trips, by taking passage across the water to new scenes, and to mix with old-country people; getting the full benefit of the great luxury of a sea-voyage to and fro, and seeing a great deal of all that is to be seen in one of the most marvellous cities of the Old World, and at a cost which can scarcely exceed the hotel-bill for a couple of

months at fashionable Saratoga. Now, let us see how this
may be done; and we will take for our purpose the case of
some hard-working man of small means, who wants to spend
a couple of months in visiting London. There is his pas-
sage-money to begin with : —

	GOLD.
First class, from Boston or New York	$80 00
Expenses on the passage (say)	10 00
Hotel and cab fares in Liverpool	5 00
Railroad-fare from Liverpool to London	10 00
Total	105 00

For $105 in gold, then, the tourist finds himself in London.
It will be convenient, perhaps, now, that we should consider,
for a moment, the question of hotel-expenses, still keeping
in view that we are dealing with a person who wants to see
as much as he conveniently can see at as little expense as
possible. There is a hotel in the Strand, for instance, frequented by Americans. and kept by one of the most popular
and attentive of London landlords, Mr. Haxell, at which a
man may board, and fare well in the English style, for about
$2.50 (gold) per day. The Royal Exeter Hotel, next door
to Exeter Hall, offers the following inducements to the traveller of moderate means : —

SUITES OF ROOMS.				
	S. D.	S. D.		GOLD.
Drawing-room with bed-room en suite .	8 0	10 6	say $2 to $2 50	
SERVICE.				
Each person, for the first day . . .		1 6	"	35
Afterwards		1 0	"	25
Breakfasts	1 6	2 6	"	.35 to 0 50
Dinners, from		2 0	"	from 50
BED-ROOMS.				
Bed-rooms for one person		2 6	"	50
" for two persons		4 0	"	1 00

These charges, of course, are to be considered irrespective
of board; but, as intimated above, arrangements can be
made by which persons may live in the hotel with use of
coffee-rooms, smoking-room, &c., and most liberal board
(exclusive of wines), for the sum of ten shillings ($2.50),
gold, each person, per day.

As it takes, upon an average, eleven days, we will say, to
cross from New York or Boston to Liverpool, and another
eleven days are spent on the return-passage, we have re-

maming, out of our two months for vacation, a little over five weeks to spend in London.

	GOLD.
To travelling-expenses to London	$105 00
Add board for five weeks at $2.50 per day	87 50
	$192 50
Return-expenses to Boston or New York, subject to fifteen per cent discount if ticket taken at Boston or New York before starting	105 00
Total	$297 50

Or, in round numbers, say $300 in gold. But even this sum may be very considerably reduced, if the tourist contents himself with "lodgings," and dining from home every day, —a manner of living much affected by the very best class of Englishmen. Rooms may be hired in some of the nicest parts of London for five dollars per week; which charge includes attendance, &c. Arrangements can also be made for taking meals at your lodgings; and if a little attention be paid to the "outlook," *i.e.*, the surroundings of the place, at the time of hiring, there is no more comfortable and inexpensive manner of living in the world than in cleanly, well-furnished London lodgings, with some eminently respectable, retired gentleman's butler to look after your personal comfort, your breakfasts, and your dinners. Then, again, a reduction may be made even upon this system of inexpensive living. In many of the streets leading off the Strand to the Thames Embankment, such as Norfolk, Salisbury, Northumberland, are houses in which London barristers and other gentlemen reside, hiring a bed-room at about ten shillings a week, and living at their clubs. This is by no means uncomfortable, even if you substitute Mr. Haxell's Coffee-Room for the more ostentatious but certainly less cosey and cheerful club parlor. All this time we have been considering chiefly the man of small means, who desires to start off with this proposition: "There are my five hundred dollars; and I don't intend to spend one cent more in getting to London and back again, seeing every thing worth seeing whilst I am there, and living like a gentleman, comfortably and respectably, the while." In England it is considered by men who do a great deal of travelling, that £1 per day should be made to include all expenses, railroad-fares, hotel-bills, and so on. The American tourist would do well to bear this in mind. And here is another hint. The second-class carriages, on some lines of railroads, are exceedingly neat, comfortable, and cool for summer travelling; and, by using them on a journey, a very respectable sum may be saved in the long-run.

As to dinners, breakfasts, and so forth, there are so many excellent restaurants in London where a man may eat a well-served meal at a moderate cost, that it would seem almost invidious to select any one particular restaurant for special notice. Blanchard's in Beak Street, off Regent Street, Simpson's in the Strand, the Rainbow in Fleet Street, Spiers and Pond's at Ludgate Hill and the Victoria Railroad Stations, the Criterion in the Haymarket, the Solferino in Rupert Street, in the Haymarket, and the Scotch Stores in Oxford Street, are each and all of them excellent places for dining in; and it will be found that a dinner may be had at any one of these places, well cooked, served hot and without stint, for half a crown, or three shillings at the outside, which sums should be made to include ale, if it is desired. The average cost of plain living in London may, we think, be safely set down as follows: —

	s.	D.
First-class hotels, such as the Grosvenor Hotel, Pimlico, the Buckingham-Palace Hotel, the Westminster, the Charing Cross, and the Langham, &c., per day	10	6
Good second-class hotels, of which there are many, and most respectable houses in London, per day	8	0
Lodgings	6	0

Thus much on the preliminary question of expense. A more detailed account of "Hotels" and "Lodgings" will be given presently, together with other matters largely entering into the question of credit at your banker's. It might be as well to state here, perhaps, that, subject to variations in the rate of exchange, —

		GOLD.
The English Sovereign equals about		$4 83
Half-Sovereign " "		2 42
Crown " "		1 20
Half-Crown " "		60
Florin " "		46
Shilling " "		23
Sixpence " "		12

and that persons intending to travel on the European continent, after remaining in London for a few days, will find it convenient to carry with them a passport, which, in Boston, may be procured of Mr. James G. Freeman (firm of W. C. Codman & Freeman), 40 Kilby Street; and, in New York, of A. C. Willmarth, 41 Chambers Street.

The best way of getting over the ocean passage with the

least possible amount of personal discomfort is to have implicit faith in the steamship company of whom you purchase your ticket. This is the first and foremost essential to the enjoyment of your trip across the Atlantic. Every thing else, — meat, drink, clothing, outside cabin, inside cabins, upper berths, lower berths, rolling propensities, pitching propensities, speed, and social excellences of commanders, — all these things are, and every thing else is, subordinate to the one thing, — faith in the steamship company.

Keeping this well in mind, and that travelling by water is not one whit more dangerous — if any thing, less so — than travelling by land, you may then safely engage a state-room or berth from any one of the well-known companies whose steamships cross the Atlantic; and may feel pretty confident also, "wind and weather permitting," that your ten days at sea will be passed, as things go at sea, tolerably comfortably.

The Cunard, Inman, White Star, Guion line, and National line of steamers sail to Liverpool, calling at Queenstown.

The Anchor line and State line of steamers sail to Glasgow, calling at Londonderry.

The North German Lloyd steamers sail to Bremen, calling at Southampton.

The Hamburg American steamers sail to Hamburg, calling at Plymouth.

————

During the time this book was going through the press, some of the steamship companies were altering their rates of fare to Liverpool; and it was found quite impossible, under the circumstances, to get at all the information necessary to complete accuracy in the table of fares. It seems that it has been found desirable to effect a reduction in the rates by some of the ocean steamships sailing on a particular day. The fares by the steamers of the Cunard line remain as heretofore.

On the following page we give a table of the fares of the ocean steamships, as far as it was possible to procure them at the time of going to press.

LIST OF THE OCEAN STEAMSHIP COMPANIES, AND THEIR FARES.

FROM NEW YORK OR BOSTON TO LONDON OR LIVERPOOL.	Single Tickets.				Return Tickets.				Steerage.
	To London.		To Liverpool.		To London.		To Liverpool.		Cur-rn'y.
	$	$	$	$	$	$	$	$	$
(a) The Cunard Line (gold)	....	....	}130 }100	80	10°.	Red	uctı	on.	30
(b) " Inman " "	95	85	90	80	170	150	160	140	30
(c) " Anchor " "	90	80	75	65	160	140	130	....	30
(d) " White Star Line "	120	80	100	80	10°.	Red	uctı	on.	30
(e) " Williams & Guion Line "	90	80	75	65	160	140	130	....	30
(f) " National " "	....	....	80	70	"At	fav'	e rat	es."	30
(g) " Transatlantic " "	125	75	To	Bre	stor	Ha	vrc.		
(i) " Hamburg " "	120	72	—	—	Not	quo	ted.		36
(k) " North German Lloyds Line (gold)	120	72	—	—	Not	quo	ted.		36
The Philadelphia and Liverpool Line "	....	....	....	....	....	....	....	....	....
" State Line of Steamers New York and Glasgow "	85	65	80	60	150	110	140	100	30

(a) Passengers booked direct to Paris.

(b) " " " Paris, Hamburg, Rotterdam, Antwerp, Sweden, Norway, Denmark, &c.

(c) " " " Havre, Hamburg, Antwerp, Gothenburg, Christiania, and Paris.

(d) " " " Paris and all parts of Europe.

(e) " " " " " "

(f) " " " " " "

(g) " " Paris direct *viâ* Havre.

(i) " " " Paris *viâ* Cherbourg.

(k) " " " Paris *viâ* Havre.

THE OCEAN STEAMSHIP SAILINGS FROM ENGLAND.

CUNARD LINE.

Tuesday and Saturday for New York, *viâ* Queenstown. Wednesday and Thursday for Boston, also *viâ* Queenstown. 15, 17, and 21 guineas.
In steamers carrying no emigrants, £26 1st Cabin, £18 2d Cabin.

INMAN LINE.

Tuesday and Thursday, Liverpool *viâ* Queenstown. Fares, 15, 18, and 20 guineas.

WHITE STAR LINE.

Thursday, Liverpool *viâ* Queenstown. Fares, £21 and £25.

NATIONAL LINE.

Wednesday, Liverpool *viâ* Queenstown. Fares, 12, 15, and 17 guineas.

GUION LINE.

Wednesday, Liverpool *viâ* Queenstown. Fares, 15, 17, and 20 guineas.

ANCHOR LINE.

Tuesday, Thursday, and Saturday, Glasgow *viâ* Moville. Fares, Wednesday steamer, 12 and 14 guineas ; Saturday steamer, 13 and 15 guineas.

ALLAN LINE.

Tuesday, *viâ* Queenstown and Quebec. Thursday, *viâ* Londonderry and Quebec. Fares, to Boston or New York, 16 and 19 guineas.

The London offices of these companies are as follows:—

Cunard.....................Henry Boggs, 6 St. Helen's Place,
                            London, E. C.
Inman.....................Eives and Allen, 61 King William
                            Street.
White Star Line...........Smalpage, 41 Maddox St., London,
                            and 7 East India Avenue, City.
National..................Smith, Sundius, & Co., 17 Grace-
                            church Street.
Guion.....................A. S. Petrie & Co., 11 Old Broad St.
Anchor....................Henderson Bros., 5 East India Ave.
Allan.....................Montgomerie and Greenhorne, 17
                            Gracechurch Street.
Philadelphia Steamship Co...G. A. Smith & Co., 23 Change
                            Alley, Lombard Street.

We would strongly recommend, where a person intends re-crossing from England within six months, and by the same line of steamers, that a *return-ticket* be taken before starting, for the simple reason that it is more economical, and certainly saves unnecessary trouble in securing the return-passage; and, in the case of a passenger going direct to London, take the ticket to London, and not to Liverpool only.

Ladies will find that wraps, and plenty of them, are indispensable necessaries for the passage, and that deck-chairs are good things to have, and will add very materially to their own comfort, and, occasionally, to other people's. Deck-chairs take as good position as babies aboard ship for securing introductions. Some people seem to have an ingrained belief that a seat at the captain's table is essential to their dignity and comfort. It is nothing of the kind. One table, in point of feeding, is quite as good as another: one man is equally so, provided he be a gentleman in his behavior; and a seat at the captain's table generally means a certain amount of discomfort in passing in and out, from the fact that the oldest sailors, in some way or another, generally manage to secure their seats nearest the captain; and these are the most regular in attendance at meal-times.

A hand-bag or small portmanteau is a useful article to have in the state-room with you as a receptacle for old things — brush, combs, and so forth — on the voyage.

All hints as to remedies for sea-sickness are practically worthless. A person, in such case, must be governed by his or her own feelings; and these will usually follow in the direction of a very decided inclination to be sick, and to lie down. Do both the one and the other, taking care, when the paroxysms have passed, to be on deck as much as possible.

There are saloon-stewards, deck-stewards, bedroom-stewards, and a stewardess, on all the ocean steamships, to attend to the wants of passengers; and these will generally be found equal to any emergency.

With these remarks on the questions of expense and the ocean passage, we will pass to the main points of our book.

LIVERPOOL.

On arriving at Liverpool, there are two things to be done forthwith, — to submit your baggage to the inspection of the custom-house officers, and to secure a cab. Better to do the latter first. And, in engaging your cabman, make a mental or other note of his number, so as to keep him to his engagement; and bear in mind that it is not in the least necessary to bargain with the man, there being an authorized table of cab-fares to all the principal hotels and points of the city, which the cabman is bound by. The customs examination of baggage is not a very tedious or prolonged process. All that is necessary is to "declare" verbally to the officer any thing you carry with you liable to duty. No protective duties are now levied by the government of the United Kingdom on goods imported from abroad : customs duties are charged merely for the sake of revenue. The chief articles charged with duty, and the sums payable, are, —

		s.	d.
Tea	per lb.	0	6
Coffee	per cwt.	84	0
Cocoa	per lb.	0	1
Sugar	per cwt.	6	0
Spirits, brandy, Geneva, rum	per gall.	10	5
Spirits, rum from British Colony	per gall.	10	2
Wine containing less than 26 degrees spirits	per gall.	1	0
Wine containing 26, and less than 42 degrees	per gall.	2	6
Tobacco, unmanufactured	per lb.	3	2
Cigars	per lb.	5	0

Reprints of English books are liable to confiscation.

Gentlemen importing cigars into England for their own use will not be permitted to pass through the customs more than one pound free of duty; and, although the manufactured tobacco made in the United States is infinitely preferable to most that is sold in English towns, it scarcely pays to import American tobacco for personal use.

If you are going to proceed direct on to London, tell the cabman to drive to the London and North-western Railway Station. Every convenience will be found here for rest, refreshment, washing, &c.; and travellers, if time permits, will be enabled to make themselves comfortable without the necessity and expense of going to a hotel before the starting of the train on its six hours' journey to London.

LIVERPOOL CAB AND PORTERAGE RATES.

CABS.

For one or more passengers, 1s. per mile, and 6d. additional for each half, or lesser portion, of a mile.

By time, 6d. for every fifteen minutes, or lesser portion thereof.

From midnight until 6, A.M., 1s. 6d. per mile, and 9d. for each additional half, or lesser portion, of a mile.

These rates are inclusive of all charges for baggage not exceeding two hundred-weight.

ERRAND, MESSAGE, AND BAGGAGE PORTERS.

Liverpool porters are licensed by the watch committee of the town, and are required to wear badges with numbers (which must be visible while plying for hire), and also a distinguishing dress.

Porters are not permitted to refuse any errand, or to carry baggage, whilst on duty.

The following are the authorized rates for porterage or carriage of baggage, or for going any errand : —

	s.	d.
For every hat-box, carpet-bag, or other small package landed from any steam-vessel or boat at any of the piers, or taken on board from the pier	0	1
If taken half a mile, for every such package	0	3
If taken one mile	0	4
Every additional half-mile	0	1
If only one such package carried half a mile	0	6
For every box, portmanteau, trunk, &c., landed	0	3
If taken half a mile, for every package, including landing	0	6
If taken one mile	0	8
Every additional half-mile	0	2

If two or more men are necessary to carry one package, each to be paid on the same scale.

	s.	d.
For every half-hour, or part thereof, a porter is detained by persons hiring him	0	3
For removing baggage from steamship to custom-house dépôt, per package	0	6

BIRKENHEAD CAB-FARES.

6d. for every half-mile, or fraction of half a mile.

LONDON AND NORTH-WESTERN COMPANY'S TRAIN SERVICE TO AND FROM LIVERPOOL AND LONDON.

LIVERPOOL TO LONDON.		LONDON TO LIVERPOOL.	
Departs.	Arrives.	Departs.	Arrives.
Lime Street Station.	Euston Square.	Euston Square.	Lime Street Station.
9.15 A.M.	2.30 P.M.	9.00 A.M.	2.45 P.M.
11.40 "	5.30 "	10 00 "	3.00 "
4.00 P.M.	9.15 "	2.45 P M.	7.45 "
5.00 "	10.30 "	5.00 "	10.00 "
11.00 "	4.30 A M.	9.15 "	3.15 A.M.

FARES:— 1st class, £1 15s.; 2d class, £1 6s.; 3d class, 16s. 9d.
The Irish Limited Mail leaves London (Euston Square) for Queenstown on Tuesdays, Thursdays, and Saturdays, at 8.25 P.M.

GREAT WESTERN COMPANY'S TRAIN SERVICE TO AND FROM LONDON AND LIVERPOOL, VIA CHESTER.

LIVERPOOL TO LONDON.			LONDON TO LIVERPOOL.		
Departs.	Arrives.	Arrives.	Departs.	Arrives.	Arrives.
Liverpool Land'g Stage.	Chester.	Paddington.	Paddington.	Chester.	Liverpool Land'g Stage.
6 00 A.M.	7.45 A.M.	7.05 P.M.	7.45 A.M.	7.25 P.M.	8.30 P.M.
8.05 "	9.10 "	4.05 "	10.00 "	4.32 "	5.40 "
11.20 "	12 20 "	7.10 "	1.00 "	8.15 "	9.25 "
3.20 P.M.	4.20 P.M.	10.45 "	3.30 P.M.	10.15 "	11.25 "

LIVERPOOL TO LONDON, AND VICE VERSA, VIA DERBY, NOTTINGHAM, AND LEICESTER.

LIVERPOOL TO LONDON.		LONDON TO LIVERPOOL.	
Departs.	Arrives.	Departs.	Arrives.
Liverpool, Brunswick Station.	St. Pancras.	St. Pancras.	Liverpool, Brunswick Station.
8.15 A.M.	2.55 P.M.	10 00 A M.	4.30 P.M.
11.40 "	6.40 "	11.45 "	6.27 "
1.30 P.M.	8.55 "	3.00 P.M.	9.31 "
3.30 "	10.00 "	5.00 "	11.25 "

2

N.B. — The ticket-offices at railway stations are open *ten minutes* before the train starts; and it would be well, to avoid inconvenience and confusion, to be there at least that time before the hour appointed for the train's departure.

Always see that your baggage is properly labelled to its destination before being put into the train. Direct the first porter you see to attend to this on arrival at the station.

In event of any altercation with a cabman at the station, refer at once to the policeman on duty.

First-class passengers are allowed 112 pounds baggage free; second-class, 100 pounds. Excess baggage is charged at the rate of 1½*d.* per pound.

Make a point of asking guard of the train (conductor) whether it is necessary to *change carriages* for your destination, and where.

If you travel direct from Liverpool to London, provide what refreshment is required before starting.

In case necessity should arise for remaining in Liverpool over night, the principal hotels are as follows : —

The Liverpool Adelphi Company's Hotel, the London and North-western, the Alexandra, the Washington, the Angel, the Stork, the Imperial, the George, the Queen's, the Royal, the Union.

For our own part, without making special recommendation of any particular hotel, we infinitely prefer, for comfort's sake, for convenience, attention, and all the other essentials which tend to promote ease in one's inn, the old-fashioned, well-supported commercial houses to the new-fashioned joint-stock company hotels in Liverpool. There are two hotels immediately fronting the premises of the London and North-western Railway, the Queen's and Imperial, which are exceedingly quiet and well managed, and quite worthy the patronage of American, as they have long since earned the patronage of English travellers.

UNITED-STATES CONSULS AT LIVERPOOL.

CONSUL-GENERAL.

Lucius Fairchild, 69 Tower Buildings, South-west.

VICE-CONSUL.

Richard Paulson, 69 Tower Buildings, South-west.

LONDON.

UNITED-STATES OFFICIALS IN LONDON.

UNITED-STATES MINISTER.

Gen. ROBERT C. SCHENCK, 58 Great Cumberland Place, Hyde Park.

SECRETARY OF LEGATION.

BENJAMIN MORAN, Esq., 20 Norfolk Terrace, Westbourne Grove, and 5 Westminster Chambers, Victoria Street.

ASSISTANT SECRETARY.

Col. WILLIAM H. CHESEBROUGH. Offices, 5 Westminster Chambers, Victoria Street, S.W.

CONSUL-GENERAL.

Gen. ADAM BADEAU, Little Boston House, Brentford.

VICE-CONSUL-GENERAL.

JOSHUA NUNN, Esq. Offices, 1 Dunster Court, Mincing Lane, E.C.

UNITED-STATES DESPATCH-AGENT.

B. F. STEVENS, Esq., 17 Henrietta Street, Covent Garden, W.C. Office Hours, 11 to 3.

19

Day of M. W.	Fasts and Festivals. — Memoranda.
1 Fr	SS. Phil. and James
2 S	
3 S	4th Sunday after Easter
4 M	
5 Tu	
6 W	
7 Th	
8 Fr	
9 S	
10 S	Rogation Sunday
11 M	Rogation Day
12 Tu	Rogation Day
13 W	Rogation Day
14 Th	Ascension Day. Holy Thursday
15 Fr	
16 S	
17 S	Sunday after Ascension
18 M	
19 Tu	
20 W	
21 Th	
22 Fr	
23 S	
24 S	Whit Sunday. Queen Victoria born 1819
25 M	Whit Monday. Bank Holiday
26 Tu	Whit Tuesday
27 W	
28 Th	
29 Fr	
30 S	
31 S	Trinity Sunday

DIARY OF EVENTS FOR MAY.

An excellent and very enjoyable way of seeing something of the rare beauties of English country scenery is to secure a seat on the "box" of one of the admirably appointed four-horse coaches, which begin to run from the White Horse Cellar, Piccadilly, about the first of this month. This season promises to be altogether rich in coaching excitement. On and after the 1st, the "Old Dorking" starts at 10, driving through the loveliest parts of Surrey, and reaching Dorking in time for dinner at — excellent of English hostelries — the Red Lion. There is an afternoon coach taking the same road, and starting at 4.15. There are two coaches for Brighton, one for Windsor, a Tunbridge Wells and Reigate coach, all starting from the same place, and taking some of the very finest scenery in England in an enjoyable three or four hours' drive. The fares are reasonable, and the enjoyment to be had incalculable.

On the 1st, the EXHIBITION OF THE ROYAL ACADEMY opens at Burlington House, Piccadilly. See "Paintings."

THE BRITISH MUSEUM closes for one week from the 1st.

QUEEN VICTORIA'S BIRTHDAY kept on the 23d. — Grand parade of the Household Troops in rear of the Horse Guards, St. James's Park, at 10, A.M: Royal Family present. See "Buckingham Palace."

WHITMONDAY, 25th. — A bank holiday: all banks closed. Great holiday at Crystal Palace.

ANNUAL FESTIVAL OF SONS OF CLERGY IN ST. PAUL'S CATHEDRAL. — Meetings of the religious societies held at Exeter Hall, Strand, during the month.

CREMORNE GARDENS. — Open for the season. Whitsuntide Holidays: the amusements commence at 2.

NORTH WOOLWICH GARDENS. — Open for the season. Great holiday entertainments.

ROSHERVILLE. — Gardens open. Numerous entertainments. By boat from Paul's Wharf, near St. Paul's.

THE GRAND FLOWER-SHOWS at the Royal Horticultural Gardens (South Kensington) and Crystal Palace begin about this time, and continue through the summer.

THE CONCERT SEASON at the Hanover-square Rooms, Queen's Concert Rooms, Hanover Square, and St. James's Hall; also Saturday-afternoon concerts at Crystal Palace: very fashionable.

Day of		Fasts and Festivals. — Memoranda.
M.	**W.**	
1	M	....
2	Tu	....
3	W	....
4	Th	....
5	Fr	....
6	S	....
7	S	1st Sunday after Trinity ....
8	M	....
9	Tu	....
10	W	....
11	Th	St. Barnabas ....
12	Fr	....
13	S	....
14	S	2d Sunday after Trinity ....
15	M	....
16	Tu	....
17	W	....
18	Th	....
19	Fr	....
20	S	Queen's Accession, 1837 ....
21	S	3d Sunday after Trinity. Longest day..........
22	M	....
23	Tu	St. John Baptist. Midsummer Day ....
24	W	....
25	Th	....
26	Fr	....
27	S	....
28	S	4th Sun. after Trinity. Coronation Day..........
29	M	St. Peter Apostle and Martyr ....
30	Tu	

22

DIARY OF EVENTS FOR JUNE.

GRAND CRICKET MATCH at Lord's Cricket-Ground, St. John's Wood. — Marylebone Cricket Club *vs.* North of England, and Rugeley Great Horse Fair, on the 1st.

ROYAL CORNWALL AGRICULTURAL SHOW on the 3d and 4th at St. Austell. — Trains from G. W. Railway Station.

THE DERBY DAY on the 3d; and the OAKS, or LADY'S DAY, at Epsom on the 5th. See " Races."

FOURTH of JUNE. — Procession of boats at Eton, and grand display of fireworks from Windsor Bridge. See " Eton."

AGRICULTURAL HALL, Islington. — Horse Show: Parade of Prize Horses, Leaping, &c. : open from 10.

ASCOT RACES (Gold-Cup Day) on the 18th. — The Prince and Princess of Wales, and other members of the Royal Family, proceed on to the course in state. See " Races."

SOCIETY OF BRITISH ARTISTS, Suffolk Street, Pall Mall, East. — The Fifty-first Annual Exhibition now open, from 9 till dusk.

HOSPITAL SUNDAY on the 14th. — Special services at Westminster Abbey, St. Paul's Cathedral, and all the London churches : select preachers, for which see daily papers.

SOCIETY OF FRENCH ARTISTS, 168 New Bond Street. — The summer exhibition open from 10 till 6.

SOCIETY OF PAINTERS IN WATER COLORS, 5 Pall Mall, East. — Open from 9 till 7.

INSTITUTE OF PAINTERS IN WATER COLORS, 53 Pall Mall. — Annual Exhibition open from 9 till dusk.

NEW BRITISH INSTITUTION, 39B Old Bond Street. — On view, Pictures and Drawings (British and Foreign).

FRENCH GALLERY, 120 Pall Mall. — Twenty-first Annual Exhibition of Pictures, the contributions of Continental Artists, open.

23d, COMMENCEMENT DAY AT CAMBRIDGE UNIVERSITY. — Train from Eastern Counties Station, Shoreditch.

HENLEY REGATTA at Henley on Thames. — The Aquatic Fête of the year. The principal public schools and the universities compete.

OXFORD AND CAMBRIDGE CRICKET MATCH at Lord's on 29th and 30th.

Day of M. W.	Fasts and Festivals. — Memoranda.
1 W	
2 Th	
3 Fr	Dog-Days begin
4 S	
5 S	5th Sunday after Trinity
6 M	
7 Tu	
8 W	
9 Th	
10 Fr	
11 S	
12 S	6th Sunday after Trinity
13 M	
14 Tu	
15 W	St. Swithin
16 Th	
17 Fr	
18 S	
19 S	7th Sunday after Trinity
20 M	
21 Tu	
22 W	
23 Th	
24 Fr	
25 S	St. James, Apostle and Martyr
26 S	8th Sunday after Trinity
27 M	
28 Tu	
29 W	
30 Th	
31 Fr	

DIARY OF EVENTS FOR JULY.

OXFORD COMMEMORATION begins in the first week of July. — An excellent time for seeing the University *en fête.* Rail from Great Western Station, Paddington.

GRAND MORNING CONCERTS at the Floral Hall, Covent Garden, by the singers of the Royal Italian Opera.

One of the most popular amusements offered to the public at the Crystal Palace during the year is the Royal Dramatic College Fête, which takes place during this month. It is a motley kind of fancy fair, originally conceived and carried out with unflagging spirit by the principal actors and actresses of the metropolitan theatres. The entertainment, for the most part, consists of a mosaic of dramatic *morceaux,* culled so as to please all tastes, — from the lovers of legitimate drama down to those who care only for mere burlesque, followed by a magnificent display of fireworks in the Palace Gardens. The *fête* is held in aid of a dramatic charity, and is worthy of all support. Admission to the palace and grounds one shilling. Date always advertised.

THE ANNUAL CRICKET MATCH between Eton and Harrow Schools takes place on the 10th and 11th, and is one of the *fêtes* of the London season : Lord's Cricket-Ground.

THE NATIONAL RIFLE ASSOCIATION PRIZE MEETING opens at the camp on Wimbledon Common about the 6th instant, and continues for a fortnight. A grand review is held on the last Saturday of the meeting. Well worth visiting. Train from Waterloo Bridge.

Season of Opera ends.

GOODWOOD RACES. — Cup Day on the 30th : Duke of Richmond's seat. By rail to Chichester from Victoria. See " Races."

ROYAL ACADEMY closes on the 31st.

| Day of | | Fasts and Festivals. — Memoranda. |
M.	W.	
1	S	
2	S	9th Sunday after Trinity
3	M	
4	Tu	
5	W	
6	Th	
7	Fr	
8	S	
9	S	10th Sunday after Trinity
10	M	
11	Tu	Dog-Days end
12	W	
13	Th	
14	Fr	
15	S	
16	S	11th Sunday after Trinity
17	M	
18	Tu	
19	W	
20	Th	
21	Fr	
22	S	
23	S	12th Sunday after Trinity
24	M	St. Bartholomew
25	Tu	
26	W	
27	Th	
28	Fr	
29	S	
30	S	13th Sunday after Trinity
31	M	

DIARY OF EVENTS FOR AUGUST.

THE PROMENADE CONCERTS at Covent-garden Theatre generally commence about the end of the month; and every American having the opportunity should not fail to be present at one of them. " The London Examiner," alluding to these pleasant entertainments, says, —
" Should any lonely Londoner, depressed by semi-deserted streets and empty club, be inclined to come to the conclusion that there is nobody in town, an evening visit to Covent-garden Theatre will convince him that 'nobody' is ' a noun of quantity signifying many, if not signifying much.' Mr. Rivière's Promenade Concerts are so crowded as to make their title somewhat unsuitable, although there is still ample room on the stage for promenaders. This part of the house is prettily adorned with fountains, grottos, and waterfalls; the management understanding, apparently, the desirability of pleasing the eye as well as the ear. Nor are the other senses neglected. An extensive and well-furnished *buffet* evinces a just appreciation of the influence of internal bodily comfort on the mind, and invites all comers to enter that blissful state 'when body gets its sop, and holds its noise, and leaves soul free a little.' The every-day programmes consist of waltzes, songs, and selections ; whilst Wednesdays are partially devoted to classical music, the selection of the first part of the programme being on each evening confined to the works of one of the great masters. Some of the first artists appear at these concerts, which receive a wide and enthusiastic patronage. Admission, 1*s.*

BANK AND GENERAL HOLIDAY on the 3d.

PARLIAMENT is prorogued about the 12th. Ceremony interesting. Application to a peer will secure admission.

A BASE-BALL MATCH at Lord's Cricket-Ground, St. John's Wood, between two American clubs, takes place about the first week of this month. Cricket-matches between English and American " Elevens " to follow.

NAPOLEONIC FÊTE at Chiselhurst on the 15th. By rail from Victoria Station. Opportunity for seeing the mausoleum of Napoleon III.

GREAT CRICKET WEEK at Canterbury. Commences on 1st. NATIONAL ARTILLERY ASSOCIATION on 10th. COWES ROYAL YACHT CLUB REGATTA about the 12th. BRITISH ASSOCIATION MEETING at Belfast on 12th. BIRMINGHAM MUSICAL FESTIVAL, 27th.

Day of M. W.	Fasts and Festivals. — Memoranda.
1 Tu	....
2 W	....
3 Th	....
4 Fr	....
5 S	....
6 S	14th Sunday after Trinity ....
7 M	....
8 Tu	....
9 W	....
10 Th	....
11 Fr	....
12 S	First Day of Jewish Year 5635 ....
13 S	15th Sunday after Trinity ....
14 M	....
15 Tu	....
16 W	....
17 Th	....
18 Fr	Ember Day ....
19 S	Ember Day ....
20 S	16th Sunday after Trinity ....
21 M	St. Matthew ....
22 Tu	....
23 W	....
24 Th	....
25 Fr	....
26 S	....
27 S	17th Sunday after Trinity ....
28 M	....
29 Tu	St. Michael. Michaelmas Day ....
30 W	....

DIARY OF EVENTS FOR SEPTEMBER.

BRITISH MUSEUM closes for a week from the 1st.

EXCURSION TRAINS every day to the seaside, and places of interest in the provinces. See daily papers.

DONCASTER RACES on the 16th, St. Leger Day.

BARNET GREAT CATTLE FAIR on 3d, 4th, and 5th. See daily papers for trains. A short distance out of London.

MANCHESTER AND LIVERPOOL AGRICULTURAL SHOW at Stalybridge, about 5th.

SOCIAL-SCIENCE CONGRESS at Glasgow, about end of the month. Special train service, for which see daily papers.

WARWICKSHIRE AGRICULTURAL SHOW at Knowle, one of the prettiest parts of the county of Warwick.

FESTIVAL OF THE THREE CHOIRS. The attention of American lovers of sacred music is especially directed to this annual musical festival, which is held in one of the cathedral cities in the west of England (see daily papers), and attracts visitors from all parts of the United Kingdom. The chief singers are selected from the more noted of the artistes of the two houses of Italian Opera, the chorus comprising the choirs of the cathedrals.

London comparatively empty during the whole of this month, and most of the theatres and places of amusement closed.

─────

The Editor desires here to direct special attention to the very great advantages offered to travellers by the different railway companies of the United Kingdom, in their admirable system of Tourist Tickets. He would impress upon Americans the desirability of selecting this month, if possible, for their English tours; and in every case, before purchasing a ticket on a line of railroad, it will be found useful to consult the monthly tourist arrangements of the company. These will oftentimes suggest an economical and pleasant plan for seeing a great deal of rural England, outside of the beaten track of ordinary travel.

HOTELS.

To our thinking, the best way of getting along in London
is to breakfast in your hotel, and occasionally to dine out;
unless, of course, where ladies are concerned, when it becomes almost necessary to dine in the hotel; and under such
circumstances, always, if possible, order your dinner in the
morning, before going out, for about six o'clock, when the
best joint is generally on the table.

As regards the mere lodging, it matters little where you
go to in London: the prices average the same, north, south,
east, and west. But there are many excellent old-fashioned
family houses off St. James Street, that, for bachelors at
least, are preferable to your modern joint-stock company's
Anglo-American hotel. It were, perhaps, invidious to make
distinction as regards these modern "big" hotels of London: but, if there are points of difference, they would be,
possibly, in favor of the Grosvenor Hotel, which is situated
in one of the very best districts of West-End London, Pimlico; is admirably managed by one of the most experienced,
courteous, and kindly of London hotel-proprietors; is quiet,
and yet within a few minutes' walk of one of the busiest
and most fashionable of London thoroughfares; and where
the service is good, the cooking equally so, and the wines,
&c., excellent. But, really to enjoy what may be termed the
thorough English hotel-life, one must mostly seek for it outside of huge London; and, to tell the truth, your American,
unless of compulsion, does not go abroad to enjoy what he
may have at home.

The expenses at London hotels average as follows, — for
one person, room, three shillings and sixpence per night, with
one shilling and sixpence attendance; breakfast, plain,
consisting of eggs, and such cold meat as may be upon the
side-table, two shillings; lunch about the same; dinner
off the joint, with vegetable and cheese, two shillings and
sixpence. Thus your daily expenses in a London hotel, feeding off fare, which, though plain, is probably the whole-
somest in the long-run, are, as has been intimated elsewhere,
ten or eleven shillings and sixpence, or about two dollars
and a half in gold, exclusive entirely of beer or wine.

There are few of the old style of inns — taverns, perhaps,
it would be more correct to term them — existing in London
at the present day. The hotel-system of the English me-

tropolis, although it has not attained the vast development which has been the case in America, yet follows close upon it. The Grosvenor, the Buckingham Palace, the Westminster Palace, the Langham, the Charing Cross hotels, are all imitations of American hotels. You have all the vastness, without those redeeming qualities common to American hotels, which make you feel disposed, in their case, to sacrifice comfort at the cost of more needful requirements. The rooms are pretty much the same with both; a bachelor in this respect certainly faring better in the London hotel. The living in the latter is ordinarily not quite up to the mark; that is to say, where you content yourself with the simple every-day bill of fare. The waiting in most London hotels is infinitely better than in America, and there is far more privacy in your London hotel than that which obtains in most American houses. "Loafers" are unheard of; transient dinners are not altogether welcome; and each party has a separate table to itself. *Tables d'hôte* are, upon the whole, discountenanced; but, when they do exist, the British *table d'hôte* dinner offers nothing at all like the variety of food of the American hotels; while the charge is as much, or more. London, with a little training, and a little borrowing of master-minds, might possibly succeed in producing once, in a way, such a dinner as you may have any day at five o'clock at the Windsor or New-York Hotels, in New York; but the true idea of the thoroughly good American hotel dinner would take at least a century to mature in England. People mostly dine late in London; and if you desire to keep your hotel-bill within limits, and at the same time dine comfortably, you should always be posted on the times "the joints" arrive in the "coffee-room" (dining-rooms are generally coffee-rooms in London hotels), otherwise you will have to fall back upon the fag-end of a leg of mutton, with the alternative of a costly dish or two of badly-cooked *entrées*. A spade is a spade in London hotels; and, if you order for breakfast a steak, you get a steak to the tune of a good honest pound and a half. Variety is not to be had but here and there, we are sorry to say, except at extravagant cost.

LONDON HOTELS RECOMMENDED TO AMERICANS.

* THE ALEXANDRA HOTEL, Hyde Park. — An excellent hotel for ladies and families.

THE ALBEMARLE, Albemarle Street, Piccadilly.

* THE BUCKINGHAM PALACE HOTEL. — Fashionable and quiet for families and gentlemen.

THE BRITISH HOTEL, Cockspur Street. — Very good indeed.

* THE CHARING CROSS HOTEL, adjoining the South-Eastern Railway Station. — Especially convenient for travellers to the Continent.

THE CLARENDON, New Bond Street. — Somewhat expensive.

* THE GROSVENOR HOTEL, Victoria Station. — Very good for families and gentlemen. Adjoining London, Chatham, and Dover Railway for Paris. Very convenient to the parks, places of amusement, &c.

* THE GOLDEN CROSS, Charing Cross. — Very quiet and respectable.

* THE GREAT NORTHERN HOTEL, King's Cross. — Very convenient for travellers to Scotland and the north of England.

* THE GREAT WESTERN HOTEL, Paddington. — Very comfortable, and convenient for travellers to Leamington, Warwick, Oxford, &c.

HAXELL'S EXETER HALL HOTEL, Strand. — Excellent and moderate.

* THE LONDON AND NORTH-WESTERN HOTEL, Euston Square. — Very convenient for travellers for Liverpool, &c.

* THE LANGHAM HOTEL, Regent Street. — Much frequented by Americans.

MORLEY'S HOTEL, Charing Cross. — A good old-fashioned house, economical and convenient.

THE QUEEN'S HOTEL, Cork and Clifford Streets, adjoining Piccadilly. — An excellent family hotel, quiet, and well managed.

THE QUEEN'S HOTEL, St. Martins-le-Grand, City. — Very good, economical, and quiet.

RADLEY'S, 10 New Bridge Street, Blackfriars. — Economical and quiet.

THE TAVISTOCK, Covent Garden. — For gentlemen only,

---

* A general tariff of prices has been adopted at all these large hotels.

most excellent, an old-fashioned house, and eminently respectable.

* The Terminus Hotel, London Bridge. — Very good, and managed by an attentive and obliging landlord.
* The Westminster Palace Hotel. — Very good for families and gentlemen; convenient to the theatres, &c.
* The New Midland Hotel, St. Pancras Station. — Very good. Convenient to underground rail for the city.
* The Inns of Court Hotel, High Holborn.

The United Hotel, Charles Street, Haymarket. — Excellent and convenient.

To those who wish to be moderate in their expenses, we would call attention to the following excellent hotels : —

The Bath Hotel, Piccadilly. — Very quiet, and economical for families.

The Bridge House Hotel, London Bridge. — Economical, and well managed.

The Castle and Falcon, St. Martins-le-Grand. — Very good indeed.

De. Keyser's Hotel, Blackfriars. — Highly recommended, well managed, and economical.

Fumiral's Inn Hotel, Holborn. — An exceedingly quiet and respectable house. Convenient to the city.

The Norfolk Hotel, Norfolk Street, Strand.

Anderton's Hotel, Fleet Street.

Hatchett's Hotel, Piccadilly. — Excellent and moderate.

The Somerset Hotel, near King's College, Strand. — Moderate.

* A general tariff of prices has been adopted at all these large hotels.

3

ENGLISH HOTELS, NOT INCLUDED IN THE FORE-GOING, PATRONIZED BY AMERICANS.

LONDON.

American Pension. — 7 Montague Street, W.C.
Berners Hotel. — Berners Street, W.
Brunswick House Hotel. — Hanover Square.
Brunswick Hotel. — Jermyn Street, S.W.
Caledonian Hotel. — Robert Street, Adelphi Terrace.
Claridge's Hotel. — Brook Street, W.
Craven Hotel. — Craven Street, Strand.
Craufurd's Hotel. — 40 Sackville Street, W.
Crystal Palace Royal Hotel. — Opposite the Crystal Palace.
Fenton's Hotel. — St. James's Street, Piccadilly.
Fischer's Hotel. — 11 Clifford Street, W.
Ford's Hotel. — Manchester Street, W.
Garlant's Hotel. — 16 Suffolk Street, Pall Mall.
Langford's Pension. — 28 Bedford Place, W.C.
Lewington's Pension. — 12 Manchester Street, Manchester Square.
Long's Hotel. — Bond Street.
M. A. Child, Osnaburgh House. — Osnaburgh Place, N.W.
Mr. Burr's. — 10, 11, and 12 Queen Square, W.C.
Mrs. Charter. — 1 Montpelier Square, South Kensington, S.W.
Mrs. Davies'. — 22 Endsleigh Street, Tavistock Square, W.C.
Mrs. Evans'. — 5 Fitzroy Square, W.C.
Mrs. Jupp. — 14 Bedford Place, W.C.
Mrs. Lloyd. — 34 Woburn Place, W.C.
Mr. A. Nodskow. — 56 Torrington Square, W.C.
Mrs. Sampson's Private Hotel. — 24 Norfolk Street, Strand, W.C.
Mrs. S. Taylor. — 51 Weymouth Street, W.
Mrs. Watson. — 51 New Bond Street, W.
Mrs. Weddle. — 8 Montague Place, Russell Square, W.C.
Mrs. Wood's. — 22 Upper Woburn Place, W.C.
Mrs. Wright. — 15 Upper Woburn Place, Tavistock Square, W.C.
Queen's Hotel. — Near the Crystal Palace, Upp Norwood.
Silvester's. — 7 Bedford Place, W.C.
St. James's Hotel. — Piccadilly.

Symond's Hotel. — 34 Lower Brook Street, Grosvenor Square.
West's Private Hotel. — 90 and 91 Guilford Street, W.C.
BRIGHTON. — The Royal Albion Hotel, David Lawrence, proprietor. Bedford Hotel, John Park, manager.
DUBLIN. — Gresham Hotel. Shelbourne Hotel.
BELFAST. — Imperial Hotel.
BIRMINGHAM. — Great Western Hotel.
SOUTHAMPTON. — South-Western Hotel.
PLYMOUTH. — Duke of Cornwall.

LODGINGS IN LONDON.

There must be a number of persons visiting London every year — a number which will inevitably increase in proportion as the facilities for crossing the Atlantic become greater — who go there mainly to transact business, but with the intention, nevertheless, of seeing as much of London as is to be seen in such spare time as they may have at their disposal. To many such persons, expense becomes a matter of some consideration; and it sometimes becomes necessary to count the chances of both ends meeting, where business, hotels, and pleasure combine to draw pretty freely upon the letter of credit in a city among strangers. Now, there is no more economical or pleasanter way of living in London than in lodgings, especially where ladies are concerned; but in the selection of them it behooves the American citizen, as well as every one else, to be wary. There are lodgings and lodgings, landladies and landladies: and some parts of London are more desirable for living in than others. For the bachelor who wants comfortable quarters at a moderate rent, say from two dollars to five, gold, a week, no district could possibly be better than the Strand. In nearly all the streets running at right angles due south from the Strand — such as Northumberland, Salisbury, Norfolk, and Adelphi Streets — are to be found excellent and comfortable lodging-houses. In most of these, single rooms may be had, with attendance, for about 12*s.* 6*d.* (three to four dollars) per week, with the option of taking breakfast at home. Dining at home, except under special agreement, is not permissible; neither is it altogether desirable, seeing that the very best dinners are to be had at Simpson's, the Rainbow, or Haxell's.

hard by, at very moderate cost, with facilities for smoking, reading, and conversation, not to be had in a private house. On entering into any agreement for renting a room or rooms, it is usual to hire by the week, and to stipify at the time of hiring what are the requirements in regard to meals, &c. Rents for lodgings in London vary very much, according to localities. The following are the best, and may be relied upon as respectable : —

REGENT-STREET DISTRICT.

Conduit Street.
Maddox Street.
Hanover Street.
New Burlington Street.
Princes St., Hanover Square.

} Rents for two rooms, with cooking and attendance, vary in this locality from 3 guineas to 1 guinea per week.

PICCADILLY DISTRICT.

Jermyn Street, St. James.
Ryder Street.*
Duke Street.*
Bury Street.*
Mount St., Berkeley Square.
Half Moon Street.
Bond Street, streets west of

} Rents same as above for two rooms, &c.
* Principally for bachelors' single rooms, which may be rented at from £1 10 to £1 per week, or less, inclusive of breakfast.

OXFORD-STREET DISTRICT, W.

Margaret Street.
Duke Street, Portland Place.
Orchard Street.
Baker Street.
Bryanston St., Portland Sq.
Welbeck St., Cavendish Sq.
Davies St., Berkeley Square.

} Rents from 2 guineas to 1½ guineas for two rooms, &c.

OXFORD-STREET DISTRICT, E.

Bloomsbury Street.
Woburn Place.
Russell Sq., streets adjoining
Gower Street, and streets adjoining.

} In nearly all the streets adjacent to Russell and Bedford Squares, lodgings may be had at very reasonable rents for £1 10 to £1 for 2 rooms, &c.

STRAND DISTRICT.

Northumberl'd St., Charing Cross.
Craven Street.
Adam Street.
Cecil Street.
Villiers Street.
Norfolk Street.*
Arundel Street.*

} Principally for bachelors, though there are some excellent private hotels on the streets marked.* Rents about £1 10 for two rooms, &c.

PIMLICO DISTRICT.

Ebury Street.
Eccleston Street.
Buckingham Palace Road.   Rents from £1 10 to £1
Gloucester Street.   per week
Coleshill St., Eaton Square.   for two rooms, &c.
Westbourne Terrace, Eat'n Sq.
Cadogan Place, Sloane Street.

EDGWARE-ROAD DISTRICT.

Oxford Terrace.   Both excellent localities, and
Cambridge Terrace.   rents very reasonable.

It must be borne in mind that these prices should include cooking as required, attendance, and boot-cleaning. Ladies and families will find excellent suites of apartments in Ebury Street, and streets out of Eaton Square, Pimlico; Conduit Street. Hanover, and Princes Streets, in Regent Street, in Baker Street, Oxford Street, and in some of the best streets about Russell, Bedford, and Manchester Squares. Nearly all lodging-house keepers display a card, — not too conspicuously, the best class, — notifying the fact of rooms being to let. At the time of hiring, say explicitly whether you dine at home or not. It is certainly advisable for ladies to arrange to do so, as there is something of home-comfort in the fashion. Dine late, if possible, and arrange with the landlady that you will order in every thing for yourself. Civil, obliging, and reliable tradespeople are to be met with everywhere in London, who will *call for orders* every day without charge, thus saving the trouble of going to market. Always make this stipulation in ordering provisions, &c. Bills are always paid weekly; and a week's notice is usual before vacating rooms, except otherwise agreed upon.

The best class of apartments to be had in London are those in private houses, let by persons of respectability, generally for the season only; i.e., from April to August. In the windows of these houses you will probably not see " Apartments to Let." A list of such apartments is to be found, however, at the nearest house-agent (inquire of any tradesman), who gives cards to view, and states terms. An advertisement in " The Times " for such rooms, stating that " no lodging-house keeper need apply," will often open to the stranger the doors of very respectable families, where he will get all the quiet and comfort of a home, so difficult to be found in the noisy, and often extortionate, professed lodging-house. Furnished houses for families also can always be obtained at the West End.

RESTAURANTS AND DINING-ROOMS RECOMMENDED.

FOR GENTLEMEN.

THE ALBION, near Drury Lane Theatre. — Highly recommended.

BLANCHARD'S RESTAURANT, Beak Street, Regent Street. — Highly recommended.

THE BURLINGTON, Regent Street. — Highly recommended.

THE COCK, 201 Fleet Street. — An old-fashioned tavern.

THE CHESHIRE CHEESE, Fleet Street. — An old-fashioned tavern.

FISHER'S RESTAURANT, Victoria Station. — Very good.

PIMMS, 3, 4, and 5 Poultry. — Excellent.

SIMPSONS, Strand. — Excellent.

SPIERS AND POND'S, Ludgate Hill, and Victoria Railway Stations. — Excellent.

SPIERS AND POND'S CRITERION. — Excellent.

THE SOLFERINO, Rupert Street, Haymarket. — Excellent for French dinners.

THE SALUTATION TAVERN, Newgate Street. — Very good.

THE SOMERSET HOTEL, near King's College, Strand. — Very good.

THE SCOTCH STORES, Oxford Street, close to Regent Circus. — Very good.

FOR LADIES.

THE ALBION, Picadilly. — Quiet and economical.

THE BURLINGTON, Regent Street. — Very good.

THE ST. JAMES'S HALL, Regent Street. — Very good.

VERREY'S, in Regent Street. — Excellent.

And in the coffee-rooms of all the best hotels.

BANKING DIRECTORY.

AMERICAN BANKERS IN LONDON.

BARING BROTHERS & Co., 8 Bishopsgate Street, E.C.
BLAKE BROTHERS & Co. of Boston.
BROWN, SHIPLEY, & Co., 5 Lothbury, E.C.
CLEWS, HABICHT, & Co., 13 Old Broad Street, E.C.
McCULLOCH & Co., 41 Lombard Street, E.C.
MORGAN, J. S. & Co., 22 Old Broad Street, E.C.
MORTON, ROSE, & Co., Bartholomew House, E.C.
PETRIE, A. S. & Co., 11 Old Broad Street, E.C.
SELIGMAN BROTHERS, 3 Angel Court, E.C.

LONDON JOINT-STOCK BANKS TRANSACTING BUSINESS WITH AMERICAN HOUSES.

BANK OF BRITISH NORTH AMERICA. — 124 Bishopsgate Street Within.

CITY BANK. — *Manager*, Alfred George Kennedy, 5 Threadneedle Street; 34 Old Bond Street; 25 Ludgate Hill; 159 Tottenham Court Road.

CONSOLIDATED BANK. — 52 Threadneedle Street; Charing Cross Branch, 450 West Strand.

GLYN MILLS, CURRIE, & Co., 67 Lombard Street.

LONDON AND COUNTY BANKING COMPANY. — *Joint General Managers*, William McKewan and Whitbread Tomson, 21 Lombard Street; 21 Hanover Square; 3 Albert Gate; 55 Barbican; 19 Islington High Street; 112 Aldersgate Street; 6 Berkeley Place, Edgware Road; 441 Oxford Street; 34 Borough High Street; 67 Kensington High Street; 181 Shoreditch High Street; 74 Westbourne Grove; 6 Henrietta Street, Covent Garden; 165 Westminster Bridge Road; Deptford Broadway; Stratford Broadway; 324 High Holborn; 1 Amhurst Road, Hackney; 1 Providence Place, Commercial Road, E.; 18 Newington Butts; 3 Victoria Street, Westminster; 193 Caledonian Road; Barnet; Blackheath; Greenwich; Hammersmith; and Woolwich.

LONDON JOINT-STOCK BANK. — *General Manager*, William Frederick Narraway, 5 Princes Street, Bank; 124 Chancery Lane; St. John Street, Smithfield; 69 Pall Mall; 28 Borough High Street; 9 Craven Road, W.; Metropolitan Cattle Market; and Cattle Market, Deptford.

ORIENTAL BANKING CORPORATION. — 40 Threadneedle Street.
SMITH, PAYNE, & SMITHS. — 1 Lombard Street.
UNION BANK OF LONDON. — *General Manager*, George Holland Milford. 2 Princes Street, Mansion House; 66 Charing Cross; 14 Argyll Place, Regent Street; Chancery Lane; and Holborn Circus.

NEW-YORK BANKS.

LONDON AGENTS.

Austin, Baldwin, & Co. . . . . City Bank.
Bank of British N. America. . . Bank of British N. America.
Bank of Montreal . . . . Union Bank of London.
Bank of New York. . . . . Union Bank of London.
Bank of California. . . . . Oriental Banking Corpor.
Babcock Brothers & Co. . . . .
Blake Brothers & Co. . . . .
Brown Brothers & Co. . . . .
Drexel, Winthrop, & Co. . . . . . . London Joint-Stock Bank.
Duncan, Sherman, & Co. . . . . . . Union Bank of London.
Eugene Kelly & Co. . . . . { Smith, Payne, & Smiths, and Consolidated Bank.
Kings & Sons . . . .
Knauth, Machod, & Kahne. . . . . Alliance Bank.
Lassing, Weiss, & Co. . . . . Alliance Bank.
Maitland, Phelps, & Co. . . . . Smith, Payne, & Smith.
H. G. Marquand. . . . . City Bank.
W. B. Shattuck. . . . .
F. Schuchardt & Sons. . . . . Union Bank of London.
M. Morgans & Sons. . . . . London Joint-Stock Bank.
John Munroe & Co. . . . . Consolidated Bank.
E. P. Morton & Co. . . . . Glyn Mills, Currie, & Co.
National Bank of Commerce . . Glyn Mills, Currie, & Co.
National Park Bank. . . . . Union Bank of London.
Stokes & Co. . . . . City Bank.
John Stuart & Co. . . . . Smith, Payne, & Smiths.
Ward & Co. . . . . Union Bank of London.
Wells, Fargo, & Co. . . . . Union Bank of London.
Winslow, Lanier, & Co. . . . . City Bank.

LONDON TRADESMEN RECOMMENDED TO AMERICAN TRAVELLERS.

BAG (TRAVELLING) MAKERS.

Allen, John William..........37 Strand, W.C.
Cave & Sons................74, 76, 78 Wigmore Street.
Asser & Sherwin............81 Strand.

BAZAARS.

Baker St. (W. & E. Boulnois)..58 Baker Street.
London Crystal Palace........108 Oxford Street.
Soho Bazaar................4 to 7 Soho Square.

BISCUIT AND CRACKERS.

A. Robb & Co...............79 St. Martins Lane.
(See advertisement.)

BONNET-MAKERS (LADIES').

(See Milliners.)

BOOKSELLERS.

Hatchard, Messrs. & Co........187 Piccadilly.
Bagster, Samuel & Sons.......15 Paternoster Row, E.C.
Bell & Daldy................4, 5, 6 York Street, Covent Garden.
Bentley, Richard & Son.......8 New Burlington Street, W.
Bohn, Henry George.........18 Henrietta Street, Covent Garden.
Cassell, Petter, & Galpin......La Belle Sauvage Yard, Ludgate Hill.
Hachette & Co. (French)......18 King William St., Strand.
Longmans................38 to 41 Paternoster Row.
Murray, John...............50A, Albemarle Street.
Quaritch, Bernard...........16 Castle St., Leicester Sq.
Routledge, George...........7 Broadway, City.
Smith, W. H. & Son..........183 to 187 Strand.
Harrison & Sons.............59 Pall Mall.

BOOT AND SHOE MAKERS.

Carter, J. S................205 Oxford Street.
Daniel, L..................206 Regent Street.
Givry, V. (for ladies)........23 Old Bond Street.
Fagg Brothers.............29 Haymarket.
Holland, J. (for ladies).......40 South Audley Street.
Frisby, Edward.............20 Eccleston St., Pimlico.
Medwin, James & Co.........86 Regent Street.
Hall, C. G.................89 Quadrant, Regent Circus.
Norman, S. W. ....3 Belgrave Mans., Pimlico.
Kerby, John................70 Haymarket.

CHEMISTS, ALLOPATHIC.

It is not necessary to mention the names of particular firms.

CHEMISTS, HOMŒOPATHIC.

Epps, James & Co. ....170 Picadilly, W.
Heath, Alfred...............114 Ebury Street, Pimlico.
Headland & Co..............15 Princes St., Hanover Sq.

CIGAR-DEALERS.

Wolff, Phillips, & Co.........77 Regent Street, W.
Carreras, Joseph ....98 Regent Street.
Cigar Divan ....101, 102 Strand.
Evans, J. N................1 Pall Mall.
Van Raalte................199 Piccadilly.
Bewlay & Co................49 Strand.

CROQUET-MANUFACTURERS.

Buchanan, James ....215 Piccadilly.
Asser & Sherwin............81 Strand.

CUTLERS.

Barron & Wilson ....436 West Strand.
Mappin Brothers............220 Regent Street.
Mappin & Webb ....76, 77, 78 Oxford Street.
Mechi, John Joseph.........112 Regent Street.
Rodgers of Sheffield.........16 Vere Street, Oxford St.

DRESSMAKERS (LADIES').

(See Milliners.)

DENTISTS.

Consult the hotel proprietor or manager.

FLORISTS AND FRUIT-SELLERS

Covent-Garden Market.

HAIR-DRESSERS AND PERFUMERS.

Cweig, B....................246 Regent Street.
Shipwright, Thomas.........10 Tichborne St. Haymarket.
Truefitt, H. P..............14 Old Bond Street and Bur-
                              lington Arcade.
Truefitt, Walter.............1 New Bond Street.
Unwin & Albert.............24 Piccadilly (W.) and 6 Bel-
                              grave Mansions, Pimlico.
Imrie, John ....420 Strand.
Douglas, Robert............21, 23 New Bond Street.

HATTERS.

Christy & Co. . . . . .1 Old Bond Street.
Lincoln, Bennett, & Co. . . . . . . .1 Sackville St., Piccadilly.
Cole, Thomas Henry. . . . . .156 Strand.

HACK PROPRIETORS.

Evans, Joseph . . . . .179 Buckingham Palace Rd.
Newman & Co. . . . . .121 Regent Street.
For private carriages.

HOSIERS AND GLOVERS (GENTLEMEN).

Bennett, E. . . . . .4 Glasshouse St., Regent St.
Baker & Co. II. . . . . .112 & 113 New Bond Street.
Burden & Keer. . . . . .51 Conduit Street, Bond St.
Capper & Waters. . . . . .26 Regent St., Waterloo Pl.
Evans, John. . . . . .18 Piccadilly.
Holbrook & Walker. . . . . .1 Burlington Gardens.
Jacobs, Lewis. . . . . .146 Strand, W.
Crouch, Henry . . . . .34 Strand, W.
Pope and Plante. . . . . .4 Waterloo Place, Pall Mall.
Thresher & Glenny. . . . . .152 Strand.
Sampson & Co. . . . . .130 Oxford Street.
Morgan & Ball. . . . . .173 Strand.

JEWELLERS.

Emanuel & Co. . . . . .1 Burlington Gardens, New
⠀⠀⠀⠀⠀⠀⠀⠀⠀⠀⠀⠀⠀⠀⠀⠀⠀⠀⠀⠀Bond Street.
Hancocks & Co. . . . . .152 New Bond Street.
Hunt & Roskell. . . . . .156 New Bond Street.
London & Ryder. . . . . .17 New Bond Street.
Streeter, Edwin W. . . . . .37 Conduit Street, W.
Watherston & Son. . . . . .12 Pall Mall, East.
Ortner & Houle. . . . . .3 St. James's Street.
Attenborough, George. . . . . . . .212 Strand.
Lambert & Co. . . . . .10, 11, 12 Coventry St., W.

KID GLOVES (LADIES').

Houbigant & Co. . . . . .216 Regent Street.

MILLINERY, AND LADIES' OUTFITTERS.

Christian, Adams, & Co. . . . . . .12 Holles St., Cavendish Sq.
Swears & Wells. . . . . .Regent Street.
Brandon's . . . . .137, 138 &c., Oxford Street.

MILLINERS, DRESSMAKERS, SILK MERCERS, &c.

It is impossible to recommend any particular house. Ladies will find the latest fashions displayed in the windows of all the fashionable shops in Regent Street, Bond Street, Piccadilly, and Oxford Street; or inquire of —

Peter Robinson ....103, 104, &c., &c., Oxford St.
Jay & Co...................259 Regent Street.
Marshall & Snelgrove.........Oxford Street.
Gask & Gask.................58 to 63 Oxford Street.
Swan & Edgar ....Regent Circus, Piccadilly.
Farmer & Rogers.............171, 173 Regent Street.
Ahlborn, Augustus ....74 Regent Street.
Hitchcock, Williams, & Co.....St. Paul's Churchyard.
Nicholson, Daniel ....St. Paul's Churchyard.
Debenham & Freebody ....27, 29, 31 Wigmore Street.
Lewis & Allenby..............193, 195, 197 Regent Street.
Redmayne, Gonner, & Co......19, 20 New Bond Street.
Shoolbred, James & Co. ....151 to 156 Tottenham Court Road.
Spence & Co. ....St. Paul's Churchyard.
Stagg & Mantle ....2, 3, 4 Leicester Square.

PERFUMERS.

Atkinson, J. & E.............24 Old Bond Street.
Breidenbach & Co. ....157 New Bond Street.
Piesse & Lubin ....2 New Bond Street.
Rimmel, Eugene..............96 Strand.

PHOTOGRAPHIC ARTISTS.

Debenham, W. E.............158 Regent Street.
London Stereoscopic Company .108, 110 Regent Street.
Elliott & Fry ....55 Baker St., Portman Sq.
Maull & Co..................187A, Piccadilly.
Mayall & Collins ....224 Regent Street.
Watkins, Herbert.............215 Regent Street.

PHYSICIANS.

In event of necessity arising for consulting a physician, — at hotels, send for the regular hotel doctor; in lodgings, inquire of a respectable apothecary in the neighborhood; in emergencies, go to the nearest to be found at night, by a colored lamp displayed over the door; in the day, upon application to any respectable tradesman.

SILVERSMITHS.

Benson, James W. . . . . .25 Old Bond Street.
Dobree, Robert J . . . . .264 Strand, W.C.
Emanuel & Co.. . . . . .New Bond Street.
Elkington & Co . . . . .22 Regent Street.
Jenner & Knewstub. . . . . .33 St. James's Street.
Ortner & Houle . . . . .3 St. James's Street.
Whistler, Edward . . . . .11 Strand.
Watherston & Son . . . . .12 Pall Mall, East.

STATIONERS, FOR NOTE PAPER, VISITING CARDS, &c.

Jenner & Knewstub . . . . .33 St. James's Street.
Parkins & Gotto . . . . .24, 25, 26 Oxford Street.
Stanford, Edward . . . . .6, 7 Charing Cross.
Harrison & Sons. . . . . .59 Pall Mall.
Holmes & Son . . . . .195 Oxford Street.

SHIRTMAKERS AND GENERAL OUTFITTERS.

William Churton & Son . . . . . .91, 92 Oxford Street.
Pope & Plante . . . . .4 Waterloo Place.
Bennett, E.. . . . . .4 Glasshouse St., Regent St.
Geoghegan & Doucet. . . . . .178 Regent Street.
Burden & Keer . . . . .51 Conduit Street.

TAILORS.

Poole . . . . .Saville Row.
Smalpage & Sons . . . . .41, 43 Maddox St., Bond St.
Johnson & Sadler . . . . .66A Vigo Street, Regent St.
Cutler & Reed . . . . .24, 25 St. James's Street.
Dombey & Son . . . . .Fenchurch Street, City.
Gillott & Hassell. . . . . .2 New Burlington Street.
Goody & Johns. . . . . .2 Clifford St., Bond St., W.
Hill Brothers . . . . .3 Old Bond Street.
Humphreys, John . . . . .3 Haymarket.
Kimpton, Henry . . . . .105 Strand.
Kino, N. M. . . . . .87 Regent Street, W.
Brown, Ambrose. . . . . .50 Strand, W.
Parfitt, Roberts, & Parfitt. . . . . .75 Jermyn Street, W.
Ralph & Son . . . . .150 Strand.
Samuel Brothers . . . . .50 Ludgate Hill.

TRUNK-MAKERS.

Allen, John William. . . . . .37 Strand.
Brewer, W. S. & Son. . . . . .120 Oxford Street.
Cave, H. J. & Sons . . . . .74, 76, 78 Wigmore Street.
Hill & Millard . . . . .21 Villiers Street, Strand.

Aldred, Thomas.............126 Oxford Street and Bur-
                    lington Arcade.
Cadman, Charles S..........Burlington Arcade.
Sangster & Co..............140 Regent Street.
Smith, James...............1, 2 Saville Pl., Regent St.
Milligen, Charles..........47 Strand, West.

WINE-MERCHANTS.

W. & A. Gilbey.............(See advertisement.)
George M. Innes............69 Strand, W.C.

NOTE. — In compiling the foregoing, care has been taken to avoid, as far as possible, placing on the list of London tradesmen recommended to Americans the name of any firm unknown to the Editor himself. It would be quite impossible to draw any hard and fast line by which ladies and gentlemen should be guided in making their purchases in London. The Editor believes that London tradesmen, as a class, are thoroughly honorable, fair-dealing, trustworthy, and courteous, — as much so as any other section of the business community of the English capital; and he feels the utmost confidence, therefore, in recommending any firm in the above list, from the fact that he has personal knowledge of their fitness to deal with strangers. But he would impress upon American visitors, nevertheless, the desirability of their being guided entirely by what it suits them to buy, and what it suits them to pay, and not by this or that person's recommendation to deal exclusively with one individual. Nearly every thing is very much cheaper in England than it is in the United States; but in London, cheapness may oftentimes be very dearly purchased at the cost of goodness. Above all, the Editor strongly advises American strangers to London not to be led astray by specious advertisements framed to entrap the unwary; and he would take it as a special favor to himself, in order to add to the value and reliability of this London Directory for American Travellers, if instances of extortion and misdealing on the part of any firm appearing or advertising in its pages were reported to him, in order to prevent their names being included in any future edition of the book.

HINTS TO AMERICANS.

Always see that your baggage is labelled to its destination, when travelling by rail, before starting. Baggage is not checked.

On arrival at any railway-station, call a porter; tell him to engage a cab forthwith, and to look after your baggage.

Do not bargain with the cabman. Request him to drive your party to the hotel you have selected, and, on arrival there, desire the hall porter of the hotel to settle with the cabman. By this means you avoid all altercation.

To find your way from point to point in London, bear in mind that the great thoroughfares (a) Cornhill, Cheapside, Newgate Street, and Oxford Street, and (b) Cornhill, Cheapside, Ludgate Hill, Strand, run from east to west to Hyde Park north and south; and that Regent Street strikes their centre near Charing Cross from south to north.

Always carry a certain amount of small change about with you, but not much money.

In any difficulty, consult a policeman.

In travelling by rail, and intending to return the same day, always buy a return-ticket. Return-tickets are available on almost all lines of railroad from Saturday to Monday morning inclusive.

Saturday is the aristocratic day for sight-seeing.

The hours of business, during which all offices, banks, &c., are open, are 10 to 4. Look out for Bank Holidays.

If you are in a hurry to go anywhere, call a Hansom-cab, and don't call one off the rank if the distance is short. It is unfair to the cabman.

Hotel proprietors will always recommend trustworthy tradesmen, on application.

In making purchases, have in mind that "best" is economy in the long-run. Ladies will generally see the latest fashions in dress from Paris at the West End of London; and gentlemen, the best styles in clothes.

If you leave any article either in an omnibus or cab, apply as soon as possible at the Police Office, Scotland Yard, opposite the Admiralty, Whitehall.

Never attempt to enter or leave a railway-carriage when the train is in motion. Railway companies in England are exceedingly strict on this point; and persons infringing the rule are liable to be prosecuted, and detained on their journey.

To find addresses, consult the London Post-Office Directory.

The proper hours for calling at private houses are from 2 to 6.

The dinner-hour in England, for the professional and upper classes, varies from 5 to 8, P.M. Guests should arrive not later than five minutes before the time named. In England, the gentlemen never hand the ladies from *table*, but remain by themselves.

It is absolutely essential to wear evening dress in attending the opera. Ladies are not permitted to wear bonnets.

In requesting permission to view any of the private galleries or mansions, always write to the owner.

CABS IN LONDON.

It should be generally understood that the safest plan, when in any doubt about a fare at a railroad-station, hotel, theatre, or other place of public amusement, is to ask one of the hackney carriage attendants (men in uniform), or the policeman on duty, to inform you of the proper fare. Tables of fares are posted conspicuously outside all railroad-stations, hotels, and theatres ; and there is really not the slightest necessity for a stranger submitting to any extortion from a cabman, if the course here suggested be followed.

The American in London will be gratified at the ease with which a cab can be had in any part of the city. "Call a cab" does not imply, as in many parts of New York and Boston, sending to a stable, and taking your chance of finding a vehicle in. In London, cab-stands, and cabs moving about, are to be seen everywhere. A shrill whistle, an upraised finger, a penny to a ragged boy, and a cab is at the curbstone in an instant. At the railroad-stations, and other places, as mentioned above, the arrangements for passengers are admirable ; and the confusion in some American cities (almost running fight), which the traveller is obliged to undergo with hack-drivers, is avoided. At the doors of theatres and other places of amusement, a good cab may always be had at the close of performance, and with speed, by the aid of two or three pence to the cab-porter or boys in waiting.

THE CAB-REGULATIONS OF LONDON ARE AS FOLLOWS : —

Fares by
Distance.

If hired and discharged *within* a Four Mile Circle from
Charing Cross, for any distance not exceeding two *s. d.*
miles,   1 0
And for every additional mile, or part of a mile,   0 6
If hired *outside* the Four Mile Circle, wherever dis-
charged, for the first and each succeeding mile, or part
of a mile,   1 0
If hired *within*, but discharged *outside*, the Four Mile   1 0
Circle, not exceeding one mile,   1 0
Exceeding one mile, then for each mile within the
circle,   0 6
And for each mile, or part of a mile, outside,   1 0

Fares by
Time.

Inside the Four Mile Circle. Four-wheeled cabs, for one *s. d.*
hour or less,   2 0
Two-wheeled cabs,   2 6
For every additional quarter of an hour, or part of a
quarter, four-wheeled cab,   0 8
If a two-wheeled cab,   0 6
If hired *outside* the Circle, wherever discharged, for one
hour or less,   2 6
If above one hour, then for every quarter of an hour or
less,   0 8
If hired *within*, but discharged *outside*, the Four Mile
Circle, the same.

EXTRA PAYMENTS. — *Hirers of cabs should be particular in
noticing these regulations, as disputes generally arise from their
not being clearly understood.*

Fares by
Distance
or by Time.

LUGGAGE. — For each package carried outside the *s. d.*
carriage,   0 2
EXTRA PERSONS. — For each above two,   0 6
For each child under ten years old,   0 3

By Distance,
waiting.

For every 15 minutes completed, —   *s. d.*
If hired within the Four Mile Circle, four wheels,   0 6
Two wheels,   0 8
If hired without Circle, two or four wheels,   0 8

4

GENERAL REGULATIONS. — Fares are according to distance or time, at the option of the hirer, expressed at the commencement of the hiring; if not otherwise expressed, the fare to be paid according to distance.

Driver is not compelled to hire his carriage for a fare according to time, at any hour after eight o'clock in the evening, and before six o'clock in the morning.

Agreement to pay more than legal fare is not binding: any sum paid beyond the fare may be recovered back.

Driver not to charge more than the sum agreed on for driving a distance, although such distance be exceeded by the driver.

If the driver agreed beforehand to take any sum less than the proper fare, the penalty for exacting or demanding more than the sum agreed upon is 40s.

The proprietor of every hackney carriage shall keep distinctly painted, both on the inside and outside, a table of fares: and the driver shall have with him, and, when required, produce, the Authorized Book of Fares.

In case of any dispute between the hirer and driver, the hirer may require the driver to drive to the nearest metropolitan police court or justice room, when the complaint may be determined by the sitting magistrate without summons; or. if no police court or justice room be open at the time, then to the nearest police station, where the complaint shall be entered, and tried by the magistrate at his next sitting.

Every driver of any hackney carriage shall, when hired, deliver to the hirer a card printed according to the directions of the commissioner of police.

All property left in any hackney carriage shall be deposited by the driver at the nearest police station within twenty-four hours, if not sooner claimed by the owner; such property to be returned to the person who shall prove to the satisfaction of the commissioner of police that the same belonged to him, on payment of all expenses incurred, and of such reasonable sum to the driver as the commissioner shall award.

CAB-FARES TO OR FROM	Acacia Road, St. John's Wood.	Adelaide Wharf, London Bridge.	Bank of England.	Berners Street, Oxford Street.	Blackfriars Road, Christ Ch'urch.	Black Lion, Bayswater.	Blackwall Railway.	Brydges Street, Covent Garden.	Buckingham Gate for Palace Hotel.	Canonbury Place, Islington.
	s. d.	s. d.	s. d.	s. d.	s. d.	s. d.	s. d.	s. d.	s. d.	s. d.
Albany Street	1 0	2 0	2 0	1 0	2 0	1 6	2 0	1 6	1 6	2 0
Aldersgate Street	2 6	1 0	1 0	1 0	1 0	2 6	1 0	1 0	1 0	1 6
BakerSt.,Portm'nSq.,KingSt.	1 0	2 0	2 0	1 0	1 6	1 0	2 0	1 0	1 0	2 0
British Museum	1 6	1 6	1 0	1 0	1 0	1 6	1 6	1 0	1 0	1 6
Charing Cross	2 0	1 6	1 0	1 0	1 0	1 6	1 6	1 0	1 0	2 0
Cheapside, Wood Street	2 6	1 0	1 0	1 0	1 0	2 6	1 0	1 0	1 6	1 6
Downing Street, Whitehall.	2 0	1 6	1 6	1 0	1 0	2 0	1 6	1 0	1 0	2 0
Elephant and Castle	2 6	1 0	1 0	1 6	1 0	2 6	1 0	1 0	1 0	2 0
Exeter Hall, Strand	2 0	1 0	1 0	1 0	1 0	2 0	1 6	1 0	1 0	2 0
Fleet Street, Fetter Lane	2 0	1 0	1 0	1 0	1 0	2 0	1 0	1 0	1 0	1 6
Gower Street, New Road	1 6	1 6	1 6	1 0	1 6	1 6	2 0	1 0	1 6	1 6
Guildhall, City	2 6	1 0	1 0	1 6	1 0	2 6	1 0	1 0	1 6	1 6
Hanover Square	1 6	1 6	1 6	1 0	1 6	1 0	2 0	1 0	1 0	2 0
Hyde Park Square	1 0	2 6	2 0	1 0	2 0	1 0	2 6	1 6	1 6	2 6
Islington, "The Angel"	2 0	1 6	1 0	1 6	1 0	2 6	1 6	1 0	2 0	1 0
Kensington Church	2 0	3 0	2 6	2 0	2 6	1 0	3 0	2 0	1 6	3 6
King William Street, City	2 6	1 0	1 0	1 6	1 0	2 6	1 0	1 0	1 6	1 6
Leicester Square	1 6	1 6	1 6	1 0	1 0	1 6	1 6	1 0	1 0	2 0
Ludgate Hill, Farringdon St.	2 0	1 0	1 0	1 0	1 0	2 0	1 0	1 0	1 6	1 6
Manchester Square	1 0	2 0	2 0	1 0	1 6	1 0	2 0	1 0	1 0	2 0
Moorgate Street	2 6	1 0	1 0	1 6	1 0	2 6	2 0	1 0	2 0	1 6
Notting Hill Square	1 6	3 0	3 0	2 0	2 6	1 0	3 0	2 0	2 0	3 0
Old Bailey, Cen. Crim. Court	2 6	1 0	1 0	1 0	1 0	2 0	1 0	1 0	1 6	1 6
Oxford Street, Regent Circus	1 6	1 6	1 6	1 0	1 6	1 0	1 6	1 0	1 0	2 0
Pall Mall, George Street	1 6	1 6	1 6	1 0	1 0	1 6	1 6	1 0	1 0	2 0
Piccadilly, Half Moon Street	1 6	1 6	1 6	1 0	1 6	1 6	2 0	1 0	1 0	2 0
Post Office, St. Martin's-le-Grand	2 6	1 0	1 0	1 0	1 0	2 6	1 0	1 0	1 6	1 6
Railways, Blackwall	3 0	1 0	1 0	1 0	1 0	2 6	—	1 0	2 0	1 6
" Eastern Counties	3 0	1 0	1 0	1 6	1 6	3 0	1 0	1 6	2 0	1 6
" Great Northern	1 6	1 6	1 6	1 0	1 6	2 0	1 6	1 0	2 0	1 0
" Great Western	1 0	2 6	2 6	1 6	2 0	1 0	2 6	1 6	1 6	2 6
" North-Western	1 6	2 0	1 6	1 0	1 6	1 6	2 0	1 0	1 6	1 6
" South-Eastern	3 0	1 0	1 0	1 6	1 0	3 0	1 0	1 0	1 6	2 0
" South-Western	2 6	1 0	1 0	1 0	1 0	2 0	1 0	1 0	1 0	2 0
Regent Street, Piccadilly	1 6	1 6	1 6	1 0	1 0	1 6	1 6	1 0	1 0	2 0
St. Paul's Churchyard	2 6	1 0	1 0	1 0	1 0	2 6	1 0	1 0	1 6	1 6
Theatres, Adelphi	2 0	1 0	1 0	1 0	1 0	2 0	1 6	1 0	1 0	2 0
" Covent Garden	2 0	1 0	1 0	1 0	1 0	1 6	1 6	1 0	1 0	1 6
" Drury Lane	2 0	1 0	1 0	1 0	1 0	2 0	1 6	—	1 0	2 0
" Haymarket	1 6	1 6	1 6	1 0	1 0	1 6	1 6	1 0	1 0	2 0
" Lyceum	2 0	1 0	1 0	1 0	1 0	2 0	1 0	1 0	1 0	2 0
" Princess's	1 6	1 6	1 6	1 0	1 0	1 6	1 6	1 0	1 0	2 0
" Strand	2 0	1 0	1 0	1 0	1 0	2 0	1 0	1 0	1 0	1 6
Tottenham Ct.Rd.,Francis St.	1 6	1 6	1 6	1 0	1 6	1 6	1 6	1 0	1 6	1 6
Tower of London	3 0	1 0	1 0	1 6	1 0	2 6	1 0	1 0	2 0	2 0
Victoria Station, Pimlico	2 0	1 6	1 6	1 0	1 0	2 0	2 0	1 0	1 0	2 6
Waterloo Br., Wellington St.	2 0	1 0	1 0	1 0	1 0	2 0	1 6	1 0	1 0	2 0
Westminster Hall	2 0	1 6	1 6	1 0	1 0	2 0	1 6	1 0	1 0	2 6
York and Albany, Regent's Park	1 0	2 0	2 0	2 0	2 0	2 0	2 0	1 6	1 6	2 0
Zoölogical Gardens, Regent's Park	1 0	2 6	2 0	2 0	2 0	1 6	2 6	1 6	2 0	2 0

CAB-FARES TO OR FROM	Chelsea, Cremorne Gardn's	City-Road Cab-Stand.	Conduit Street, Regent Street.	Cumberland Gate, Hyde Park.	Dover-Road Cab-Stand.	E. Counties Rlw., Shoreditch.	Edgware Road, Aberdeen Place.	Fulham Road, Pelham Crescent.	Goswell St., City, Cab-Stand.	Gt. Northern Rd., King's Cross.
	s. d.	s. d.	s. d.	s. d.	s. d.	s. d.	s. d.	s. d.	s. d.	s. d.
Albany Street	2 6	1 6	1 0	1 6	2 0	2 6	1 6	2 0	1 6	1 0
Aldersgate Street	2 6	1 0	1 6	1 6	1 0	1 0	2 0	2 6	1 0	1 0
BakerSt,Portm'nSq.,KingSt.	2 0	2 0	1 0	1 0	2 0	2 0	1 0	1 6	2 0	1 6
British Museum	2 6	1 0	1 0	1 0	1 6	1 6	1 6	1 6	1 0	1 0
Charing Cross	2 0	1 6	1 0	1 0	1 6	1 6	1 6	1 6	1 0	1 6
Cheapside, Wood Street	2 6	1 0	1 6	1 6	1 0	1 0	2 6	2 6	1 0	1 0
Downing Street, Whitehall	2 0	1 6	1 0	1 6	1 0	2 0	2 0	1 6	1 6	1 6
Elephant and Castle	2 6	1 6	1 6	2 0	1 0	1 6	2 6	2 0	1 6	2 0
Exeter Hall, Strand	2 0	1 6	1 0	1 6	1 0	1 6	2 0	1 6	1 0	1 0
Fleet Street, Fetter Lane	2 6	1 0	1 0	1 6	1 0	1 0	2 0	2 0	1 0	1 0
Gower Street, New Road	2 6	1 6	1 0	1 0	1 6	2 0	1 6	2 0	1 6	1 0
Guildhall, City	3 0	1 0	1 6	2 0	1 0	1 0	2 6	2 6	1 0	1 6
Hanover Square	2 0	1 6	1 0	1 0	1 6	2 0	1 0	1 6	1 6	1 0
Hyde Park Square	2 0	2 0	1 0	1 0	2 6	2 6	1 0	1 6	2 0	1 6
Islington, "The Angel"	3 0	1 0	1 6	2 0	1 6	1 0	2 0	2 6	1 0	1 0
Kensington Church	1 6	3 0	1 6	1 6	2 6	3 0	1 6	1 0	2 6	2 6
King William Street, City	3 0	1 0	1 6	2 0	1 0	1 0	2 6	2 6	1 0	1 6
Leicester Square	2 0	1 6	1 0	1 0	1 6	1 6	1 6	1 6	1 6	1 0
Ludgate Hill, Farringdon St.	2 6	1 0	1 0	1 6	1 0	1 0	2 0	2 0	1 0	1 0
Manchester Square	2 0	2 0	1 0	1 0	2 0	2 0	1 0	1 6	1 6	1 0
Moorgate Street	3 0	1 0	1 6	2 0	1 0	1 0	2 6	2 6	1 0	1 6
Notting Hill Square	2 0	3 0	1 6	1 0	3 0	3 0	1 0	1 6	2 6	2 6
Old Bailey, Cen. Crim. Court	2 6	1 0	1 6	1 6	1 0	1 0	2 0	2 0	1 0	1 0
Oxford Street, Regent Circus	2 0	1 6	1 0	1 0	1 6	2 0	1 0	1 6	1 6	1 0
Pall Mall, George Street	1 6	1 6	1 0	1 0	1 6	2 0	1 6	1 6	1 6	1 6
Piccadilly, Half Moon Street	1 6	2 0	1 0	1 0	1 6	2 0	1 6	1 6	1 6	1 6
Post Office, St. Martin's-le-Grand	2 6	1 0	1 6	1 6	1 0	1 0	2 0	2 6	1 0	1 0
Railways, Blackwall	3 0	1 0	2 0	2 0	1 0	1 0	2 6	2 6	1 0	1 6
" Eastern Counties	3 6	1 0	2 0	2 0	1 0	—	3 0	3 0	1 0	1 6
" Great Northern	3 0	1 0	1 0	1 6	2 0	1 6	1 6	2 6	1 0	—
" Great Western	2 0	2 6	1 0	1 0	2 6	2 6	1 0	2 0	2 6	1 6
" North-Western	2 6	1 6	1 0	1 6	2 0	2 0	1 6	2 0	1 0	1 0
" South-Eastern	2 6	1 0	2 0	2 0	1 0	1 0	2 6	2 6	1 0	1 6
" South-Western	2 0	1 6	1 0	1 6	1 0	1 6	2 0	2 0	1 0	1 6
Regent Street, Piccadilly	2 0	1 6	1 0	1 0	1 6	2 0	1 6	1 6	1 6	1 6
St. Paul's Churchyard	2 6	1 0	1 6	1 6	1 0	1 0	2 0	2 0	1 0	1 0
Theatres, Adelphi	2 0	1 6	1 0	1 0	1 0	1 6	1 6	1 6	1 0	1 0
" Covent Garden	2 0	1 6	1 0	1 0	1 0	1 6	1 6	1 6	1 0	1 0
" Drury Lane	2 0	1 6	1 0	1 0	1 0	1 6	1 6	1 6	1 0	1 0
" Haymarket	2 0	1 6	1 0	1 0	1 6	2 0	1 6	1 6	1 0	1 0
" Lyceum	2 0	1 6	1 0	1 0	1 0	1 6	2 0	1 6	1 0	1 0
" Princess's	2 0	1 6	1 0	1 0	1 6	1 6	1 6	1 6	1 0	1 0
" Strand	2 0	1 6	1 0	1 6	1 0	1 6	2 0	2 0	1 0	1 0
Tottenham-ct.Rd.,Francis St.	2 6	1 6	1 0	1 0	1 6	2 0	1 6	2 0	1 6	1 0
Tower of London	3 0	1 0	2 0	2 0	1 0	1 0	2 6	2 6	1 0	1 6
Victoria Station, Pimlico	1 6	2 0	1 0	1 6	1 6	2 0	2 0	1 0	1 6	2 0
Waterloo Br., Wellington St.	2 0	1 6	1 0	1 6	1 0	1 6	2 0	1 6	1 0	1 0
Westminster Hall	2 0	2 0	1 0	1 6	1 0	2 0	2 0	1 6	1 6	1 6
York and Albany, Regent's Park	3 0	1 6	1 0	1 6	2 0	2 0	1 0	2 0	1 6	1 0
Zoölogical Gardens, Regent's Park	3 0	2 0	1 6	1 6	2 6	2 6	1 0	2 6	2 0	1 0

CAB-FARES TO OR FROM	Great Western Railway.	Grosvenor Street, West.	Guildford Street, Foundling Hosp'l.	Hampstead Road, Cab-Stand.	Haymarket.	High St., Camberwell.	High St., Camden Town.	Holborn, Chancery Lane.	Islington, Clark's Place.	Kennington Cross.
	s. d.	s. d.	s. d.	s. d.	s. d.	s. d.	s. d.	s. d.	s. d.	s. d.
Albany Street	1 6	1 6	1 0	1 0	1 0	3 0	1 0	1 6	1 6	2 0
Aldersgate Street	1 6	2 0	1 0	2 0	1 0	2 0	1 6	1 0	1 0	1 6
BakerSt.,Portm'nSq.,KingSt.	1 0	1 0	1 0	1 6	1 0	2 6	1 6	1 6	1 6	2 0
British Museum	1 6	1 6	1 0	1 6	1 0	2 0	1 0	1 0	1 0	1 6
Charing Cross	1 6	1 0	1 0	1 6	1 0	2 0	1 6	1 0	1 6	1 0
Cheapside, Wood Street	2 0	1 6	1 0	2 0	1 0	2 0	1 6	1 0	1 0	1 6
Downing Street, Whitehall	2 0	1 0	1 0	2 0	1 0	2 0	1 6	1 0	1 0	1 0
Elephant and Castle	2 6	1 6	1 6	2 6	1 0	1 0	2 0	1 0	1 6	1 0
Exeter Hall, Strand	2 0	1 0	1 0	1 6	1 0	2 0	1 6	1 0	1 6	1 0
Fleet Street, Fetter Lane	2 0	1 6	1 0	2 0	1 0	2 0	1 6	1 0	1 6	1 6
Gower Street, New Road	1 6	1 6	1 0	1 0	1 0	2 6	1 0	1 0	1 0	2 0
Guildhall, City	2 6	2 0	1 0	2 0	1 6	2 0	2 0	1 0	1 0	1 6
Hanover Square	1 0	1 0	1 0	1 6	1 0	2 6	1 6	1 0	1 6	1 6
Hyde Park Square	1 0	1 0	1 6	1 6	1 6	2 6	1 6	1 6	2 0	2 0
Islington, "The Angel"	2 0	2 0	1 0	1 6	1 6	2 6	1 0	1 0	—	2 0
Kensington Church	1 0	1 6	2 6	2 6	1 6	3 0	2 6	2 0	3 0	2 6
King William Street, City	2 6	2 0	1 0	2 0	1 6	1 6	2 0	1 0	1 0	1 0
Leicester Square	1 6	1 0	1 0	1 6	1 0	2 0	1 6	1 0	1 6	1 6
Ludgate Hill, Farringdon St	2 0	1 6	1 0	2 0	1 0	1 6	1 6	1 0	1 0	1 0
Manchester Square	1 0	1 0	1 0	1 6	1 0	2 6	1 6	1 0	1 6	2 0
Moorgate Street	2 6	2 0	1 0	2 0	1 6	2 0	2 0	1 0	1 0	1 6
Notting Hill Square	1 0	2 0	2 0	2 6	2 0	3 6	2 6	2 0	2 6	3 0
Old Bailey, Cen. Crim. Court	2 0	1 6	1 0	2 0	1 0	2 0	1 6	1 0	1 0	1 6
Oxford Street, Regent Circus	1 0	1 0	1 0	1 6	1 0	2 6	1 0	1 0	1 6	1 6
Pall Mall, George Street	1 0	1 0	1 0	2 0	1 0	2 0	1 6	1 0	1 6	1 6
Piccadilly, Half Moon Street	1 6	1 0	1 0	2 0	1 0	2 0	1 6	1 0	1 6	1 6
Post Office, St. Martin's-le-Grand	2 0	1 6	1 0	2 0	1 0	2 0	1 6	1 0	1 0	1 6
Railways, Blackwall	2 6	2 0	1 6	2 6	1 6	2 0	2 0	1 0	1 6	1 6
" Eastern Counties	2 6	2 6	1 6	2 6	2 0	2 0	2 0	1 0	1 6	1 6
" Great Northern	1 6	2 0	1 0	1 0	1 6	2 6	1 0	1 0	1 0	2 0
" Great Western	—	1 6	2 0	2 0	1 6	3 0	2 0	2 0	2 0	2 6
" North-Western	1 6	2 0	1 0	1 0	1 0	2 6	1 0	1 0	1 0	2 0
" South-Eastern	2 6	1 6	1 6	2 6	1 6	1 6	2 0	1 0	1 6	1 0
" South-Western	2 0	1 0	1 0	2 0	1 0	1 6	1 6	1 0	1 6	1 0
Regent Street, Piccadilly	1 6	1 0	1 0	1 6	1 0	2 0	1 6	1 0	1 6	1 6
St. Paul's Churchyard	2 0	1 6	1 0	2 0	1 0	2 0	1 6	1 0	1 0	1 6
Theatres, Adelphi	1 6	1 0	1 0	2 0	1 0	2 0	1 6	1 0	1 6	1 0
" Covent Garden	1 6	1 0	1 0	1 6	1 0	2 0	1 6	1 0	1 0	1 0
" Drury Lane	1 6	1 0	1 0	1 6	1 0	2 0	1 6	1 0	1 6	1 0
" Haymarket	1 6	1 0	1 0	1 6	1 0	2 0	1 6	1 0	1 6	1 0
" Lyceum	1 6	1 0	1 0	1 6	1 0	2 0	1 6	1 0	1 0	1 0
" Princess's	1 6	1 0	1 0	1 6	1 0	2 0	1 0	1 0	1 6	1 6
" Strand	2 0	1 0	1 0	2 0	1 0	2 0	1 6	1 0	1 0	1 0
Tottenham-ct. Rd.,Francis St.	1 6	1 6	1 0	1 0	1 0	2 6	1 0	1 0	1 0	1 6
Tower of London	2 6	2 0	1 6	2 6	1 6	2 0	2 0	1 0	1 0	1 6
Victoria Station, Pimlico	2 0	1 0	1 6	2 0	1 0	1 6	2 0	1 6	2 0	1 0
Waterloo Br., Wellington St.	2 0	1 0	1 0	1 6	1 0	1 6	1 6	1 0	1 6	1 0
Westminster Hall	2 0	1 0	1 6	2 0	1 0	1 6	1 6	1 0	2 0	1 0
York and Albany, Regent's Park	1 6	2 0	1 0	1 0	1 6	3 0	1 0	1 6	1 6	2 6
Zoölogical Gardens, Regent's Park	1 6	2 0	1 6	1 0	1 6	3 0	1 0	1 6	1 6	2 6

CAB-FARES TO OR FROM	King's Road, Gray's Inn	Knightsbridge Green	Leicester Square	Manor Place, Walworth	North-Western Railway	Old Kent Road, Bricklayers'Arms	Oxford Street, Orchard Street	Palace Yard, Westminster	Park Lane, Stanhope Gate	Penton Street, Pentonville
	s. d.	s. d.	s. d.	s. d.	s. d.	s. d.	s. d.	s. d.	s. d.	s. d.
Albany Street	1 6	1 6	1 0	2 6	1 0	2 6	1 0	1 6	1 6	1 6
Aldersgate Street	1 0	2 0	1 0	1 6	1 6	1 6	1 6	1 6	1 6	1 0
BakerSt.,Portm'nSq.,KingSt.	1 6	1 0	1 0	2 0	1 0	2 6	1 0	1 6	1 0	1 6
British Museum	1 0	1 6	1 0	1 6	1 0	1 6	1 0	1 0	1 0	1 0
Charing Cross	1 0	1 0	1 0	1 6	1 0	1 6	1 0	1 0	1 0	1 6
Cheapside, Wood Street	1 0	2 0	1 0	1 0	1 6	1 0	1 6	1 6	1 6	1 0
Downing Street, Whitehall	1 0	1 0	1 0	1 0	1 6	1 6	1 0	1 0	1 0	1 6
Elephant and Castle	1 6	2 0	1 0	1 0	2 0	1 6	2 0	1 0	2 0	1 6
Exeter Hall, Strand	1 0	1 0	0 6	1 0	1 0	1 6	1 0	1 0	1 0	1 6
Fleet Street, Fetter Lane	1 0	1 6	1 0	1 6	1 0	1 6	1 6	1 0	1 6	1 0
Gower Street, New Road	1 0	1 6	1 0	2 0	1 0	2 0	1 0	1 0	1 0	1 0
Guildhall, City	1 0	2 0	1 0	1 0	1 6	1 0	1 6	1 6	2 0	1 0
Hanover Square	1 0	1 0	1 0	2 0	1 0	2 0	1 0	1 0	1 0	1 6
Hyde Park Square	1 6	1 0	1 6	2 6	1 0	2 6	1 0	1 6	1 0	2 0
Islington, "The Angel"	1 0	1 0	1 6	2 0	1 0	2 0	1 0	1 6	2 0	1 0
Kensington Church	2 0	1 0	1 6	2 6	2 0	3 0	1 6	2 0	1 6	2 6
King William Street, City	1 0	2 0	1 0	1 0	1 6	1 0	2 0	1 0	2 0	1 6
Leicester Square	1 0	1 0	—	1 6	1 0	1 6	1 0	1 0	1 0	1 6
Ludgate Hill, Farringdon St.	1 0	1 6	1 0	1 0	1 6	1 0	1 6	1 0	1 0	1 0
Manchester Square	1 0	1 0	1 0	2 0	1 0	2 0	2 0	1 6	1 0	1 6
Moorgate Street	1 0	2 0	1 6	1 6	1 0	1 0	1 0	1 6	2 0	1 0
Notting Hill Square	2 6	1 6	2 0	3 0	2 0	3 0	3 0	2 6	1 6	2 6
Old Bailey, Cen. Crim. Court	1 0	1 6	1 0	1 0	1 6	1 6	1 6	1 0	1 6	1 0
Oxford Street, Regent Circus	1 0	1 0	1 0	2 0	1 0	2 0	1 0	1 0	1 0	1 6
Pall Mall, George Street	1 0	1 0	1 0	1 6	1 6	1 6	1 0	1 0	1 0	1 6
Piccadilly, Half Moon Street	1 0	1 0	1 0	2 0	1 6	2 0	1 0	1 0	1 0	1 6
Post Office, St. Martin's-le-Grand	1 0	2 0	1 0	1 6	1 6	1 0	1 6	1 6	1 6	1 0
Railways, Blackwall	1 0	2 6	1 6	1 6	2 0	1 0	2 0	1 6	2 0	1 6
" Eastern Counties	1 6	2 6	1 6	1 6	2 0	1 6	2 0	2 0	2 6	1 0
" Great Northern	1 0	2 0	1 6	2 0	1 0	2 0	1 6	1 6	1 6	1 0
" Great Western	2 0	1 6	1 6	2 6	1 6	3 0	1 0	2 0	1 0	2 0
" North-Western	1 0	1 6	1 0	2 0	—	2 0	1 0	1 6	1 6	1 0
" South-Eastern	1 0	2 0	1 6	1 0	2 0	1 0	2 0	1 6	2 0	1 6
" South-Western	1 0	1 6	1 0	1 0	1 6	1 0	1 6	1 0	1 6	1 6
Regent Street, Piccadilly	1 0	1 0	1 0	1 6	1 0	1 6	1 0	1 0	1 0	1 6
St. Paul's Churchyard	1 0	1 6	1 0	1 6	1 6	1 6	1 6	1 0	1 6	1 0
Theatres, Adelphi	1 0	1 0	1 0	1 6	1 0	1 6	1 0	1 0	1 0	1 6
" Covent Garden	1 0	1 0	1 0	1 6	1 0	1 6	1 0	1 0	1 0	1 0
" Drury Lane	1 0	1 6	1 0	1 6	1 0	1 6	1 0	1 0	1 0	1 0
" Haymarket	1 0	1 0	1 0	1 6	1 0	1 6	1 0	1 0	1 0	1 6
" Lyceum	1 0	1 6	1 0	1 0	1 0	1 6	1 0	1 0	1 0	1 0
" Princess's	1 0	1 0	1 0	1 6	1 0	2 0	1 0	1 0	1 0	1 6
" Strand	1 0	1 6	1 0	1 6	1 0	1 6	1 0	1 0	1 0	1 0
Tottenham-ct.Rd.,FrancisSt.	1 0	1 6	1 0	1 6	1 0	2 0	1 0	1 0	1 0	1 0
Tower of London	1 0	2 0	1 6	1 6	2 0	1 0	2 0	1 6	2 0	1 6
Victoria Station, Pimlico	1 6	1 0	1 0	1 6	1 6	1 0	1 0	1 0	1 0	2 0
Waterloo Br.,Wellington St.	1 0	1 6	1 0	1 0	1 6	1 0	1 0	1 0	1 0	1 6
Westminster Hall	1 0	1 0	1 0	1 0	1 6	1 6	1 6	—	1 0	1 6
York and Albany, Regent's Park	1 6	2 0	1 6	2 6	0 6	2 6	1 0	1 6	1 6	1 0
Zoölogical Gardens, Regent's Park	1 6	2 0	1 6	2 6	1 0	2 6	1 0	2 0	1 6	1 0

CAB-FARES TO OR FROM	Piccadilly, "The Albany."	Piccadilly, Apsley House.	Pitfield Street, Hoxton.	Portland Road, New Road.	Richmond Road, Islington.	St. Clement's Church, Strand.	St. Luke's, Old Street.	St. Paul's Church-yard.	Sloane Square.	Southampton Row.
	s. d.	s. d.	s. d.	s. d.	s. d.	s. d.	s. d.	s. d.	s. d.	s. d.
Albany Street	1 0	1 6	2 0	1 0	1 6	1 6	2 0	2 0	2 0	1 0
Aldersgate Street	1 6	1 6	1 0	1 6	1 0	1 0	1 0	1 0	2 0	1 0
BakerSt.,Portm'n Sq.,KingSt.	1 0	1 0	2 0	1 0	1 6	1 6	2 0	1 6	1 6	1 0
British Museum	1 0	1 0	1 6	1 0	1 0	1 0	1 0	1 0	1 6	1 0
Charing Cross	1 0	1 0	1 6	1 0	1 6	1 0	1 6	1 0	1 0	1 0
Cheapside, Wood Street	1 6	1 6	1 0	1 0	1 6	1 0	1 0	1 0	2 0	1 0
Downing Street, Whitehall	1 0	1 0	2 0	1 0	2 0	1 0	2 0	1 0	1 0	1 0
Elephant and Castle	1 6	1 6	1 6	1 6	2 0	1 0	1 6	1 0	1 6	1 6
Exeter Hall, Strand	1 0	1 0	1 6	1 0	1 6	1 0	1 0	1 0	1 6	1 0
Fleet Street, Fetter Lane	1 0	1 6	1 0	1 0	1 0	1 0	1 0	1 0	1 6	1 0
Gower Street, New Road	1 0	1 6	1 6	1 0	1 0	1 0	1 6	1 6	2 0	1 0
Guildhall, City	1 6	2 0	1 6	1 6	1 6	1 0	1 0	1 0	2 0	1 0
Hanover Square	1 0	1 0	2 0	1 0	1 6	1 0	1 6	1 6	1 6	1 0
Hyde Park Square	1 0	1 0	2 0	1 0	2 0	1 6	2 0	2 0	1 6	1 6
Islington, "The Angel"	1 6	2 0	1 0	1 0	1 0	1 0	1 0	1 0	2 6	1 0
Kensington Church	1 6	1 0	3 0	2 0	3 0	2 0	3 0	2 6	1 6	2 0
King William Street, City	1 6	2 0	1 0	1 6	1 0	1 0	1 0	1 0	2 0	1 0
Leicester Square	1 0	1 0	1 6	1 0	1 6	1 0	1 6	1 0	1 6	1 0
Ludgate Hill, Farringdon St.	1 0	1 6	1 0	1 6	1 6	1 0	1 0	1 0	2 0	1 0
Manchester Square	1 0	1 0	2 0	1 0	1 6	1 6	2 0	1 6	1 6	1 0
Moorgate Street	1 6	2 0	1 0	1 6	1 6	1 0	1 0	1 0	2 6	1 0
Notting Hill Square	1 0	1 6	3 0	1 6	2 6	2 6	3 0	2 6	1 6	2 0
Old Bailey, Cen. Crim. Court.	1 0	1 6	1 0	1 6	1 0	1 0	1 0	1 0	2 0	1 0
Oxford Street, Regent Circus.	1 0	1 0	2 0	1 0	1 6	1 0	1 6	1 6	1 6	1 0
Pall Mall, George Street	1 0	1 0	2 0	1 0	2 0	1 0	1 6	1 0	1 0	1 0
Piccadilly, Half Moon Street	1 0	1 0	2 0	1 0	2 0	1 0	2 0	1 6	1 0	1 0
Post Office, St. Martin's-le-Grand	1 6	1 6	1 0	1 6	1 0	1 0	1 0	1 0	2 0	1 0
Railways, Blackwall	1 6	2 0	1 0	2 0	1 6	1 0	1 0	1 0	2 6	1 6
" Eastern Counties	2 0	2 0	1 0	2 0	1 6	1 6	1 0	1 0	2 6	1 6
" Great Northern	1 6	1 6	1 0	1 0	1 0	1 0	1 0	1 0	2 0	1 0
" Great Western	1 6	1 6	2 6	1 0	2 0	2 0	2 6	2 0	2 0	1 6
" North-Western	1 0	1 6	1 6	1 0	1 0	1 0	1 6	1 6	2 0	1 0
" South-Eastern	1 6	2 0	1 0	2 0	1 6	1 0	1 0	1 0	2 0	1 6
" South-Western	1 0	1 6	1 6	1 6	2 0	1 0	1 6	1 0	1 6	1 0
Regent Street, Piccadilly	1 0	1 0	2 0	1 0	1 6	1 0	1 6	1 0	1 0	1 0
St. Paul's Churchyard	1 0	1 6	1 0	1 6	1 6	1 0	1 0	—	2 0	1 0
Theatres, Adelphi	1 0	1 0	1 6	1 0	1 6	1 0	1 6	1 0	1 6	1 0
" Covent Garden	1 0	1 0	1 6	1 0	1 6	1 0	1 6	1 0	1 6	1 0
" Drury Lane	1 0	1 0	1 6	1 0	1 6	1 0	1 6	1 0	1 6	1 0
" Haymarket	1 0	1 0	2 0	1 0	1 6	1 0	1 6	1 0	1 0	1 0
" Lyceum	1 0	1 0	1 6	1 0	1 6	1 0	1 6	1 0	1 6	1 0
" Princess's	1 0	1 0	1 6	1 0	1 6	1 0	1 6	1 0	1 6	1 0
" Strand	1 0	1 0	1 6	1 0	1 6	1 0	1 0	1 0	1 6	1 0
Tottenham Ct.Rd.,Francis St.	1 0	1 0	1 6	1 0	1 0	1 0	1 6	1 0	1 6	1 0
Tower of London	1 6	2 0	1 0	2 0	1 6	1 0	1 6	1 0	2 6	1 6
Victoria Station, Pimlico	1 0	1 0	2 0	1 6	2 0	1 0	2 0	1 6	1 0	1 6
Waterloo Br., Wellington St.	1 0	1 0	1 6	1 0	1 6	1 0	1 6	1 0	1 6	1 0
Westminster Hall	1 0	1 0	2 0	1 0	2 0	1 0	2 0	1 6	1 0	1 6
York and Albany, Regent's Park	1 6	1 6	2 0	1 0	2 6	1 6	2 0	2 0	2 0	1 0
Zoölogical Gardens, Regent's Park	1 6	1 6	2 0	1 0	1 6	2 0	2 0	2 0	2 0	1 0

CAB-FARES TO OR FROM	South-Eastern Railway.	South-Western Railway.	Stockwell Place, Brixton.	Tottenham Ct. Rd., Francis Street.	Tower Hill, East Side.	Tower Hill, West Side.	Uxbridge Road, White Swan.	White Chapel, High Street.	Whitehall.	York and Albany, Regent's Park.
	s. d.	*s. d.*	*s. d.*	*s. d.*	*s. d.*	*s. d.*	*s. d.*	*s. d.*	*s. d.*	*s. d.*
Albany Street	2 6	1 6	2 6	1 0	2 6	2 0	1 6	2 6	1 6	1 0
Aldersgate Street	1 0	1 0	2 0	1 0	1 0	1 0	1 6	1 0	1 0	2 0
Baker St.,Portm'n Sq..King St.	2 0	1 6	2 6	1 0	2 6	2 0	1 0	2 6	1 0	1 0
British Museum	1 6	1 0	2 0	1 0	1 6	1 6	1 6	1 6	1 0	1 0
Charing Cross	1 6	1 0	1 6	1 0	1 6	1 6	1 6	1 6	1 0	1 6
Cheapside, Wood Street	1 0	1 0	2 0	1 6	1 0	1 0	2 0	1 0	1 0	2 0
Downing Street, Whitehall	1 6	1 0	1 6	1 0	2 0	1 6	1 6	2 0	1 0	1 6
Elephant and Castle	1 0	1 0	1 0	1 6	1 6	1 0	2 6	1 6	1 0	2 0
Exeter Hall, Strand	1 0	1 0	2 0	1 0	1 6	1 6	1 6	1 6	1 0	1 6
Fleet Street, Fetter Lane	1 0	1 0	2 0	1 0	1 0	1 0	2 0	1 0	1 0	1 6
Gower Street, New Road	2 0	1 6	2 6	1 0	2 0	2 0	1 6	2 0	1 0	1 0
Guildhall, City	1 0	1 0	2 0	1 6	1 0	1 0	2 0	1 0	1 6	2 0
Hanover Square	2 0	1 6	2 0	1 0	2 0	2 0	1 0	2 0	1 0	1 0
Hyde Park Square	2 6	2 0	2 6	1 0	2 6	2 6	1 0	2 6	1 6	1 6
Islington, "The Angel"	1 6	1 6	2 6	1 0	1 6	1 6	2 0	1 6	1 6	1 0
Kensington Church	3 0	2 6	2 6	2 0	3 0	3 0	1 0	3 0	2 0	2 6
King William Street, City	1 0	1 0	2 0	1 6	1 0	1 0	2 6	1 0	1 6	2 0
Leicester Square, N.W.	1 6	1 0	2 0	1 0	2 0	1 6	1 6	1 6	1 0	1 6
Ludgate Hill, Farringdon St.	1 0	1 0	2 0	1 0	1 0	1 0	2 0	1 0	1 0	1 6
Manchester Square	2 0	1 6	2 6	1 0	2 6	2 0	1 0	2 0	1 0	1 0
Moorgate Street	1 0	1 6	2 0	1 6	1 0	1 0	2 6	1 0	1 6	2 0
Notting Hill Square	3 0	2 6	3 0	2 0	3 6	3 0	1 0	3 0	2 0	2 0
Old Bailey, Cen. Crim. Court.	1 0	1 0	2 0	1 0	1 0	1 0	2 0	1 0	1 0	1 6
Oxford Street, Regent Circus.	2 0	1 0	2 0	1 0	2 0	2 0	1 0	2 0	1 0	1 0
Pall Mall, George Street	1 6	1 0	2 0	1 0	2 0	1 6	1 6	2 0	1 0	1 6
Piccadilly, Half Moon Street	2 0	1 0	2 0	1 0	2 0	2 0	1 0	2 0	1 0	1 6
Post Office, St. Martin's-le-Grand	1 0	1 0	2 0	1 0	1 0	1 0	2 0	1 0	1 0	2 0
Railways, Blackwall	1 0	1 6	2 0	1 6	1 0	1 0	2 6	1 0	1 6	2 0
" Eastern Counties	1 0	1 6	2 6	2 0	1 0	1 0	2 6	1 0	1 6	2 0
" Great Northern	1 6	1 6	2 6	1 0	2 0	1 6	1 6	2 0	1 6	1 0
" Great Western	2 6	2 0	2 6	1 6	3 0	2 6	1 0	3 0	1 6	1 6
" North-Western	2 0	1 6	2 6	1 0	2 0	2 0	1 6	2 0	1 0	1 0
" South-Eastern	—	1 0	1 6	1 6	1 0	1 0	2 6	1 0	1 6	2 6
" South-Western	1 0	—	1 6	1 6	1 0	1 0	2 0	1 6	1 0	2 0
Regent Street, Piccadilly	1 6	1 0	2 0	1 0	2 0	1 6	1 6	2 0	1 0	1 6
St. Paul's Churchyard	1 6	1 0	2 0	1 0	1 0	1 0	2 0	1 0	1 0	2 0
Theatres, Adelphi	1 6	1 0	2 0	1 0	1 6	1 6	1 6	1 6	1 0	1 6
" Covent Garden	1 6	1 0	2 0	1 6	1 6	1 6	1 6	1 6	1 0	1 6
" Drury Lane	1 6	1 0	2 0	1 6	1 6	1 6	1 6	1 6	1 0	1 6
" Haymarket	1 6	1 0	2 0	1 0	2 0	1 6	1 6	1 6	1 0	1 6
" Lyceum	1 0	1 0	2 0	1 0	1 6	1 0	1 6	1 6	1 0	1 6
" Princess's	1 6	1 0	2 0	1 0	2 0	1 6	1 6	2 0	1 0	1 0
" Strand	1 0	1 0	2 0	1 0	1 6	1 6	1 6	1 6	1 0	1 6
Tottenham Ct. Rd., Francis St.	1 6	1 0	2 0	—	2 0	1 6	2 0	1 0	1 0	1 0
Tower of London	1 6	1 6	2 0	1 6	1 0	—	2 6	1 0	1 6	2 6
Victoria Station, Pimlico	1 6	1 0	1 6	1 6	2 0	2 0	1 6	2 0	1 0	2 0
Waterloo Br., Wellington St.	1 0	1 0	1 6	1 0	1 6	1 6	1 6	1 6	1 0	1 6
Westminster Hall	1 6	1 0	1 6	1 0	2 0	1 6	2 0	2 0	1 0	1 6
York and Albany, Regent's Park	2 6	2 0	3 0	1 0	2 6	2 6	1 6	2 6	1 6	—
Zoological Gardens, Regent's Park	2 6	2 0	3 0	1 0	2 6	2 6	1 6	2 6	1 6	1 0

OMNIBUS ROUTES.

The most convenient and the cheapest form of travelling from one London street to another, or from one point of London to another, in the suburbs, — except where both points rest on a direct line of metropolitan or underground railroad, — is by omnibus; and these useful vehicles traverse the streets not only north and south, but east and west, central and otherwise, from eight in the morning until twelve at night. The chief centres from which omnibus routes radiate are the following; and it may help to know, that to make for any one of these fixed points, when any doubt arises, and the distance is not too great, will be found to be economy in the long-run : —

All the railroad-stations.
The Bank of England.
Charing Cross, at the corner of Trafalgar Square.
Oxford Street, corner of Tottenham Court Road.
Oxford Street, Regent Circus.
Piccadilly, Regent Circus and White Horse Cellar, — a little to the right of Bond Street.
Sloane Street, near Hyde Park.
Bishopsgate Street, Flower Pot.
Gracechurch Street.
The Angel, Islington.
The Elephant and Castle, in the Surrey Road.
London Bridge.
Westminster Bridge.

COLORS OF OMNIBUSES.

BLUE, DARK. — "Royal Blue." — Blackwall Railway, by Cheapside, Ludgate Hill, Strand, Charing Cross, Piccadilly, to Pimlico.

BLUE, DARK. — "Waterloo." — Waterloo Bridge, by Charing Cross, Regent Street, Portland Road, to Zoölogical Gardens, Regent's Park.

GREEN, DARK. — "Favorite." — Victoria Station, Pimlico, by Whitehall, Charing Cross, and Strand, to Chancery Lane and Islington.

GREEN, LIGHT. — "City Atlas." — Charing Cross, through

Regent and Baker Streets (past Madame Tussaud's), to Regent's Park, for Zoölogical Gardens. ⋅

GREEN, OLIVE. — London Bridge, through Cheapside, Holborn, Oxford Street, Edgware Road, to Bayswater.

RED. — "Royal Oak." — Charing Cross, through Regent Street, Oxford Street, and Edgware Road, to Bayswater.

RED. — "Hammersmith and Kensington." — Bank, by Cheapside, Ludgate Hill, Strand, Piccadilly, to Hammersmith and Kensington (for Museum).

WHITE. — "Chelsea." — Bank, by Ludgate Hill, Strand, Charing Cross, and Piccadilly, to King's Road, Chelsea, for Cremorne Gardens.

WHITE. — "Brompton." — London Bridge, by Cheapside, Ludgate Hill, Strand, Charing Cross, Piccadilly, to Brompton.

WHITE. — "Richmond." — White Horse Cellar, Piccadilly, to Richmond, Kew, &c.

YELLOW, BRIGHT. — Victoria Station, through Whitehall, by Charing Cross, St. Martin's Lane, Tottenham Court Road (for British Museum), to Camden Town.

The fares from terminus to terminus never exceed sixpence, except in the case of the Richmond omnibuses. The fares are painted inside the door.

STEAMBOATS ON THE THAMES.

The London visitor should make a point of ascending or descending the Thames by a steamboat, say from Westminster to Kew, from Chelsea to Blackwall; or in this latter case, almost as well, and more convenient, from Westminster Bridge to Greenwich; and if he be a man of some niceness in his feeding, and who, as Dr. Johnson expressed it, " likes to dine," let him, if he goes that way, take care of his appetite for a dinner of whitebait, either at the East-India-Dock Tavern, at Blackwall, or the Ship at Greenwich.

All river boats have their names painted conspicuously on the paddle-boxes; and at the foot of nearly every one of the London bridges is a wharf for the arrival and departure of passengers. The steamers plying on the Thames are as follows: —

" CITIZENS " AND " IRON STEAMBOATS." — Leave London, and nearly all the other bridges, every ten minutes, for stations on both sides of the Thames, from 9, A. M., till dusk.

The points of arrival and departure are, Paul's Wharf (St. Paul's Cathedral), Blackfriars Bridge, Temple, Waterloo Bridge, Hungerford Bridge (Charing Cross), Westminster Bridge, Lambeth (Lambeth Palace), Vauxhall, Pimlico, Chelsea, Battersea, Cremorne Gardens, Kew, &c.

Fares from London Bridge to Lambeth .... 1*d.*
    "   "   "   " Pimlico.................. 2*d.*
    "   "   "   " Chelsea.................. 3*d.*
    "   "   "   " Kew.................. 6*d.*

WATERMAN'S COMPANY. — All boats of this company have a separate and distinct name, such as Sylph, Plover, &c., and run from Westminster Bridge to Greenwich, Woolwich, Blackwall, Erith, Rosherville, Gravesend.

Fares from Westminster to Greenwich................ 4*d.*
    "   "   "   " Woolwich.................. 4*d.*
    "   "   "   " Gravesend.............. 1*s.* 2*d.*

LONDON TRAINS, METROPOLITAN OR UNDERGROUND.

THE METROPOLITAN OR UNDERGROUND SYSTEM OF RAILROAD in London provides most admirably for rapid transit between stations in the city, and stations in the suburbs. A stranger may experience some little difficulty at first in mastering the details of the time-bills ; but if he will only bear in mind that the trains run every five and ten minutes, from early morning until close upon midnight, there need be little or no anxiety about catching a particular train. This system of railroad makes an almost complete circuit of London ; so that a passenger may start from Moorgate Street, near the Bank, and, after travelling for an hour, find himself back at Moorgate Street again. Always inquire where you should change carriages.

The direct lines underground are nearly as follows : —
From Mansion House, in the city, to Blackfriars.
  "   "   "   "   " the Temple.
  "   "   "   "   " Charing Cross.
  "   "   "   "   " Westminster Bridge.
  "   "   "   "   " St. James's Park.
  "   "   "   "   " Victoria Station.
  "   "   "   "   " Sloane Street.
  "   "   "   "   " South Kensington, &c.

From Broad or Moorgate St., city, to King's Cross.
"   "   "   "   "   Gower Street.
"   "   "   ".   "   Near Albany Street,
                                                Regent's Park.
"   "   "   "   "   Baker Street.
"   "   "   "   "   Edgware Road.
"   "   "   "   "   Paddington, &c., to
.   Kensington.

N.B. — The Mansion House line takes stations along the Strand district to Victoria Station, and so to Kensington; the Moorgate Street system, stations to the north of Oxford Street, to Kensington.

CONTINENTAL TRAINS.

N.B. — THE EXPRESS MAIL SERVICES, *via* Dover and Calais, of the London, Chatham, and Dover Railway, are now completely established to Paris, Brussels, and Switzerland, Geneva, Como, Interlacken, Mont Blanc, the Austrian Tyrol, and Salzburg.

PARIS, VIA DOVER AND CALAIS. — Fare, first class, £3; second class, £2 5s.

Leave.	Morning.	Evening.
	1*st*, 2*d class.*	1*st class.*
Charing Cross, or Victoria Station, or		
Ludgate Hill Station................	7.40, A.M.	8.45, P.M.
Dover, departs.......................	9.35, A.M.	10.45, P.M.
Calais, "	12.25, P.M.	1.55, A.M.
Amiens, "	3.52, P.M.	5.10, A.M.
Paris, arrives	6.05, P.M.	7.20, A.M.

PARIS VIA FOLKESTONE AND BOULOGNE. — Fare, first class, £2 16s.; second class, £2 2s. This is a tidal service, the hours of departure varying each day.

From Charing Cross or Cannon Street. See Bradshaw for the month.

PARIS VIA NEWHAVEN AND DIEPPE. — Fare, first class, £1 11s.; second class, £1 3s. This, also, is a tidal service.

From Victoria Station or London Bridge. See Bradshaw for the month.

PARIS VIA SOUTHAMPTON AND HAVRE. — Fare, first class, £1 11s.; second class, £1 2s. 9d.

Every Monday, Wednesday, and Friday, from Waterloo Station, latest train, 9, P.M; arriving in Paris, — first class, 4.23, P.M., next day; second class, 6.20, P.M.

RATES FOR THROUGH TICKETS TO THE EUROPEAN CONTINENT.

LONDON TO	SINGLE TICKETS.			Period for which Available.	By what Route Available.
	1st Cl.	2d Cl.	Mixed 1, 2 Cl.		
	£ s. d.	£ s. d.	£ s. d.		
Aix-la-Chap.	3 1 6	2 5 9	.....	1 Month	Calais and Herbesthal.
Aix-la-Chap.	2 17 6	2 1 3	.....	"	Ostend and Herbesthal.
Aix-la-Chap.	3 1 6	2 5 9	.....	30 Days	Calais and Bleyberg.
Aix-la-Chap.	2 17 6	2 1 3	.....	"	Ostend and Bleyberg.
Amiens	2 3 6	1 12 6	.....	7 Days	Boulogne.
Antwerp	2 11 0	1 18 3	.....	1 Month	Calais.
Antwerp	2 7 3	1 13 6	.....	"	Ostend.
Baden Baden	5 16 3	.....	.....	30 Days	Calais and Paris.
Baden Baden	5 1 3	.....	4 11 9	"	Ostend and Cologne.
Baden Baden	5 5 6	.....	4 16 3	"	Calais and Cologne.
Bâle	5 7 3	3 10 0	.....	15 Days	Boulogne and Paris.
Bâle	5 11 3	4 2 0	.....	"	Calais and Paris.
Bâle (R. B.)	5 16 3	.....	5 0 3	30 Days	Ostend and Cologne.
Bâle (R. B.)	6 0 9	.....	5. 4 9	"	Calais and Cologne.
Bâle	5 3 6	3 13 6	.....	1 Month	Calais and Luxemburg.
Bâle	4 19 0	3 9 0	.....	"	Ostend and Luxemburg.
Barmen	3 13 0	2 14 6	.....	30 Days	Calais and Bleyberg.
Barmen	3 8 9	2 9 9	.....	"	Ostend and Bleyberg.
Berlin	5 19 3	.....	5 5 0	1 Month	Calais, Cologne, & Brunswick.
Berlin	5 19 3	.....	5 5 0	"	Calais, Cologne, and Stendal.
Berlin	5 19 3	.....	5 5 0	"	Calais, Bleyberg, and Aix-la-Chapelle.
Berlin	5 15 0	.....	5 0 9	"	Ostend, Cologne, & Brunswick.
Berlin	5 15 0	.....	5 0 0	"	Ostend, Cologne, and Stendal.
Berlin	5 15 0	.....	5 0 0	"	Ostend, Bleyberg, and Aix-la-Chapelle.
Berne	6 3 3	.....	5 9 0	30 Days	Ostend and Cologne.
Bonn	3 12 9	2 13 9	.....	1 Month	Calais and Cologne.
Bonn	3 8 9	2 9 6	.....	"	Ostend and Cologne.
Bordeaux	5 13 0	4 4 9	.....	15 Days	Boulogne and Paris.
Bordeaux	5 17 0	4 7 9	.....	"	Calais and Paris.
Boulogne	1 10 9	1 2 6	1 4 6	7 Days	Folkestone.
Bremen	5 3 9	.....	4 17 6	1 Month	Calais and Cologne.
Bremen	4 19 3	.....	4 13 0	"	Ostend and Cologne.
Brindisi	11 17 7	8 14 4	.....	17 Days	Boulogne or Calais, Paris, and Mont Cenis Tunnel.
Do.(Childr'n)	5 18 10	4 7 2	.....	"	" " " [ner.
Brindisi	13 2 0	.....	10 9 6	1 Month	Calais, Cologne, and the Bren-
Brindisi	12 16 9	.....	10 4 9	"	Ostend, Cologne, and the Bren- [ner.
Bruges	1 19 6	1 7 9	.....	"	Ostend.
Brussels	2 10 0	1 17 3	.....	"	Calais.
Brussels	2 6 6	1 13 0	.....	"	Ostend.
Calais	1 10 9	1 2 6	1 4 6	7 Days	Dover.
Cassel	4 12 9	3 9 9	.....	30 Days	Calais and Bleyberg.
Cassel	4 8 6	3 5 0	.....	"	Ostend and Bleyberg.
Coblence	3 17 3	2 17 6	.....	1 Month	Calais and Cologne.
Coblence	3 13 3	2 13 0	.....	"	Ostend and Cologne.
Cologne	3 10 6	2 12 0	.....	"	Calais and Herbesthal.
Cologne	3 6 6	2 7 9	.....	"	Ostend and Herbesthal.
Crefeld	3 9 3	2 11 9	.....	30 Days	Calais and Bleyberg.
Crefeld	3 5 0	2 7 0	.....	"	Ostend and Bleyberg.

RATES FOR THROUGH TICKETS. — *Continued.*

LONDON TO	SINGLE TICKETS.			Period for which Available.	By what Route Available.
	1st Cl.	2d Cl.	Mixed 1, 2 Cl.		
	£ s. d.	£ s. d.	£ s. d.		
Darmstadt..	4 10 6	....	4 5 3	1 Month	Calais and Cologne.
Darmstadt..	4 6 0	....	4 0 9	"	Ostend and Cologne.
Dortmund...	3 16 9	2 17 3	....	30 Days	Calais and Bleyberg.
Dortmund...	3 12 3	2 12 6	....	"	Ostend and Bleyberg.
Dresden	6 7 3	....	5 9 6	1 Month	Calais,Col'gne, & Brunsw'k.
Dresden.....	6 7 3	... ...	5 9 6	"	Calais, Bleyberg, and Aix-la-Chapelle.
Dresden.....	6 3 0	....	5 5 3	"	Ostend,Col'gne,&Brunsw'k.
Dresden.....	6 3 0	....	5 5 3	"	Ostend, Bleyberg, and Aix-la-Chapelle.
Dusseldorf..	3 10 6	2 12 6	....	30 Days	Calais and Bleyberg.
Dusseldorf..	3 6 0	2 7 9	....	"	Ostend and Bleyberg.
Elberfeld....	3 12 9	2 14 3	....	"	Calais and Bleyberg.
Elberfeld....	3 8 6	2 9 9	....	"	Ostend and Bleyberg.
Ems.........	4 1 0	....	3 18 6	"	Calais and Cologne.
Ems.........	3 16 0	....	3 14 0	"	Ostend and Cologne.
Essen.......	3 12 6	2 14 3	....	"	Calais and Bleyberg.
Essen.......	3 8 3	2 9 6	....	"	Ostend and Bleyberg.
Florence	9 2 10	6 17 2	....	17 Days	Boulogne or Calais, Paris, and Mont Cenis Tunnel.
Francf't O.M.	4 9 9	....	4 5 0	1 Month	Calais and Cologne.
Francf't O.M.	4 5 9	....	4 1 0	"	Ostend and Cologne.
Geneva......	5 17 9	....	....	"	Boulogne and Paris.
Geneva......	6 1 9	....	....	"	Calais and Paris.
Genoa.......	7 14 6	5 14 8	....	17 Days	Boulogne or Calais, Paris, and Mont Cenis Tunnel.
Ghent.......	2 7 0	1 14 9	....	1 Month	Calais.
Ghent	2 2 9	1 10 0	....	"	Ostend.
M. Gladbach	3 7 3	2 10 3	....	30 Days	Calais and Bleyberg.
M. Gladbach	3 3 0	2 5 6	....	"	Ostend and Bleyberg.
Hagen	3 15 0	2 16 0	....	"	Calais and Bleyberg.
Hagen	3 10 9	2 11 3	....	"	Ostend and Bleyberg.
Hamburg ...	5 13 0	....	5 4 6	"	Calais, Cologne, & Harburg.
Hamburg ...	5 8 6	....	5 0 0	"	Ostend, Cologne, & Harb'rg.
Hanover	4 19 0	....	4 13 9	1 Month	Calais and Cologne.
Hanover	4 14 6	....	4 9 6	"	Ostend and Cologne.
Heidb'g,R.B.	4 16 3	....	4 9 6	30 Days	Calais and Cologne.
Heidb'g,R.B.	4 11 9	....	4 5 0	"	Ostend and Cologne.
Homburg....	4 12 0	....	4 6 6	"	Calais and Cologne.
Homburg....	4 8 0	....	4 2 6	"	Ostend and Cologne.
Leghorn	9 7 6	7 0 11	....	17 Days	Boulogne or Calais, Paris, and Mont Cenis Tunnel.
Leipsic......	5 15 6	....	5 1 9	1 Month	Calais,Col'gne, & Brunsw'k.
Leipsic......	5 15 6	....	5 1 9	"	Calais, Bleyberg, and Aix-la-Chapelle.
Leipsic......	5 11 3	....	4 17 3	"	Ostend,C'l'gne,& Brunsw'k.
Leipsic......	5 11 3	....	4 17 3	"	Ostend, Bleyberg, and Aix-la-Chapelle.
Liege.......	2 17 0	2 2 3	....	"	Calais.
Liege.......	2 13 6	1 18 0	....	"	Ostend.
Lille........	2 1 6	1 11 0	....	7 Days	Calais.
Louvain.....	2 8 6	1 14 3	....	1 Month	Ostend.

RATES FOR THROUGH TICKETS. — *Continued.*

LONDON TO	SINGLE TICKETS.			Period for which Available.	By what Route Available.
	1st Cl.	2d Cl.	Mixed 1, 2 Cl.		
	£ s. d.	£ s. d.	£ s. d.		
Lucerne.....	6 2 0	....	5 8 0	30 Days	Ostend.
Lyons........	5 8 0	....	....	15 Days	Boulogne or Calais & Paris.
Marseilles...	7 1 3	....	....	"	Boulogne and Paris.
Marseilles...	7 5 0	....	....	"	Calais and Paris.
Mayence	4 6 0	....	4 2 3	1 Month	Calais and Cologne.
Mayence ...	4 1 9	....	3 18 0	"	Ostend and Cologne.
Milan........	7 13 6	5 14 2	....	17 Days	Boulogne or Calais, Paris, and Mont Cenis Tunnel.
Munich	7 7 6	....	....	1 Month	Boulogne and Paris.
Munich	7 11 6	....	....	"	Calais and Paris.
Munich	6 8 3	....	5 11 6	30 Days	Calais and Cologne.
Munich	6 3 9	....	5 7 0	"	Ostend and Cologne.
Naples	12 0 3	8 16 10	....	17 Days	Boulogne or Calais, Paris, and Mont Cenis Tunnel.
Neuss........	3 8 9	2 11 3	....	30 Days	Calais and Bleyberg.
Neuss........	3 4 6	2 6 6	....	"	Ostend and Bleyberg.
Nice.........	8 5 3	6 4 0	....	1 Month	Boulogne or Calais.
Ostend.......	1 17 6	1 6 6	....	7 Days	Dover.
Paris	2 16 0	2 2 0	....	"	Boulogne.
Paris........	3 0 0	2 5 0	....	"	Calais.
Paris*.	....	1 11 6	†1 1 0	3 Days	Boulogne or Calais.
Rheydt.......	3 6 9	2 9 0	....	30 Days	Calais and Bleyberg.
Rheydt.......	3 2 3	2 5 0	....	"	Ostend and Bleyberg.
Rome	10 15 9	8 0 0	....	17 Days	Boulogne or Calais, Paris, and Mont Cenis Tunnel.
Rotterdam...	3 1 9	2 6 0	....	1 Month	Calais.
Rotterdam..	2 17 0	2 1 0	....	"	Ostend.
Ruhrort.....	3 10 9	2 12 9	....	30 Days	Calais and Bleyberg.
Ruhrort.....	3 6 6	2 8 0	....	"	Ostend and Bleyberg.
Spa.........	2 19 3	2 4 0	....	"	Calais.
Spa.........	2 15 9	1 19 9	....	"	Ostend.
St. Petersb'g	13 6 3	....	10 17 0	"	Calais, Cologne,& Brunsw'k.
St. Petersb'g	13 6 3	....	10 17 0	"	Calais, Cologne, and Stendal.
St. Petersb'g	13 6 3	....	10 17 0	"	Calais and Bleyberg.
St Petersb'g	13 2 0	....	10 12 9	"	Ostend, C'l'gne, & Brunsw'k.
St. Petersb'g	13 2 0	....	10 12 9	"	Ostend, Cologne, & Stendal.
St. Petersb'g.	13 2 0	....	10 12 9	"	Ostend and Bleyberg.
Strasburg...	5 5 0	3 18 0	....	15 Days	Boulogne and Paris.
Strasburg....	5 9 0	4 1 0	....	"	Calais and Paris.
Strasburg...	4 10 9	3 5 6	....	1 Month	Calais and Luxemburg.
Strasburg....	4 7 0	3 0 9	....	"	Ostend and Luxemburg.
Stuttgart....	5 7 3	....	4 17 6	30 Days	Calais, Cologne, & Bruchsal.
Stuttgart....	5 2 9	....	4 13 0	1 Month	Ostend, C'l'gne, & Bruchsal.
Turin......	6 19 11	5 4 7	....	17 Days	Boulogne or Calais, Paris, and Mont Cenis Tunnel.
Venice......	9 3 11	6 16 3	....	"	" " "
Verviers....	2 18 9	2 3 9	....	1 Month	Calais.
Verviers....	2 15 3	1 19 6	....	"	Ostend.
Vienna	9 18 0	....	....	"	Boulogne and Paris.
Vienna	10 2 0	....	....	"	Calais and Paris.
Vienna	8 8 0	....	7 0 9	"	Calais, C'logne, and Passau.
Vienna	8 3 6	....	6 16 3	"	Ostend, C'logne, and Passau.

* Night services only.   † Third class.

RATES FOR THROUGH TICKETS. — *Continued.*

LONDON TO	SINGLE TICKETS. 1st Cl.	2d Cl.	Mixed 1, 2 Cl.	Period for which Available.	By what Route Available.
	£ s. d.	£ s. d.	£ s. d.		
Vierzen.....	3 8 0	2 10 9	....	30 Days	Calais and Bleyberg.
Vierzen.	3 3 9	2 6 0	....	"	Ostend and Bleyberg.
Wiesbaden..	4 7 0	....	4 2 6	"	} Calais, Cologne, and Rudesheim. [heim.
Wiesbaden..	4 2 6	....	3 18 0	"	Ostend, C'logne, and Rudes-
Zurich	6 2 0	....	5 7 6	"	Ostend and Cologne.

DOVER TO	SINGLE TICKETS. 1st Cl.	2d Cl.	Mixed 1, 2 Cl.	Period for which Available.	By what Route Available.
	£ s. d.	£ s. d.	£ s. d.		
Aix-la-Chap	2 1 6	1 10 9	....	1 Month	Calais and Herbesthal.
Bâle........	4 11 3	3 7 9	....	15 Days	Calais and Paris.
Bâle (R. B.)	5 0 9	....	4 4 9	30 Days	Calais and Cologne.
Berlin.......	4 19 3	....	4 5 0	1 Month	Calais,Cologne,and Stendal.
Brussels ..	1 10 0	1 2 3	....	"	Calais.
" (return)	2 2 9	1 12 6	....	"	Calais.
Cologne.....	2 10 6	1 17 0	....	"	Calais and Herbesthal.
Francfort ...	3 9 9	....	3 5 0	30 Days	Calais and Herbesthal.
Hamburg ...	4 13 0	....	4 4 6	"	Calais,C'logne,and Harb'rg.
Munich	6 11 6	....	....	1 Month	Calais and Paris.
Munich	5 8 3	....	4 11 6	30 Days	Calais and Cologne.
Paris........	1 17 9	1 8 6	....	7 Days	Calais.
Spa..........	1 19 3	1 9 0	....	1 Month	Calais.
Verviers	1 18 9	1 8 9	....	"	Calais.
Vienna......	9 2 0	....	....	"	Calais and Paris.
Vienna......	7 8 0	....	6 0 9	"	Calais,Cologne, and Passau.

RETURN TICKETS.

LONDON TO	SINGLE TICKETS. 1st Cl.	2d Cl.	3d Cl.	Period for which Available.	By what Route Available.
	£ s. d.	£ s. d.	£ s. d.		
Boulogne....	2 7 6	1 17 6	....	7 Days	Folkestone.
Brussels	3 16 0	2 16 6	....	1 Month	Dover and Calais.
Brussels	3 11 0	2 10 6	....	"	Dover and Ostend.
Calais.......	2 7 6	1 17 6	....	7 Days	Dover.
Paris........	4 15 0	3 15 0	....	1 Month	Folkestone or Dover.
Paris*	....	2 7 0	1 11 6	14 Days	Folkestone or Dover.

STOPPING-PLACES. — Passengers can stop at each of the intermediate points for which there is a separate coupon; and the tickets are available between those points by any train of the same class.

* By night services only.

• EXCURSION-TRAINS.

From or about the middle of August to the 30th of September, all the principal railway-companies run excursion-trains from London to points of interest inland, and on the coast. A trip to Brighton, Ramsgate, or Margate, is a desirable change from the heat and bustle of the London streets during the hot season, and will be certain to repay a stranger who is unfamiliar with the manners and customs of Englishmen at the sea-side. Brighton possesses an Aquarium which certainly ought to be seen; and the Margate Sands, at bathing-time, present a sight not to be met with out of England. Excursion-trains run as follows; but, for details of other excursions, see London daily papers: —

To BRIGHTON AND BACK. — Every Sunday and Monday, from Victoria Station and London Bridge Station, at 9, A.M. Fares 7s. and 3s.

To RAMSGATE, MARGATE, BROADSTAIRS, AND HERNE BAY, AND BACK. — Every Sunday, from Victoria Station and Ludgate Hill Station, at 8.30, A.M. Fare 10s.

To RAMSGATE, MARGATE, BROADSTAIRS, AND HERNE BAY. — Three cheap fast trains daily, at 10.10, A.M., 12.30, P.M., and 3.15, P.M. Fares, return-ticket, 15s. and 8s.

To PORTSMOUTH (DOCKYARD), ISLE OF WIGHT, QUEEN'S RESIDENCE AT OSBORNE. — Every Saturday, from Victoria, at 2.50, P.M., returning the following Tuesday. Fares 11s. and 7s. 6d.

Every Saturday in September, excursion-trains run from London as follows, returning in each case on the Monday week or Monday fortnight following date of departure: —

Leave Paddington Station at 7.30, and Reading 8.55, A.M., for Clevedon, Weston-super-Mare, Bridgewater, Taunton, Ilminster, Chard, Watchett, Wiveliscombe, Tiverton, Exeter, Torquay, Plymouth, Truro, Falmouth, Penzance, and other intermediate stations in the most beautiful parts of Devon and Cornwall.

Leave Paddington at 1.05, and Reading, 2.20, P.M.; for Trowbridge, Wells, Yeovil, Dorchester, Weymouth, and other intermediate stations. Passengers taking tickets to Weymouth will have the privilege of going from Weymouth to Guernsey or Jersey at single fares for the double journey.

5

TRAINS. — CHIEF RAILWAY-STATIONS IN LONDON.

GREAT WESTERN RAILWAY. — Paddington.
LONDON AND NORTH-WESTERN. — Euston Square.
GREAT NORTHERN RAILWAY. — King's Cross.
EASTERN COUNTIES. — Shoreditch.
LONDON, BRIGHTON, AND SOUTH COAST. — London Bridge,
Cannon Street, Charing Cross, Victoria Station.
LONDON AND SOUTH-WESTERN. — Waterloo Bridge.
LONDON, CHATHAM, AND DOVER. — Victoria Station.
THE BLACKWALL RAILWAY. — Mark Lane.
N.B. — The best Railway Time-Tables to consult are
the A. B. C. Railway Guide, price 6*d.*; and Cassell's Time-
Tables, price 2*d.* To be had at all railway book-stalls.

POSTAL ARRANGEMENTS.

Mails are made up in London, for the United States, every
Tuesday, Thursday, and Saturday evening.

POSTAGE FOR LETTERS : ½ oz., 3*d.*; 1 oz., 6*d.*; and 3*d.* for
every additional ½ oz. NEWSPAPERS : 4 oz., 1*d.*; 8 oz., 2*d.*
BOOKS AND PATTERNS : 1 oz., 1*d.*; 2 oz.. 2*d.*: 3 oz., 3*d.*

CONTINENTAL POSTAGE: To France, 3*d.* for ⅓ oz.; Bel-
gium, Switzerland, and Germany, 3*d.* for ½ oz.; Italy, 6*d.* for
½ oz.

INLAND LETTERS or packets sent to or from any part of
the United Kingdom are charged as follows : —
Not exceeding 1 oz. in weight, 1*d.*; exceeding 1 oz., but
under 2 oz., 1½ *d.*; exceeding 2 oz.. but under 4 oz., 2*d.*; exceeding 4 oz.. but under 6 oz., 2½ *d.*; exceeding 6 oz., but under 8 oz., 3*d.*; exceeding 8 oz., but under 10 oz., 3½*d.*; exceeding 10 oz., but under 12 oz., 4*d.*; over 12 oz., the rate is 1*d.*
per oz.; e.g., a prepaid letter weighing 17 oz., and under 18
oz., is charged 1*s.* 6*d.*, and so on.

If the postage be not paid in advance, a *double postage* will
be demanded on delivery; and, if the prepaid postage be in-
sufficient, *double the amount of the deficiency* will be charged.

NEWSPAPERS : A postage of one halfpenny is charged for
the transmission of each newspaper within the United Kingdom. Such newspaper posted for inland circulation must
be prepaid by adhesive stamp or stamped wrapper. The

prepaid rate for a packet containing two or more newspapers is one halfpenny for each newspaper; or if under two ounces, then at the book-rate of one halfpenny for every two ounces, or fraction of two ounces. The newspaper must be folded so that its title can be inspected, must contain no enclosure except its supplement, nor any writing except the address. A tick, however, may be made to call attention to any part of its contents.

Newspapers for the United States or abroad must be posted within seven days of publication. The rates for eight ounces and under are given above.

POSTAL CARDS are available solely for transmission between places in the United Kingdom. Nothing may be attached. If the card be folded, cut, or otherwise altered, it will be charged on delivery as an insufficiently-paid letter. The cards are sold in packets only, at sixpence halfpenny per dozen.

BOOK POST: The prepaid postage for a packet of books, paper, printed matter, manuscript, circulars, or photographs, including binding and mounting, is one halfpenny for every 2 oz. or fraction of that weight. No book-packet may contain any thing sealed, or otherwise closed against inspection. Any such prohibited enclosure will be taken out, and forwarded to the address on the packet, charged with postage as an unpaid letter; and the remainder of the packet, if duly prepaid, will be forwarded to its address. There must be no letter, nor any communication of the nature of a letter, written on any part of a book-packet or its cover. If this rule be infringed, the entire packet will be treated as a letter. Entries, however, stating to whom a book is given, or by whom sent, are not regarded as a letter; and, in order to secure the return of book-packets which cannot be delivered, the name and address of the sender should be printed or written on the top, at the left hand, and *outside* the packet. Newspapers and such documents as are allowed to pass at the book-rate of postage, must, in order to secure that privilege, be sent either entirely open, or in wrappers open at the ends, so as to admit of the contents being readily removed for inspection. If wrappers be used, it is not enough that they be partly, but they must be *entirely*, open at the ends; and the privilege of transmission at the low rate of postage applicable to printed matter is forfeited by any packet the contents of which are in any way fastened to the cover, or the cover of which cannot from any cause be withdrawn without diffi-

culty. A string to confine separate MSS. is not considered
an invasion of this rule. The privilege is similarly forfeited
by circulars, &c., sent without covers, if they are fastened
at some point by means of gum, wafers, seals, or even postage labels. No packet of "printed matter of any kind"
must exceed five pounds in weight, or eighteen inches in
length, or six inches in depth, or nine inches in width. An
infringement of any of these rules will cause the packet to
be treated as an unpaid letter. The rates to the United
States are given above.

PATTERN POST: The regulations in regard to these are
similar to those above given in respect to Inland Book Post.
In no case will any thing likely to injure other letters, &c.,
be forwarded. The articles must be so packed as to be
readily examined. Limits of weight vary; and articles of
intrinsic value are not admitted to the United States, as being liable to customs dues.

LONDON DISTRICT POST: It may facilitate letters addressed to persons living within London if Americans will
bear in mind that London called the metropolis is divided
into eight districts; viz., the Eastern Central (E.C.), the
Eastern (E.), Northern (N.), North-western (N.W.), South-
eastern (S.E.), South-western (S.W.), Western (W.), Western Central (W.C.). The use of the initials at the bottom
of the address facilitates the delivery of letters, &c. In the
E.C., or city districts, — that is to say, within Temple Bar, —
there are twelve deliveries daily; within the town districts —
that is, three miles of the general post-office — there are
eleven. The suburban districts have six deliveries daily.
Inland and many colonial and foreign mails are delivered
at from 7.30 to 9.30, A.M. The times for despatch, &c., of
letters between the districts for London letters, are generally
exhibited in the windows of the local offices and their
branches. On Sunday, letters can only be posted at the head
office of the district and at the pillar posts, the branch offices
being closed. In the Central districts, on week-days, letters
for the country and abroad must be posted before 6, P.M.; an
earlier hour being fixed in suburban places. Letters for the
morning mails may be posted until 5.30, A.M., in London; and
from 3.30 to 5.00, A.M., in the town and suburban districts.

REGISTRATION OF LETTERS: The fee for registration, in
addition to the ordinary postage, is *fourpence* for a letter,
newspaper, book, or other packet, to any place within the
United Kingdom or the Colonies. The registration and

postage fee must be prepaid, if inland, by stamps; but if for abroad, either by money or stamps. If letters enclosing coin are *sent unregistered*, they will be *charged on delivery with a double registration-fee*, viz., *eightpence;* and may, on press of business, be delayed in delivery.

POSTAL TELEGRAMS AND CABLE TELEGRAMS.

THE ATLANTIC TELEGRAPHS. — In June, 1873, another submarine cable was laid between England and the United States, making a total of four which have been successfully laid, and are really at work. The rates for cable telegrams to the United States are as follows: To New York, Boston, and New-England States generally, 4*s.* per word; to Philadelphia, Baltimore, Washington, 4*s.* 3*d.* per word; to St. Louis and Chicago, 4*s.* 9*d.* per word; to San Francisco, 5*s.* 3*d.* (address and signature included).

THE POST-OFFICE DEPARTMENT collects and delivers messages throughout the United Kingdom for the Submarine Telegraph Company, the Anglo-American Telegraph Company, the French Atlantic Telegraph Company, The Indo-European Telegraph Company, the Falmouth, Malta, and Gibraltar Telegraph Company, and the Great Northern Telegraph Company; and there are offices for the receipt of such messages in nearly all the principal thoroughfares in London.

TARIFF. — The charge for the transmission of messages by telegraph throughout the United Kingdom is 1*s.* for the first twenty words, and 3*d.* for each additional five words or part of five words. The names and addresses of the sender and receiver are not charged for.

Telegrams may be repeated at the request of the sender, if he desires to adopt this extra security against risk of error, by being sent back from the office at which they are received to the office from which they are forwarded. The charge for repetition is one-half the ordinary tariff, fractions of 3*d.* being reckoned as 2*d.*

The cost of a reply to a telegram may be prepaid.

Copies of a telegram directed to more than one firm or person in the same free delivery will be delivered separately at an additional charge of 3*d.* per copy.

Telegrams may be re-directed from town to town at an extra charge of *one-half* the ordinary tariff, fractions of 3*d.* being reckoned as 2*d.*

All numbers, and fractions of numbers, must be written in words, and will be charged for accordingly. For example, "365" should be written "*three hundred and sixty-five,*" and, when so written, will be charged for as five words; and "⅜" should be written "*three-eighths,*" and, when so written, will be charged as two words.

Porterage is charged only when the addressee does not reside within one mile of the terminal telegraph-office.

The Central Station — open day and night, Sundays and week-days, throughout the year — of the whole telegraph system of the United Kingdom is in the handsome edifice opposite the General Post-office in St. Martins-le-Grand, which we strongly advise the stranger to see before leaving London.

The following are the most important collecting offices in the London districts, ranged in order of importance : —

In the East Central, or city proper, the Stock Exchange, Fenchurch Street, Gresham House, Leadenhall Street, Cornhill, and Lothbury offices ; in the West Central or Charing Cross District, the West Strand, West Central District, Somerset House, and Covent Garden Market offices ; in the Western, or Regent Street District. the Piccadilly Circus, Western District, and Paddington offices ; in the South-western, or Pall Mall District, the St. James Street, Parliament Street, and Knightsbridge offices ; in the South-eastern District, the Borough and Crystal Palace offices ; in the Eastern District, the Aldgate, Shoreditch, and St. Catherine's Dock offices ; in the North-western, the Euston and Camden Road offices ; and, in the Northern, the King's Cross and the Cattle Market offices. An application to a policeman, however, will always insure attention, and he will readily point the way to the nearest office for receiving telegrams. All railroad-stations have telegraph-offices.

Visitors will find that they can procure blank postal-telegraph forms at all hotels in London, and elsewhere in England, on application at the office. The message may, of course, be sent by one of the porters of the hotel, obviating the inconvenience of attending at the telegraph-office in person.

SUBMARINE TELEGRAPH COMPANY.

Head office, 58 Threadneedle Street, City. Open day and night.

International service between London and the Continent.

Charge for twenty words, including address : —

Austria..	.....6s. 0d.	Italy	..7s. 6d.
Belgium	....2 6	Norway	..5 0
Denmark	....5 0	Portugal	..8 0
France	....3 4	Russia	..10 0
Germany	....6 0	Spain	..7 0
Greece	...10 0	Sweden	..7 0
Holland	....3 9	Switzerland	..5 10
	Turkey.....9s.		

DIFFERENCE OF TIME between London and the following cities : —

When it is noon in London, it is

1h.	35m.	18s.	afternoon	at Athens.
12	17	49	"	at Brussels.
12	53	58	"	at Berlin.
1	56	19	"	at Constantinople.
12	50	43	"	at Copenhagen.
12	24	59	"	at Geneva.
11	23	49	morning	at Lisbon.
5	24	2	"	at Mexico.
11	45	40	"	at Madrid.
7	4	23	"	*at New York.*
12	50	12	afternoon	at Rome.
1	12	38	"	at Stockholm.
2	1	37	"	at St. Petersburg.

RACES DURING THE SUMMER SEASON NEAR LONDON.

Following is a calendar of some of the principal Race Meetings to be held during this summer within easy reach of London. They are set down here merely to afford opportunity to a stranger for seeing England's "national sport" on English ground, if there should be the inclination. The Derby — "the Isthmian Games of England" — is one of the sights of the world. A writer in a London evening paper, "The Globe," says of it, that it is literally the truth to say, that the race is a sort of London and All-England picnic. "Thousands attend it for the simple purpose of being present at a wonderful fair, and of realizing a scene which they have read of in books, and gazed at in pictures, and have even witnessed caricatured in theatres. The abundant literature which has instructed us so persistently in the more quaint and suggestive elements of the gathering has forced an almost universal enthusiasm and curiosity on every class, except the very poorest, in connection with the contest on the Downs. And, as a rule, the Derby does not, weather permitting, disappoint expectation. . . . The real Derby is, on the whole, strangely like the Derby of books and of newspapers. This is the very first sensation felt by a spectator who sees a Derby for the first time. It is an experience certainly worth realizing: and not one of the least striking or stirring emotions developed by it in a new-comer is the odd familiarity of the pageant to his mind, and the sharp distinct fashion in which his imaginary conceptions of the scene, both personal and borrowed, are brought before him in a concrete, visible shape."

Ascot, or, as it is termed, "Royal Ascot," should be visited, if possible, though for different reasons to those which would take a man on to Epsom Downs. Ascot Course, on the Cup-Day, receives the very cream of English society. The royal family are present in state ; and there is a gathering of notabilities such as are only to be seen once in a year, or perhaps in a lifetime. A drive by the road is a delicious outing for those fond of English scenery ; and is not very expensive, compared with what would be charged for the luxury of a twenty-miles' drive in America. Goodwood, too, should tempt the stranger. It is one of the prettiest race-grounds in England, planted in the midst of most charming scenery, at the bottom of a valley overlooked by the famous country-seat of the Duke of Richmond. Chichester is the nearest railroad-station, and a cathedral-town worth visiting, — to be reached easily, it may be noted, from Victoria Station, Pimlico. Ascot is on a direct line of railway from Waterloo Bridge : the same may be said of Epsom. But, for the latter races, hire a seat on a four-in-hand, and go down by road, if possible.

MAY.

5th. NEWMARKET. Excellent for sport.
12th. CHESTER.   "   "
19th. NEWMARKET.   "   "
26th. BATH. Very beautiful city and country.
27th. WYE. Pretty country town, near Canterbury (for Cathedral).

JUNE.

2d. EPSOM RACES begin. Off-day.
3d. DERBY DAY. The great carnival.
4th. EPSOM. Off-day.
5th. THE OAKS. A great event.
11th. CROYDON. Pretty country.
16th. ASCOT. Scenery lovely.
18th.   "   Race for the Gold Cup (the grand day).
23d. WINDSOR. Good, and charming scenery.
25th. HAMPTON. Well worth attending.

JULY.

7th. NEWMARKET. Excellent.
14th. WEST DRAYTON. Country well worth going to see.
28th. GOODWOOD. The Cup-Day.

AUGUST.

3d. CROYDON. Well worth going to.
4th. BRIGHTON. Excellent.
7th. LEWES. Pretty scenery.
11th. EGHAM. Pretty scenery.
25th. OXFORD. Good.
27th. READING. Good.

SEPTEMBER.

1st. SUTTON PARK, near Birmingham.
3d. CANTERBURY. Very good.
8th. RICHMOND. Excellent for an outing.
8th. WARWICK. Well worth attending.
22d. HENDON. Pretty country.

LONDON CHURCHES, WITH TIMES OF SERVICE.

The following are the churches in London which attract
some of the largest congregations ; doubtless, among other
reasons, because of the fame or eloquence of the preachers
occupying the pulpit. As a rule, morning service commences at 11, afternoon at 3, and evening at 7, at all
churches in London.

WESTMINSTER ABBEY. — 10, A.M. (generally one of the
canons preaches); 3, P.M., almost always the dean. Dr.
Arthur Penrhyn Stanley, from May until the end of July.
It would be well for persons desirous of securing seats in the
choir, where the service takes place, to reach the Abbey at the
opening of the doors, half an hour at least before the service
begins. On Sunday evenings, during the summer months,
special services are held in the nave, which attract very
large congregations.

ST. PAUL'S CATHEDRAL. — 9.45, A.M., when it is usual for
one of the canons to preach, — Drs. Gregory, Liddon, Light-
foot, or Claughton ; 3.15, P.M., when the dean, Dr. Church,
preaches ; and 7, P.M., special services under the dome.

TEMPLE CHURCH, Fleet Street. — 11, A.M., when the Rev.
Dr. Vaughan, Master of the Temple, officiates ; and 3, P.M,
preacher, the Rev. Alfred Ainger, the Reader at the Temple.
This little church is one of the most famous in the world.
It was built 1185, in the times of the Crusades. Application must be made to what is termed a Bencher for admission to the service on Sundays ; but no doubt an application
to the Rev. the Master, by letter, would secure a seat to a
stranger.

THE CHAPEL ROYAL, Whitehall, opposite the Horse
Guards. — Service at 11, A.M., and 3, P.M. The preachers here
are selected by the Queen, and are always men of eminence
in the Church.

CHAPEL ROYAL, ST. JAMES'S PALACE. — Service commences at noon on Sundays. The princes usually attend
this service. Admission can be had by application at the
lord-chamberlain's office, St. James's Palace.

CHAPEL ROYAL, SAVOY, in the Strand, within a stone's-
throw of Waterloo Bridge. — Service at 11. A.M., when the
preacher is usually the Rev. Henry White, chaplain to the
House of Commons ; and at 7, P.M.

ST. JAMES'S CHURCH, Piccadilly, very near to Regent

Street.—Services, 11, A.M, 3, P.M., and 7, P.M. The Rev. J. E. Kempe is the rector, and usually preaches in the morning.

ALL SAINTS', Margaret Street, near to the Langham Hotel.—Services at 11, A.M., 3, P.M., and 7, P.M. The most beautiful of the modern London churches. The services are extremely "ritualistic."

ST. ANDREW'S, Wells Street, Oxford Street.—Services at 11, A.M., 3 and 7, P.M.; also very "High Church;" but the music is possibly the finest to be heard in any London church outside of a cathedral.

ST. ALBAN'S, Brooke Street, Holborn.—A very famous modern church, of which the Rev. Mr. Maconchy is rector. Services (extreme ritualist) at 11, A.M., 3 and 7, P.M.

THE FOUNDLING, Foundling Hospital, Guilford Street, Russell Square.—Services at 11, A.M., and 3, P.M. The singing by the children is beautiful in the extreme.

ST. BARTHOLOMEW'S, West Smithfield, near to St. Bartholomew's Hospital.—The oldest church of "Old London," and the scene of the Smithfield martyrdoms. Built 1102. Services at 11, A.M., 3 and 7, P.M.

CHRIST CHURCH, Newgate Street, in the city.—The boys of Christ's Hospital (Charles Lamb's old school) attend the services at 11, A.M., and 3, P.M. Singing very good.

ST. MARTIN-IN-THE-FIELDS, Trafalgar Square.—A grand old church, the burial-place of several eminent persons. Services at 11, A.M., 3 and 7, P.M.

MR. SPURGEON'S TABERNACLE, Newington Butts.—The best way to get there is by any omnibus passing over Westminster Bridge. About twenty minutes' ride. Services at 10.45, A.M., and 6.30, P.M.

SCOTCH CHURCH, Drury Lane.—Rev. Dr. Cumming (author of "The Coming Struggle"). The services commence at 11, A.M., and 7, P.M.

The stranger will find it interesting to visit some of the quaint old chapels of the Inns of Court. The services are choral, and the preachers are eminent divines. Those chapels are as follows:—

THE ROLLS CHAPEL, Chancery Lane.—Service at 11, A.M.

LINCOLN'S INN CHAPEL, Chancery Lane.—Services at 11, A.M., and at 3, P.M.

GRAY'S INN CHAPEL, at the top of Chancery Lane.—Services at 11, A.M., and at 3, P.M.

"Unorthodox London" is well represented by eloquent

preachers every Sunday in some of the larger halls, — such as St. James's, Regent Street; Exeter, in the Strand; and St. George's Hall, Langham Place. The third column of the first page of " The London Times " usually announces the names of the preachers every preceding Saturday.

The following may be found interesting in studying church architecture in London and elsewhere in England: —

STYLES OF ENGLISH ARCHITECTURE.

Name.	Prevailed.	Characteristics.
NORMAN	1066 to 1154	Round-headed doorways and windows, heavy pillars, and zigzag ornaments.
TRANSITION	1154 to 1189	Same, but with pointed windows.
EARLY ENGLISH	1189 to 1272	Narrow-pointed windows, usually plain; clustered pillars.
TRANSITION	1272 to 1307	Tracery introduced into windows.
DECORATED	1307 to 1377	Geometrical tracery in windows, enriched doorways, beautifully arranged mouldings.
TRANSITION	1377 to 1399	Lines not quite so flowing.
PERPENDICULAR	1399 to 1547	Upright lines of mouldings in windows and doorways; combination of square heads with pointed mouldings.
TUDOR	1550 to 1600	A debased species of Perpendicular, mostly employed in domestic architecture.
JACOBEAN	1603 to 1641	An admixture of Classical with all kinds of Gothic or Pointed.

GARDENS.

BOTANIC, Regent's Park. — Accessible by orders from Fellows only, which may usually be had by a civil application to the secretary of the society, stating the fact that it is an American lady or gentleman who applies. Open daily and on Sundays.

CREMORNE, Chelsea. — Daily during the summer. Admission, 1s. A very pleasant way of getting to this spot is by steamboat from Westminster Bridge. Fare, 3d.

HORTICULTURAL, South Kensington. — Accessible by order from Fellows. Daily, except Sundays, by payment at the gates. Free on Aug. 26, Prince Consort's birthday, and on certain other days during the summer.

KEW, BOTANICAL. — Accessible by railway, omnibus, and

steamboat, at a cost of 6*d.* to 1*s.* Open from 1 till sunset on week-days, and 2 to dusk on Sundays. Free. Palace by order. The most direct way of getting here is from the Waterloo Bridge Station of the London and South-western Railway.

North Woolwich, north bank of the Thames. — Varied entertainments; fine esplanade. Access by rail and steam-boat, 4*d.* and 6*d.*

People's, Willesden. — Admission daily, by introduction of shareholder.

Rosherville Gardens, near Gravesend. — Access by railway and steamboat. Fare by boat, 1*s.*, during summer season, from Westminster Bridge.

Temple Gardens. — Quite worth a casual visit when walking down Fleet Street. Entrance by passing through the Temple.

Zoölogical Gardens, Regent's Park. — Admission on Monday, 6*d.*; the rest of the week, 1*s.* The band of one of the cavalry regiments stationed in London plays on Satur-day afternoons. Admittance may be had to these beautiful gardens on Sundays, when all the fashionable world of London go there. Admission on Sunday by order from a Fellow of the Society.

LONDON HOSPITALS.

St. Bartholomew's Hospital, West Smithfield. — Ordinary cases admitted from 9 to 10 daily; accidents at all times. Visiting-days: Sundays, 2 to 3; Tuesdays and Fri-days, 3 to 4, P.M. Clerk, W. H. Cross, Esq.

St. Thomas's, Albert Embankment. — Out-patients daily at 11, A.M.; accidents and urgent cases at all times. Visit-ing-days: Sundays, Tuesdays, and Fridays, from 3 to 5. A Samaritan Society for relief of the poor is attached to the hospital. Steward, F. Walker, Esq.

Guy's, St. Thomas's Street, Borough. — Accidents and urgent cases at all times, day and night. Taking-in day, Wednesdays, at 10.30. Secretary, M. Shattock, Esq.

London, Whitechapel Road. — Medical cases every day, except Sundays; surgical cases daily, except Wednesdays and Sundays. Out-patients, ophthalmic, Wednesdays and Saturdays; aural, Saturdays; skin, Wednesdays, from 8.30

to 9.30, A.M. Visiting-days : Tuesdays, Fridays, and Sundays, from 3 to 5. Assistant Secretary, Mr. M. A. G. Snellgrove.

MIDDLESEX, Charlotte Street. — Urgent cases at all times; out-patients, with a Governor's letter, must apply before 11, A.M. Resident Medical Officer, R. H. Lucas, Esq. Secretary and Superintendent, R. H. Lucas, Esq.

WESTMINSTER, near Westminster Abbey. — Urgent cases at all times ; out-patients, with Governor's letter, apply on Tuesdays, at 12 o'clock. Visiting-days : Sundays, between 2 and 4; and Mondays, Wednesdays, and Fridays, between 3 and 4, P.M. Secretary, F. J. Wilson, Esq.

UNIVERSITY COLLEGE, or NORTH LONDON, Gower Street. — In-patients daily, at 11, A.M.; out-patients daily, at 1 o'clock ; midwifery cases, Mondays and Thursdays, at 1 o'clock ; dental cases, Wednesdays, at 10, A.M.; eye, Mondays, Wednesdays, and Fridays, at 1 o'clock. Resident Medical Officer, W. Rigden, Esq. Secretary, H. J. Kelly, Esq., R.N.

KING'S COLLEGE, Portugal Street, Lincoln's-Inn-Fields. — Urgent cases at all times ; out-patients daily, at 1, P.M. Secretary, J. W. Waldron, Esq. Steward, Mr. D. G. Gray.

CHARING CROSS, Agar Street, Strand. — Urgent cases at all times ; others at 12.30 on Wednesdays; out-patients seen daily, at 12.30. Visiting-days : Tuesdays, Thursdays, and Sundays, 3 to 4. Secretary, H. Woolcott, Esq.

ROYAL FREE, Gray's-Inn-Road. Open at all times for accidents, &c.

ST. GEORGE'S, Hyde Park Corner. — Open at all times for accidents.

ST. MARY'S, Cambridge Place, Paddington, W. — In-patients, by letter of recommendation, on Fridays, at 1 o'clock ; urgent cases at all times ; out-patients daily at 1. Visiting-days : Tuesdays, Thursdays, and Sundays, from 3 to 4. Secretary, J. G. Wilkinson, Esq.

All the above have medical schools attached to them ; but it should be understood that they by no means represent the actual number of hospitals provided for the sick poor in London. There are a great many others for the treatment of special diseases. The foregoing are selected as the largest and chief medical schools of the metropolis.

MUSEUMS.

BRITISH, Bloomsbury. — National collections of objects of natural history, sculpture, &c. Entirely free. Open Monday, Wednesday, and Friday, from 10, and on Saturdays from 12 till dusk. To view the magnificent reading-room, apply in the Great Hall.

BETHNAL GREEN. — In the east of London. A branch of South Kensington Museum, specially organized for the poorer classes of London's citizens. Collection of pictures and art objects, animal products, food, &c. Most interesting. Open under same regulations as South Kensington Museum, for which see below.

COLLEGE OF SURGEONS, Lincoln's-Inn-Fields. — Admission to the museum only by order of members of the College, first four days of the week, from 12 to 5, in summer; and from 12 to 4, October to March.

PRACTICAL GEOLOGY, Jermyn Street, Piccadilly. — Open every day but Friday; free from 10 to 5. Closed from 10th of August to 10th of September.

INDIA, NEW INDIA OFFICE, Charles Street, St. James's Park. — Free on Monday, Tuesday, Wednesday, and Saturday, from 12 to 5.

KENSINGTON, SOUTH. — Free Mondays, Tuesdays, and Saturdays, from 10 to 10; on other days, from 10 to 6, on payment of 6d. See "Public Exhibitions of Paintings."

SOANE'S, SIR JOHN, Lincoln's-Inn-Fields. — Hogarth's paintings and other art treasures. Open from February to August inclusive on Wednesdays, and every Thursday and Friday in April, May, and June, from 10 to 4. Apply to Curator, by letter, for an order.

LINNÆAN MUSEUM, BURLINGTON HOUSE, Piccadilly. — Natural history. Free by order from Secretary.

ROYAL INSTITUTION, Albemarle Street, Piccadilly. Minerals. By order.

SOCIETY OF ARTS, John Street, Adelphi. — Paintings by Barry, in the great hall. Free on application.

ROYAL SOCIETY, Burlington House, Piccadilly. — General Museum. Free.

UNITED SERVICE INSTITUTION, Whitehall Yard. — Naval and military museum. Admission free, on application to the Secretary.

MUSIC HALLS, ETC.

THE OXFORD, near corner of Oxford Street and Tottenham Court Road. — Miscellaneous entertainments nightly. Admission, 1s.

LONDON PAVILION, Haymarket. — New programme of miscellaneous entertainments each night. Admission, 1s.

CANTERBURY HALL, Westminster Bridge Road. — Miscellaneous entertainments. Admission, 1s.

METROPOLITAN MUSIC HALL, Edgware Road. — Ballet and miscellaneous entertainment. Admission, 1s.

EVANS'S, Covent Garden. — Open every evening at 8. Excellent for suppers after the opera and theatres.

THE ARGYLL ROOMS, Haymarket. — Open for dancing every evening at 8.30. Admission, 1s.

SOUTH LONDON PALACE, Lambeth Road. — Ballet, &c. Admission, 1s.

---◆---

PLACES AND SIGHTS WHICH MUST BE SEEN BY A STRANGER BEFORE LEAVING LONDON.

THE TOWER OF LONDON. — The crown jewels, armories, &c. Admission by fee of 6d. to see the armories and the Beauchamp Tower, and 6d. to the jewel house. Daily, except Sundays, from 10 to 4.

The best way of getting to the Tower, and the one least likely to cause trouble or annoyance, is by cab. The fare from Charing Cross is 2s. See Appendix, *Tower of London.*

WESTMINSTER ABBEY, near the Houses of Parliament and Westminster Bridge. — Free to the chief parts of the building; to other parts by fee of 6d. No fee on Mondays from 11 till 2.30, P.M. Daily service is performed in the Abbey chorally. See Churches, also Appendix, *Westminster Abbey.*

ST. PAUL'S CATHEDRAL. — The masterpiece of Sir Christopher Wren. Splendid architecture, whispering-gallery, cross and ball, monuments to famous men. Nave and transepts free; choir closed except during divine service. Whispering-gallery, 6d.: ball, 1s. 6d.; clock, bell, library, and staircase, 6d.; crypt, 6d. See Churches.

BRITISH MUSEUM, Bloomsbury. — See Museums, also Appendix, *British Museum.*

NATIONAL GALLERY, Trafalgar Square.— See Public Exhibitions of Paintings.

HOUSES OF PARLIAMENT, near Westminster Bridge.— Admission on Saturdays free, by order of the lord-chamberlain, obtained at a neighboring office, for which ask a policeman on duty; also during the hearing of appeals in the House of Lords. Admission to the Strangers' Gallery, by member's order only, obtained through the embassy.

HOUSE OF COMMONS. — This branch of the British Legislature used to sit in St. Stephen's Chapel until the year 1834, when that building was destroyed by fire. St. Stephen's Hall now occupies the site of the former House of Commons. The original basement-story of St. Stephen's Chapel still exists in the ancient crypt of St. Stephen's, which has been superbly embellished, and restored for use as the Palace Chapel. The representatives of the people of the United Kingdom, in February, 1852, first assembled in their present chamber, which is not far from the north end of the Palace. The Strangers' Gallery, and below it the Speaker's Gallery, are placed opposite the speaker's chair, and command a full view of the House. Behind the chair is a gallery appropriated to the reporters. The side-galleries were intended to be strictly reserved for members; but, during great debates, peers are tacitly permitted to occupy the benches farthest removed from the speaker. Persons usually obtain access to the Strangers' Gallery through the written order of a member. Admission to the Speaker's Gallery is a more coveted privilege; and this is generally effected by a personal application on the part of some member of parliament to the sergeant-at-arms. These two galleries for non-members are opened as soon as the speaker takes the chair; but on Budget Nights, and other interesting occasions, the candidates for admission to the Strangers' Gallery range themselves in St. Stephen's Hall several hours before the doors are opened. The House used to adjourn to 10 o'clock in the morning; but the practice now is, that, a few minutes before 4 o'clock, the speaker takes his seat at the table, and the chaplain reads prayers. The Strangers', Speaker's, and Reporters' Galleries are then opened; the members present are counted; and, as forty generally attend, business begins.* If, after 4 o'clock, there are not forty members present when the House is counted, the House is

* See Appendix, *House of Commons.*

6

adjourned to the next day at the customary hour. The first
half-hour is devoted to private business and petitions. At
half-past four public business begins, when the leading
members of the Government are expected to be in their
places to answer the questions of which notice has been
given. On Wednesdays the House meets at noon, and sits
till 6, if the orders of the day are not sooner disposed of.
Towards the latter end of the session, the House not unfre-
quently holds what are called "day sittings," in order to
expedite the bills before it. On these occasions, the speaker
takes the chair at 12 o'clock : at 4, the sitting is suspended
until 6, when business is resumed; and the sitting is generally continued until after midnight. The House does not
usually sit on Saturday. Peers and distinguished foreigners
are accommodated with seats below the bar. The foreign
ministers usually sit in the gallery opposite the speaker,
which is also resorted to by members of the other House of
Parliament.

House of Lords. — The Strangers' Gallery, as in the
Commons, is not opened till after prayers. Their lordships
frequently sit during the day as a court of appeal; but do
not usually assemble in their legislative capacity until 5
in the afternoon, unless upon the opening or closing of the
session, which generally takes place at 2 o'clock; or when
the royal assent is to be given to bills by commission, on
which occasion their lordships meet earlier than the customary hour; but for this purpose no precise time has been
established by usage. While sitting in their judicial capacity, the House, like other courts of justice, is open to the
public.

Westminster Hall, adjacent to the Houses of Parliament. — Free. Contains Courts of Chancery, Queen's Bench,
Common Pleas, and Exchequer. One of the largest and
oldest buildings in the kingdom. A point should be made
of entering one of the courts of law to watch the proceedings. See Appendix, *Westminster Hall.* N.B. — Do not
leave before seeing St. Stephen's Crypt, under the House
of Commons.

Bank of England. — The business portion free. The
private portions, as the safes, printing machinery, only by
order of a governor; 10 till 4. See Appendix, *Bank of
England.*

South Kensington Museum. — See Public Exhibitions.

International Exhibition, South Kensington. — See
Public Exhibitions.

St. James's Park and Palace, foot of Pall Mall. — None of the apartments are to be seen. At 11 every morning a color-guard of one of the regiments of Guards mounts in the Palace yard. The ceremony is interesting, and the military music always exceedingly good.

Marlborough House. — Residence of the Prince of Wales, east end of St. James's Palace. The red brick house adjoining.

Lambeth Palace. — The official residence of the Archbishop of Canterbury, on south bank of Thames, Lambeth. Library, &c.; free, by order from the archbishop. Better take steamboat from foot of Westminster Bridge to Lambeth, 1*d.*

Apsley House. — The residence of the Duke of Wellington, corner of Piccadilly and Hyde Park. May be viewed by permission.

Rotten Row and Hyde Park. — Be sure to go there between 12 and 2, or 5 and 7, during May, June, or July.

Kensington Gardens (the Albert Memorial). — A continuation of Hyde Park. The Memorial is one of the most costly and grand monuments in London.

Kensington Palace (private) and Gardens. — Free every day. At the West of Hyde Park.

Buckingham Palace, west end of St. James's Park. — Admision, in the absence of Royalty, by special order only of the lord-chamberlain, which it is very difficult to procure.

Clubs in Pall Mall. — Admission obtained through a member's order. The Carlton (with the large and massive polished granite columns), the Junior Carlton (opposite), the Reform, the Army and Navy, the Athenæum, and the United Service, are large and elegant buildings, and well worth seeing. See Appendix, *London Clubs.*

Government Offices. — Magnificent new Home, Colonial, Foreign, and India offices, Downing Street and St. James's Park; Admiralty, Horse Guards, Treasury, &c. Interior free, by order from heads of departments. A walk past Whitehall, on the right-hand side from Charing Cross, will enable the visitor to take in all the above buildings; passing the Admiralty first, Paymaster-General's next, Horse Guards next, and so on.

Whitehall, opposite Horse Guards. — Erected by Inigo Jones; intended for a banqueting-house, now used as the Chapel Royal. King Charles I. was beheaded in front of it. See Churches.

Inns of Court, the abode of the practisers of the law. — The chief are the Temple, in Fleet Street; Lincoln's Inn, between Chancery Lane and Lincoln's-Inn-Fields; Gray's Inn, north of Holborn; and New Inn, Wych Street. The halls and chapels are very interesting in most of the Inns. The Temple Church open to strangers from 10 to 12, and from 1 to 4; service daily at 10, A.M., and on Sundays at 11, A.M., and 3, P.M. See Churches and Appendix, *Inns of Court.*

The Guildhall, in King Street, City. — The most interesting and grandest civic hall in the kingdom. The library is especially fine. Strangers are received with the greatest courtesy by the officials in charge, and every part of this fine old building may be seen. Ask for the Council Chamber.

Mansion House, City. — The official residence of the lord-mayor. The Egyptian hall and ball-room are the chief attractions. Admission by order and a small fee.

Times Printing Office, Printing House Square, Blackfriars Road. — From 11 to 1, by order only from the editor.

Christ's Hospital (Elia's old school), Newgate Street, City. — Do not fail to visit this wonderful relic of the monastic institutions of Old England. The hall is one of the finest in London, and the cloisters are especially interesting. St. Bartholomew's Hospital, close by. See Churches. Appendix, *Christ's Hospital.*

Royal Exchange, Cornhill. — Free. Statue of Queen inside, Wellington in front, Peabody behind, and Queen Elizabeth, Sir Thomas Gresham, and others, on the walls of the building. 'Change, the busy time, from 3 to 4, P.M.

Post Office, St. Martin's-le-Grand, — Should be visited a little before 6, P.M., when the business of letter-posting is greatest. Make a special point of visiting the Central Telegraph Office, opposite.

Monuments. — Albert, South Kensington; finest in the country. London, to commemorate great fire, near London Bridge; fine views of the city; admission 3*d.* Duke of York, St. James's Park; view of Park and West End; admission, 6*d.* Nelson's, Trafalgar Square. Guards, Waterloo Place. Crimean, Broad Sanctuary, Westminster.

Docks. — St. Katharine's, London, East and West India, Commercial, Victoria, &c. All accessible by steamboat or railway at about 4*d.* Wine-tasting orders may be obtained through the leading wine-merchants; otherwise, free.

Law Courts. — In Westminster Hall are the courts of

Chancery, Queen's Bench, Common Pleas, Exchequer, &c.; in Lincoln's Inn, Chancery and Vice-Chancery courts. Courts of law and equity are also held at Guildhall in the city. Central Criminal Court, Old Bailey.

MARKETS.— Metropolitan Meat Market, Smithfield: to see the market, go early on a Monday morning. Leadenhall Market (poultry). Billingsgate (fish), Thames Street. Columbia, near Shoreditch Church. Covent Garden (fruit, flowers, &c.): go on a Saturday morning early. Farringdon, Borough, and Spitalfields (vegetables, &c.). Cattle Market and Abattoirs, Caledonian Road. Foreign Cattle Market, Deptford.

STATUES. — Equestrian statue of the Duke of Wellington, on the Arch opposite Apsley House; Charles I., Charing Cross; Peel, Cheapside; Albert, Holborn Circus; Guards' Memorial, Pall Mall; Cobden, High Street, Camden Town; Peabody, William IV., and others, in city and West End.

SUGGESTIONS FOR SEEING THE FOREGOING.

Before setting out for a day's sight-seeing in London, it would be very advisable for the stranger to consult his map for a moment, and take, let us say, a "district" for the day. Thus the following places (A), lying within a half-mile radius of each other, might very well be set down for one day; and the other places, if convenient, in groups as follows: —

A. 1. Westminster Abbey.
   2. Westminster Hall.
   3. Houses of Parliament.
   4. Whitehall.
      The Government offices, to be seen as suggested above.

If possible, on a Saturday; the Houses of Lords and Commons being open to the public on that day only.

B. 1. St. Paul's Cathedral.
   2. Christ's Hospital.
   3. Guildhall.
   4. Tower of London.
   5. Post - Office (on the way back).

The first two are within five minutes' walk of each other; the third, about a hundred yards from the second. The Tower is a one-shilling cab-fare from Guildhall.

C. 1. The National Gallery.
2. The British Museum.
3. The Polytechnic Institution.
4. The Clubs.
5. St. James's Park.

Take a *yellow* omnibus at the church at corner of Trafalgar Square, and ask to be set down at British Museum. The remaining two on the way home, or in the evening.

D. 1. The South Kensington Museum.
2. The National Portrait Gallery.
3. The International Exhibition.
4. The Horticultural Gardens.
5. The Albert Memorial. Hyde Park, if not too tired. (*Rotten Row from 5 to 7, P. M.*)

Ask for nearest *Metropolitan Railway* Station, and take ticket to *South* Kensington. Each place is within stone's-throw of the other.

E. 1. The Royal Academy, Burlington House.
2. The Doré Gallery, 35 New Bond Street.
3. Buckingham Palace.
4. Crystal Palace at Sydenham.

The Academy opens at 8, A.M. Walk down Piccadilly, across Park, to the Palace, and ask for Victoria Railroad Station for the Crystal Palace.

F. (*Steamboat at foot of Westminster Bridge for view of Thames, Docks, and Shipping; and for*)
1. Greenwich, Painted Hall, Nelson relics, &c.
2. Woolwich Arsenal, Artillery, &c.
3. London Bridge (*land on way back*) for
4. Royal Exchange.
5. Bank of England.
6. Mansion House.

Fares, 6*d.* and 3*d.*

G. 1. Zoölogical Gardens, Regent's Park.
 2. Madame Tussaud's Waxworks.
 3. Regent Street and the shops, about 4 in the afternoon.

Take omnibus marked *"City Atlas"* at corner of Regent's Circus, Piccadilly, for Regent's Park. Mad. Tussaud's on way back.

H. 1. Lambeth Palace.
 2. Kew Gardens.
 3. Richmond.

Take steamboat from foot of Westminster Bridge for Lambeth. On leaving Palace, ask for Vauxhall Bridge Railroad Station, and take ticket for Kew or Richmond, where dine.

I. 1. Temple Bar.
 2. The Temple, Hall, and Church.
 3. Lincoln's Inn.
 4. Gray's Inn.
 5. Holborn Viaduct, &c.
 6. Newgate, and the Strand, home.

K. 1. Windsor Castle.
 2. Virginia Water.
 (Tickets to be had at Colnaghi, Publisher, 13 Pall Mall.)

From Waterloo Bridge Railroad Station to Windsor. Take Return-Ticket.

L. 1. Hampton Court and the Palace.
 2. Gardens, &c. &c.

Rail from Waterloo Bridge. Return-Ticket.

These groups will furnish the tourist with a pretty general idea of how he should set about sight-seeing in London so as to economize time and money. Many of the places here set down are, of course, worth whole days of study; but they have been grouped together so as to bring them within a day's not too tedious work.

PRIVATE COLLECTIONS OF PAINTINGS.

Only to be seen by special permission of the owners, which may generally be had upon courteous application by letter.

BRIDGEWATER GALLERY, St. James's.

GROSVENOR GALLERY (the Marquis of Westminster's), Upper Grosvenor Street. By tickets, in May, June, and July.

DUKE OF SUTHERLAND'S PICTURES by Murillo, Van Dyck, and P. Delaroche, Stafford House, St. James's Palace.

DUKE OF BEDFORD'S DUTCH PICTURES, 6 Belgrave Square.

THE CORREGGIO (Christ in the Garden), and other pictures, at Apsley House, the residence of the Duke of Wellington.

THE VAN DYCK PORTRAITS AND SKETCHES (*en grisaille*), fine Canalétti (View of Whitehall), at Montague House.

LADY GARVAGH'S RAPHAEL, THE ALDOBRANDINI MADONNA, 26 Portman Square.

DUKE OF GRAFTON'S Van Dyck, of Charles I. standing by his horse, at 47 Clarges Street, Piccadilly.

EARL DE GREY'S COLLECTION, by Van Dyck, in St. James's Square.

LORD LANSDOWNE'S COLLECTION, Lansdowne House.

THE DUKE OF DEVONSHIRE'S GALLERY, Devonshire House, Piccadilly.

LORD ASHBURTON'S COLLECTION, at Bath House, Piccadilly.

MARQUIS OF HERTFORD'S COLLECTION, 'Hertford House, Manchester Square.

BARON ROTHSCHILD'S MURILLO (Infant Saviour), at Gunnersbury, five miles from Hyde Park Corner.

Mr. R. S. HOLFORD'S COLLECTION, at Dorchester House, Park Lane.

PUBLIC EXHIBITIONS OF PAINTINGS, ETC.

ACADEMY ROYAL, Burlington House, Piccadilly. — Exhibition of modern paintings by the Royal Academicians and eminent painters, thirteen weeks from first Monday in May, from 8, A.M., to 7, P.M. Admission 1s.; catalogue 1s. Americans in London during the time this exhibition is open to the public would do well to make a point of seeing it. The collection of paintings embraces works of art from all the most celebrated painters in the United Kingdom. Beyond this, Burlington House itself is quite worth a visit.

NATIONAL GALLERY, Trafalgar Square. — The National Collection of Great Britain, comprising paintings from some of the most famous of the old masters, many of which have been purchased by the nation at fabulous sums. Open Monday, Tuesday, Wednesday, and Saturday, from 10 to 6. Closed entirely during October. Admission free.

SOUTH KENSINGTON MUSEUM. — Collection of art treasures, manufactures, useful arts, paintings, inventions. Possibly the most interesting exhibition, taken as a whole, in London. The tourist must not neglect to spend, if possible, one whole day at this charming institution. Beyond a most interesting and priceless collection of art treasures, here are original paintings of Landseer, Rosa Bonheur, David Wilkie, Maclise, Frith (the celebrated Derby Day), Lance, and a whole host of other great artists, and the well-known paintings of the Vernon Gallery. Every convenience is to be found. An admirable and exquisitely decorated suite of dining-rooms, where meals may be had at most reasonable prices, and well served; and there can be no hesitation about saying that the South Kensington Museum is one of the most delightful resorts, both for the student and sight-seer, to be found anywhere in London. Free Mondays, Tuesdays, and Saturdays, from 10, A.M., to 10, P.M.; on other days from 10, A.M., to 6, P.M., on payment of sixpence.

The courts and corridors of South Kensington are full of work, and much of it very beautiful work, well worth careful inspection, done by the students, either during their course of study or after it, when they have been engaged at good wages to design and model, to paint on porcelain, wood, or other material. With a few exceptions, all the decorative art at South Kensington has been or is being done by the students. In the refreshment-rooms, the South Court, and on the staircases, there are pillars, panels, and ceilings which may claim a visitor's attention equally with the contents of the Museum. In the Competition Gallery the upper part of the wall is decorated with lunettes, some of which are after designs by Yeames, Marks, Leslie, Pickersgill; and others by Messrs. Godfrey Sykes and Moody, two of the most distinguished students the School of Art has produced; while the reproduction in full size of all the designs is the work of the students. These panels, in the actual beauty of the figures, as well as in the excellence of the execution, are real works of high art. The decoration of the arches over the gallery of the South Court, and of the north staircase windows and ceiling, is home-made. The figures in mosaic on the walls of the South Court were most of them executed by the female students, and some of them designed by the male. The decoration of two of the three refreshment-rooms is the product of the schools; the designs on the panels of the grill-room having been done in small by Mr. Poynter, and enlarged by the students.

NATIONAL PORTRAIT GALLERY. — A branch of the above institution at South Kensington, open free on Mondays, Tuesdays, and Saturdays, as above; on other days, on payment of sixpence. The National Portrait Gallery originated with the late Lord Derby, who advised a collection of historical portraits, which, when chronologically arranged, "might not only possess great historical interest by bringing together portraits of all the most eminent contemporaries of their respective eras, but might serve also to illustrate the progress and condition at various periods of British art." The gallery contains about three hundred and fifty portraits, the earliest of which is an old panel picture of Henry IV. (born 1366; died 1413). Admission free.

INTERNATIONAL EXHIBITION, South Kensington. — Within five minutes' walk of either of the above institutions. This is another exhibition which must be visited by the American tourist. Admission 1s. Wednesdays, 2s. 6d.

The three divisions of the South Kensington International Exhibition of 1874 will consist of, —

I. — FINE ARTS. FINE ARTS APPLIED, OR NOT APPLIED, TO WORKS OF UTILITY.
   There will be an exhibition of the works of deceased artists in 1874.

II. — MANUFACTURES. Machinery and Processes as follows: —

Lace, Hand, and Machine Made.
Civil Engineering, Architectural, and Building Contrivances · *and Tests.*
  a. Civil Engineering, and Building Construction.
  b. Sanitary Apparatus and Constructions.
  c. Cement and Plaster Work, &c.
Leather, including Saddlery and Harness.
  a. Leather, and Manufactures of Leather.
  b. Saddlery and Harness.
Bookbinding of all kinds.
Heating by all methods.
Machinery in general for the group.
Raw materials used for all the above-mentioned objects.

III. — RECENT SCIENTIFIC INVENTIONS AND NEW DISCOVERIES OF ALL KINDS.

IV. — FOREIGN WINES.

Any modifications which may have been found necessary will be found duly announced in the daily press.

ART EXHIBITIONS. — The daily papers will always advertise the principal collections on view during the summer season in London. The usual period for the best to be opened is between May and the end of August; and they are as follows: —

SOCIETY OF BRITISH ARTISTS, Suffolk Street, Charing Cross.

THE BRITISH INSTITUTION, Pall Mall.

SOCIETY OF PAINTERS IN WATER COLORS, Pall Mall, East.

INSTITUTE OF PAINTERS IN WATER COLORS, Pall Mall.

THE DORÉ GALLERY, 35 New Bond Street. — "Genius of the most comprehensive, the boldest, and the loftiest type, is the verdict that must be passed by the most hypercritical beholder of the few pictures which make up the Doré Gallery in Bond Street. We say few, in the comparative sense of numbers, when contrasting it with other exhibitions; but when we examine the vast execution of these paintings, and consider, besides, the vast amount of smaller and desultory undertakings in the way of engraving and book-illustration which the artist has effected, we are led to marvel at the industry as well as power he possesses. In half a dozen of these oil paintings there is enough to stamp the reputation of a life; nay, in even one there is such a world of wealth, such a prodigality of art, that a painter might reasonably say,

"I have succeeded; I have done enough." To the student and the lover of pictorial art, more genuine enjoyment is to be found in the contemplation of this limited collection than in wearily travelling over acres of gaudily-covered canvas on the walls of an annual exhibition. There the eye pauses only occasionally on a production of true genius, gulfed in a maze of mediocrity: here the superabundance of power almost dazzles: the spectator and he reverts from one picture to another, taking in fresh points of beauty and excellence at every glance." —*London Examiner.*

PUBLIC EXHIBITIONS.

CRYSTAL PALACE, Sydenham. — Access by several lines of railroad from Victoria Station, Charing Cross, Waterloo Bridge, and London Bridge, and all the principal stations of the Metropolitan Railroad. Admission, including first-class return-ticket by·rail, 2s. 6d. on every day· but Saturday, when the single admission to the Palace is 5s. The Crystal Palace is now an established institution in England. It belongs to every class; and all can enjoy themselves within its delightful precincts just as the humor suits. Throughout its vast extent the keenest point of individual satisfaction can be realized, and at a cost that suits the humblest resources. It is undoubtedly the cheeriest place of popular resort about London; and the managers, from their tact, skill, and variety of enterprises, are well entitled to that commendation which an appreciative public are not chary to bestow. In all seasons, the Crystal Palace affords a genial welcome to every description of comer. The gardens in which the building stands, the scenery which surrounds them, the grand system of fountains (second only to those of Versailles), offer, without any exception whatever, the most charming attractions to the strangers to be found anywhere inside or outside of London. The Saturday-afternoon Concerts and the Flower Shows, during the summer season, attract the very *élite* of London fashionable society; and the displays of fireworks on special occasions are exceptionally grand. It may be mentioned, that, for dinner-giving, the Crystal Palace is one of the most popular resorts near London.

One of the chief attractions of the place is the Aquarium.

The tanks are well filled with a representative British fauna; and the arrangement is thoughtful and systematic, and such as enables even a casual visitor, hand-book in hand, .to.gain, in passing from tank to tank, a very large amount of knowledge with wonderful ease and pleasure.

N.B. — In going by rail, be sure to ask for *First-class Return, and Admission* to the Palace.

ALEXANDRA PARK, Muswell Hill. — This extensive park offers many attractions, and abounds in beautiful scenery. See Appendix, *Suburban Resorts.*

MADAME TUSSAUD'S WAX-WORK. 58 Baker Street, Portman Square. — Latest additions, portrait models of Marshal MacMahon (President of the French Republic), and the distinguished novelist, the late Mr. Charles Dickens. Admission, 1s.; children under ten, 6d.; extra rooms, 6d. Open from 10, A.M. till 10, P.M.

POLYTECHNIC INSTITUTION, 309 Regent Street. — Admission 1s. Variety of entertainments, scientific, musical, and general. Open from 12 to 5, and 7 till 10, daily.

SUBURBAN RESORTS.

Much frequented by Londoners during the summer months, and to which the tourist should, if possible, pay a visit, if only to make himself acquainted with the manners and customs of Londoners "out for the day," and how they manage to get a great deal of real enjoyment out of the expenditure of very little money.

BROXBOURNE in Hertfordshire. — On the Great Eastern Railway. Fine gardens, boating, fishing, amusements, &c. Close to the scene of the Rye-House Plot. Fare, by railway, 1s. and upwards.

DULWICH. — By railway or omnibus, fare 6d. Fine gallery of paintings at the college, free. Ride outside an omnibus, and get a glimpse of South London streets.

ERITH. — By Gravesend boats or North Kent Railway, Charing Cross. Garden. Regattas in the summer.

GRAVESEND. — Access from London by steamboat (30 miles), and railway from Charing Cross. Fares, 1s. to 1s. 6d. Windmill Hill, Springhead Gardens, Cobham Park, fine views of the Thames (here a mile wide), shipping, sea-water bathing. Near are *Rosherville Gardens*, admission 6d. Opposite is *Tilbury Fort.* By going to Gravesend by steamboat, a fine view of the Thames, Docks, &c., may be had.

GREENWICH. — The Naval Hospital, commonly known as Greenwich Hospital, the Painted Hall, Nelson's Relics, &c., the Observatory, Park, Blackheath. Fare, 4*d.* from Charing Cross, by boat or railway; tramway from Blackfriars Bridge.

HAMPSTEAD HEATH. — Fine view of London. Access by railway and omnibus. Fare, 6*d.* Well worth a visit.

HAMPTON COURT. — Built by Cardinal Wolsey; 13 miles from London. Railway fare, 1*s.* from Waterloo Bridge Station. Steamboats, with beautiful view of river, in summer. Gardens and splendid gallery of pictures, free daily (including Sunday), 2 to 4 winter, 2 to 6 summer, except Friday, from 10 till dusk. It would be well to try the trip by steamboat, if the day be fine, from foot of Westminster Bridge. Kew Gardens not a great way off.

HARROW. — Great public school. View from churchyard. Access by rail, 1*s.*

EPPING FOREST, LOUGHTON, BUCKHURST HILL, &c., on Great Eastern Railway. — Fare, 1*s.* Beautiful forest-scenery. A favorite resort for picnic-parties, and what are called, by the London artisan and his better half, " bean-feasts."

MOULSEY, near Hampton Court. — Fine view of the Thames, boating, and fishing. Rail from Waterloo Bridge.

RICHMOND. — The Park and adjacent villages, &c., — as Twickenham, Sheen, Mortlake, Teddington, Thames Ditton, Pope's Villa, Strawberry Hill, — afford views of some of the most lovely scenery to be found in any part of England. The stranger to London must not leave it without going to Richmond. The best way of getting there is by rail from Waterloo Bridge ; or a very enjoyable but somewhat long ride may be had " outside " an omnibus, starting from the White Horse Cellar, Piccadilly, every half-hour or hour. Dine at Richmond at the Star and Garter, and don't omit to eat a " Maid of Honor."

WINDSOR. — Twenty-two miles from London by Southwestern (Waterloo Bridge), North London, or Great Western Railways. Castle, in the absence of the Queen, free four days a week. Eton College, and, close by, Runnymede, celebrated in connection with Magna Charta. See appendix, *Windsor Castle.*

WOOLWICH. — Extensive barracks for artillery. The Arsenal, by order only, on Tuesdays and Fridays.

THEATRES: PRICES OF ADMISSION, AND LOCALITIES.

Doors open generally at 6.30, P.M., performances commencing at 7; except in the case of the Royal Italian Operas at Covent Garden and Drury Lane, where 8 is the usual hour for the doors being opened, and 8.30 for the performances to commence.

DRURY LANE. — Drama, and, in May and June, opera, &c. Private boxes from 1 to 4 guineas each; stalls, 7*s.*; dress circle, 5*s.*; first circle, 4*s.*; balcony, 3*s.*; pit, 2*s.*; lower gallery, 1*s.*; upper gallery, 6*d.* During the season of opera, the prices are considerably higher.

HAYMARKET. — Private boxes, 42*s.*, 31*s.* 6*d.*; orchestra stalls, 7*s.*; dress boxes, 5*s.*; upper boxes, 3*s.* and 2*s.*; pit and amphitheatre, 2*s.*; gallery, 1*s.* Half-price at 9, P.M.

ADELPHI, Strand. — Pit and dress-circle boxes, for six, 52*s.* 6*d*; first circle, for six, 42*s.*; family boxes, for four, 21*s.*; orchestra, single, 6*s.*; balcony, 5*s.*; first circle, 3*s.*; pit, 2*s.*; amphitheatre, 1*s.*; gallery, 6*d.*

PRINCESS'S, Oxford Street, five minutes' walk from Regent Street. — Private boxes, from 21*s.* to 73*s.* 6*d.*; stalls, 7*s.*; dress circle, 4*s.*; pit stalls, 2*s.*; pit, 1*s.* 6*d.*; amphitheatre, 1*s.*; gallery, 6*d.*

ST. JAMES'S, King Street, St. James's. — Dramatic and opera seasons. Boxes, 31*s.* 6*d.* to 5 guineas; orchestra stalls, 7*s.*; dress circle, 5*s.*; family circle, 2*s.* 6*d.*; amphitheatre, 1*s.*; no pit.

QUEEN'S, Long Acre, near Covent Garden. — Private boxes, 31*s.* 6*d.*, 42*s.*, 52*s.* 6*d.*; orchestra, 7*s.* 6*d.*; balcony, 4*s.*; upper circle, 2*s.*; pit, 2*s.*; amphitheatre, 1*s.*; gallery, 6*d.*

ROYALTY, Dean Street, Soho. — Private boxes, 42*s.*, 52*s.* 6*d.*; stalls, 7*s.*; dress circle, 4*s.*; boxes, 2*s.*; pit, 1*s.* 6*d.*; gallery, 6*d.*

GAIETY, Strand. — Opera, farce, and burlesque. Private boxes, from 21*s.*; orchestra stalls, 7*s.*; balcony stalls, 5*s.*; upper boxes, 3*s.*; pit, 2*s.*; amphitheatre, 1*s.*; gallery, 6*d.*

LYCEUM, Wellington Street, Strand. — Drama. Private boxes, 31*s.* 6*d.*, 42*s.*, 63*s.*; stalls, 7*s.*; dress circle, 5*s.*; boxes, 3*s.*; pit, 2*s.*; gallery, 1*s.*

GLOBE, Newcastle Street, Strand. — Comedy, &c. Private boxes, from 1 to 3 guineas; stalls, 7*s.*; dress circle, 5*s.*; upper boxes, 3*s.*; pit, 2*s.*; gallery, 6*d.*

OLYMPIC, Wych Street, Drury Lane. — Private boxes, 21s. to 52s. 6d.; stalls, 6s.; dress circle, 4s.; boxes, 4s.; pit, 2s.; amphitheatre, 1s.; gallery, 6d.

OPERA COMIQUE, 299 Strand. — Private boxes, from 1 to 3 guineas; orchestra stalls, 7s.; balcony stalls, 5s.; upper circle, 3s.; amphitheatre stalls, 2s.; gallery, 1s.

STRAND, a few doors east of Somerset House. — Various, burlesque and farce. Private boxes, 31s. 6d. and 42s.; stalls, 7s.; dress circle, 4s.; boxes, 3s.; pit, 2s.; gallery, 6d.

PHILHARMONIC, Islington Green. — Opera, burlesque, ballet, &c.; 5s., 3s., 2s., 1s. 6d.

PRINCE OF WALES'S, Tottenham Court Road. — Stalls, 7s. 6d.; dress circle, 5s.; boxes, 4s.; upper circle, 3s.; pit, 2s. 6d.; amphitheatre, 1s.

COURT, Sloane Square. — Private boxes, 1 to 3 guineas; stalls, 7s. 6d.; dress circle, 5s.; boxes, 3s.; pit, 2s.; amphitheatre, 1s. 6d.; first gallery, 1s.; second gallery, 6d.

VAUDEVILLE, Strand. — Comedy and burlesque. Private boxes, 42s.; stalls, 7s.; balcony stalls, 5s.'; boxes, 3s.; upper circle, 2s.; pit, 2s.; gallery, 6d.

HOLBORN. — Private boxes, 21s., 42s., 63s., 84s.; stalls, 10s. 6d.; dress circle, 5s.; boxes, 3s. 6d.; pit, 2s.; gallery, 1s.

SURREY, Blackfriars Road. — Melodrama, farce, &c. Stalls, 3s.; dress circle, 2s.; upper boxes, 1s. 6d.; pit, 1s.; gallery, 6d.

CHARING CROSS, King William Street. — Stalls, 7s.; boxes, 5s.; pit, 2s.

ASTLEY'S (now Sanger's), Westminster Bridge Road. — Circus, &c. Stalls, 5s.; private boxes, 21s. and upwards; lower boxes, 3s.; upper boxes, 1s. 6d.; pit, 1s.; gallery, 6d.

HENGLER'S CIRCUS, Palais Royal, Argyll Street. — Horsemanship, &c.; 5s., 4s., 3s., 2s., 1s., and 6d.

ALHAMBRA, Leicester Square. — Farce, ballet, and burlesque. Boxes, 21s. to 42s., 6s., 5s., 3s., 2s., 1s. 6d.

It is usual, during the months of May, June, and July, to appear in full dress (especially where ladies are concerned) in the stalls and boxes of the best London theatres. In visiting the Royal Italian Opera, either at Covent Garden or Drury Lane, full dress is absolutely necessary both for gentlemen and ladies.

The daily papers always give the performances for each evening, together with the hours at which they commence. The time is liable to be changed during the continuance of the London season, from May to August.

APPENDIX.

INTRODUCTION.

The Editor has endeavored, in this portion of his book, to awaken an interest in a place or event, not by giving a detailed account of objects apparent to the eye, and which an ordinary amount of thought, or reading at home, or a word of inquiry, should enable a person to distinguish at once, and to connect with this circumstance in a man's life, or that event in history, but by writing a short general sketch of the chief points of interest in and near London, leaving the reader to fill in whatever blanks are left for himself. "If you are not a thinking man, to what purpose are you a man at all?" asks Coleridge. Judge for yourselves with the objects before you; think, and then go home to learn and to venerate, and to improve the heart and the understanding both, by studying history.

There are few things so exhilarating to the spirits, especially in the season of ardent and buoyant youth, as the first visit to a foreign land. Amongst things purely pleasurable, it is, perhaps, one of the most unalloyed gratifications which occur in the course of a lifetime. Like all other pleasures, however, it may be made, according as we use it, a source of present vanity and future regret;· or, on the other hand, of lasting and solid improvement.

It is to be hoped that few persons undertake a journey to London — that city, taken altogether, perhaps the most wonderful in the world, and possessing some of the world's rarest historic treasures — for the sole purpose of gratifying an idle curiosity, and seeking mere temporary amusement. We should set out with an intention of profiting to the utmost by the visit, both physically and mentally, and of laying up such a treasury of thought as shall serve us in good stead, and prove an inexhaustible source of pleasure by and by, when the days come creeping on for counting up the pleasures of a lifetime.

Where is the profit in that modern abomination known as "doing" such and such a place?

"Have you been in London?" we asked of a man the other day. "Been in London? Why, I staid there three weeks!" "Did you see any thing in that time?" "'Did' the place thoroughly, my dear sir." And how dangerous is the little learning that man possesses! — nay, how worthless it is! He has been to the Tower of London, of course. For the life of him, though, he couldn't discourse upon the trifling facts of history connected with

> "That gate misnamed, through which before
> Went Sidney, Russell, Raleigh, Cranmer, More."

Your modern traveller in London walks through corridors of the Houses of Parliament. He stays to admire the beautiful frescoes which adorn their walls. One especially attracts his attention: it is Speaker Lenthall claiming privilege for the Commons when Charles attempted to seize the five members. You question him upon that most important passage in the life of Charles the First. What does he know about it? What does he care to know? Yet it was one of the most important events in parliamentary history; and that was the one most serious error of Charles's life, when he went on his bootless errand to the House of Commons in quest of the five members. It was then that Speaker Lenthall, making way for him in the chair, spoke those memorable words which live in history: "I have neither eyes to see, nor tongue to speak, in this place, but as the House is pleased to direct me, whose servant I am here." The Commons claimed "privilege;" and the King perforce granted it, though signing his own death-warrant the while.

By accident, your modern tourist drops into the chapel of the Foundling Hospital for service on a Sunday. He hears the rich tones of a magnificent organ, which he is told was the gift of the great Handel; which was erected, in fact, under his immediate supervision. "Oh!" he says, and passes out, not caring to inquire what were the circumstances which led to the gift being made, or how it was that Handel became connected with this hospital for foundlings in London. Yet Handel, if we mistake not, wrote his glorious oratorio, "The Messiah," for that institution. He played it time and time again upon the chapel organ. And we believe that he presented its copyright to the governors, and by that means became one of the greatest benefactors the institution has known. Look, too, at that wonderful little church in the Temple: we mean the Temple off Fleet Street. Have any of us who have passed it by, and who have stood to gaze at the quaint little structure planted in the midst of Old London, the least conception of the enormous wealth of history that lies buried within its walls? Do we even know why the place where it stands is called the Temple?

The best of all ways, good reader, for seeing London, is through the light of history.

Most of the sketches which appear here have been condensed from articles written by the Editor, and published from time to time in "Appleton's Journal," "Hearth and Home," and "The Boston Commercial Bulletin;" and the present opportunity is taken for thanking the proprietors of those journals for permitting the republication of the articles in this form.

APPENDIX.

THE BANK OF ENGLAND.

The Bank of England was the first joint-stock bank established in England; and having exclusive privileges in the capital of England, granted by royal charter, it continued the only joint-stock bank in London until 1834. At this date the London and Westminster Bank was founded, and proceeded so successfully, that it was quickly followed by the formation of the London Joint-Stock Bank and the Union Bank of London. Some of the privileges claimed by the Bank of England, in opposition to the new banks, were found, after litigation, to be untenable. The Old Lady of Threadneedle Street was born A.D. 1694, in the reign of good King William of pious and immortal memory, — that King William whose memory gentlemen of Orange-loving tendencies most fondly cherish. She was an especial favorite of this good king; adopted his Whig principles; and dutifully acted a daughter's part in supplying him with cash when he was fighting the cause of civil and religious freedom, much to the disgust, be it said, of his own loving subjects on foreign soil. It was not until the middle of the last century that the Bank of England dropped many of her aristocratic ideas, and began really to facilitate banking. Hitherto that money-bringing occupation had been confined entirely to the goldsmiths, who lent the money lodged in their hands for security to government and individuals.

In the course of time, business came to be transacted in houses given up wholly to banking, and nothing else; and it is this which has made the Bank of England what it now is,— so important an institution in London city circles. All the London banks keep their principal reserves on deposit at the Bank. The London bill-brokers do the same. In fact, it is the Bank of England which keeps Lombard Street going. All the spare money of Scotch and Irish and country banks finds its way to Threadneedle Street; and, since the Franco-German war, there has been an increase in the Bank's liabilities. As has been somewhere observed, the Bank of England may, indeed, be said to keep the European reserve also. Formerly there were two such stores in Europe, — the Bank of England and the Bank of France; but, since the suspension of specie payments by the Bank of France, its use as a reserve of specie is at an end. Accordingly, London has become the great settling-house of exchange transactions in Europe.

These increased responsibilities do not, however, seem to have brought to the Bank of England much increase of profits. In 1844 the dividend on the bank stock was seven per cent, and the price 212. The dividend is nine now, and the stock sells at 232; an increase by no means commensurate with the profits made by other London joint-stock banks. Take the London and Westminster, for instance, where the shares, in addition to one hundred per cent of the capital, have risen from twenty-seven to sixty-six, and the dividend from six to twenty per cent.

The most material duties of the Bank of England seem to be, first, the management of the national debt of the United Kingdom; secondly, the issue of bank-notes; thirdly, discount and private banking. The whole amount of the national debt of Great Britain is close upon $3,466,773,790, the dividends of which are paid at the Bank of England half-yearly. For looking after this little matter of three billion odd dollars, the government pays one million dollars; and the Old Lady, in connection with the same, keeps the accounts of nearly 240,000 persons, who hold that debt as stock. Department No. 2 relates to the issue of notes. According to the last half-year's return, the amount of all bank-notes of every description in circulation in England, Scotland, and Ireland, was about $217,500,000 worth. Of the gold which the Bank of England receives in exchange for its notes, it is permitted to invest as much as $75,000,000 in government securities, and to receive the benefit of the interest, which is three per cent, the rest of the gold being kept in reserve in its cellars; and it would be easy to see on any day of the week sacks full of it, so heavy as to be drawn about the floor in little wagons.

No. 3 department of the Bank of England is very important, — perhaps the most important of all. The whole of the income of the United Kingdom finds its way into the coffers of the Old Lady at the rate of $6,500,000 a week ; and the deposits of private customers amount to about $140,000,000 more.

In another way, also, the Bank of England is serviceable to the country to a very large extent. All the balances daily at the clearing-house between banker and banker are settled by check on the great bank; and in this way the year before accounts, to the amount of $29,467,230,000, were settled. It is calculated that the amount of gold and silver in circulation in Great Britain is represented by about $500,000,000 of American money.

The management of the Bank of England is vested in a board of twenty-four directors, a governor, and a deputy-governor. Nominally, the election of the directors is in the hands of the stockholders; virtually, they are self-elected. In theory, a certain portion retire annually; but, if the board recommends it, they are re-elected. The elder members of the board, those who have passed the chair, constitute an important body, called the Committee of Treasury, which settles many vital questions affecting the money-market. It may be mentioned that the qualification for governor is $20,000 worth of stock; deputy-governor, $15,000 worth; and director, $10,000 worth.

In the Bank of England upwards of a thousand persons are employed, the salaries and wages of whom amount to nearly $1,300,000 a year, besides pensions to superannuated officers of about $175,000. The clerks are, as a rule, an obliging, gentlemanly lot of men, not perhaps overworked, but performing what they do in a trustworthy, careful manner. Inside the building is a well-filled library for their benefit, where they may sit and read, or write, or play chess, till seven o'clock, when the subaltern's guard of the Regiment of Guards stationed in London take possession for the night.

Like nearly all large employers of labor in England, the bank directors encourage thrift among their people; and one of the most noteworthy features of the Bank of England is its Clerks' Insurance Company. It may be mentioned that an examination is requisite for all clerks entering the Bank of England's service.

Without staying to describe all the departments comprised in the Old Lady's establishment at Threadneedle Street, some of which are quite worth a long attention, it will be sufficient to allude to one or two special attractions of the place. First of all, the room where the sovereigns are weighed, and the bad separated from the good. Here are twelve machines of wonderful mechanism,·two of them being for half-sovereigns, and they weigh at the rate of twenty-eight a minute. The way of working is somewhat as follows: Three hundred sovereigns are placed at once on a slide, as it were, at the lower end of which is the weighing and separating apparatus, which has two bolts placed at right angles to each other; and, on each side of the platform or scale, there is a part cut away so as to admit of the bolts striking so far into the interior as to remove any thing that would nearly fill it. These bolts are made to strike at different elevations, the under striking a little before the upper one. If the sovereign be full weight, the scale remains down ; and then the under bolt, which strikes a little before the upper, knocks it off into the full-weight box. If the sovereign be light, it rises up, and the first bolt strikes under it, and misses it; but the higher bolt then strikes, and knocks it off into the light box. A very pretty and delicate operation, and difficult to describe.

As regards the light sovereigns, in ·less time than it took to write this they are chopped in two by a machine, and sent back to the bankers whence they came, to re-appear in a short time in the vaults of the Bank of England as "bullion" to be re-coined.

In another room, near this weighing-machine room, is the treasury, where millions worth of Bank-of-England notes are stored in iron safes, with bags full of a thousand sovereigns each, for ready use by the bank as called for.

Another exceedingly interesting sight at the Old Lady's is the bullion-room. Here you may see little bars of gold, of the value of $4,000 each, placed on trucks for delivery. There is sometimes as much as $400,000 worth of bars on each truck, to be gazed at and admired, but not run away with. In the same cellar are piles on piles of bags of French and Russian coins; and here, also, may be seen the light coins in bags·returned from the outside bankers. As for bank-notes which have been paid, we are afraid to say how many there are in the vaults. Seven years they are allowed to accumulate before destruction; and they come in at the rate of $230,000 worth a day. Perhaps a reader would like to calculate what he can see in pounds value.

No Bank-of-England note ever goes out of the bank parlors when once it has come in. You present a bank-note for payment, when the signature is torn off, and your note, with the day's accumulations, is tied up in a bundle, to be kept for seven years, when the whole are burned, as many as are burned corresponding with the numbers that are issued. There are 16,500 boxes of paid notes in this chamber, and the quantity of notes in them amounts to ninety-three millions; and it has been stated, that, placed flat one upon another, a million of Bank-of-England notes would reach as high as the London Monument.

THE BRITISH MUSEUM.

This magnificent building, which contains some of the most wonderful ancient sculptures in the world, and priceless collections of MSS., prints, and geological, zoölogical and other curiosities, is situated in Great Russell Street, Bloomsbury. It should be borne in mind, that, the first week in May, the Museum is wholly closed for a week; that it is closed for a like period the first week in September; and again, for the same period, in January.

It is difficult to obtain admission to the reading-room. Still it is worth some trouble to do so; for it happens to be unique of its kind, and one of the noblest rooms in the world. It stands in the inner quadrangle of the Museum itself; was finished at a cost somewhere in the neighborhood of $750,000, gold; and is probably the most ingenious application of glass and iron, for the purposes of economizing space and providing effectual accommodation for and sufficient light to the enormous number of books it contains, that was ever invented. It occupies an area of forty-eight thousand superficial feet, and is circular in form, not occupying the whole quadrangle, there being a clear interval of from twenty-seven to thirty feet all round, to give light and air to the surrounding buildings, and to guard against possible destruction by fire from the outer parts of the building. The dome of this reading-room, one of the most prominent and grandest portions of the British Museum architecturally, is a hundred and six feet in height, having a diameter of a hundred and forty feet; in the last dimension being only inferior to the Pantheon at Rome by two feet. For sake of comparison, it may be mentioned that the dome of St. Peter's, at Rome, is one hundred and thirty-nine feet; that of Santa Maria, at Florence. being the same; the dome of St. Paul's Cathedral is one hundred and twelve feet in diameter; that of St. Sophia, at Constantinople, being one hundred and seven feet; and of the glorious old church at Darmstadt, one hundred and five feet.

The reading-room itself contains 1,250,000 cubic feet of space; and the surrounding libraries, 750.000. Its shelves contain about sixty thousand volumes; and the building will accommodate altogether one million five hundred thousand volumes. The building contains three lineal miles of book-shelves, eight feet high; and. assuming them all to be spaced for the average octavo book size, the entire ranges form no less than twenty-five miles of book-shelves. Assuming, again, the shelves to be filled with books of paper of average thickness, the leaves, placed edge to edge, would extend about twenty-five thousand miles, or more than three times the diameter of the globe. Mr. Winter Jones, the present distinguished principal librarian of the Museum, in his guide to the printed books, dated February, 1858, remarks that the library has been twice counted; the first time on the 25th of July, 1838, when the number of printed books was found to be 235,000; and again on the 13th of December, 1849, at which period they had increased to 435,000. They are now, he adds, in 1858, about 550,000; and the annual increase is not less than 20,000. The number of volumes now in the library exceeds a million. To obtain the great privilege of what is termed a "reader's ticket" of admission, which holds good for one year, and may be renewed, the applicant must be furnished with a testimonial in the shape of a letter from some well-known person, — a member of parliament, or clergyman, barrister, or head of some public department, — stating that the person making the application is well known to the writer, and that he is a fit person to be allowed to read in the library. The number of "readers" who visit the room annually, armed with such authority, is seventy thousand. See MUSEUMS.

BURLINGTON HOUSE, PICCADILLY.

In this noble new building, on the right-hand side of Piccadilly, a few doors east of Bond Street, are to be found the rooms of the Royal Academy, — the headquarters of art, — and suites of apartments belonging to the six principal learned and scientific societies of Great Britain; viz., the Royal Society, the Society of Antiquaries, the Linnæan, the Geological, the Royal Astronomical, and the Chemical Societies.

The oldest of these learned bodies, having rooms on the eastern side of the quadrangle, is the Royal Society, which was incorporated by royal charter more than two hundred years ago, and had for its first patron Charles II., who appears to have found in the experiments of the philosophers an agreeable change from the frivolities and dissipation of his court, and at whose hands the society received the silver-gilt mace which still graces the table of the council-chamber at all meetings. This illustrious body numbers some six hundred of the foremost scientific men of the day; and, ever since its foundation, it has been the adviser of the British Government on all matters of a scientific nature. ·

The library comprises nearly 35,000 volumes, and is in all respects one of the most complete scientific libraries in existence. On the side of the quadrangle immediately facing the Royal Society are apartments belonging to the Antiquaries, the next to the Royal Society in point of age. It was, indeed, originally established in 1572; but it appears to have subsequently dissolved. It was not till 1751 that it was incorporated by charter; and about thirty years afterwards it was established in free quarters at Somerset House, in the Strand, where it remained till its removal to the present elegant suite of rooms in Burlington House.

The suite devoted to the Geological Society lies between the Royal Society and Piccadilly, thus forming the south-eastern corner of the block. Besides a library, meeting-room, &c., it comprises a small but prettily-decorated museum, divided into two parts by an intervening row of oak cases, the larger section having two galleries round it. The whole is fitted with cases suitable for the reception of objects of interest. The Geological Society was established in 1807.

The Chemical Society are located in the front of the building, between the corner occupied by the geologists and the central gateway. The accommodation provided here is very similar to that elsewhere. Belonging to the society is a well-selected chemical library : it is the youngest of the six, and was incorporated as recently as the year 1818, and numbers now five hundred members.

The whole of the western front of the new building (the part, that is, extending from the central gateway to the west corner) is occupied by the Linnæan Society, — a body which took its rise as an offshoot of the Royal Society in 1788. It has a very valuable library and collection of natural objects, for the latter of which a well-appointed herbarium has been provided.

The suite of rooms over the central gateway is, for the present, not appropriated. Those set apart for the reception of the Royal Astronomical Society lie between the apartments of the Linnæan Society in front and the Antiquaries behind, and on the western side of the quadrangle.

BUCKINGHAM PALACE.

During the London season, — in the months of May, June, and July, — there is a great deal to be seen of very considerable interest to a stranger, entirely outside of public exhibitions, art galleries, museums, and so forth. On the 24th of May, for instance, the Queen's birthday, there is a review of the Brigade of Guards by the commander-in-chief, the Prince and Princess of Wales, and other members of the royal family, in the parade-ground of the Horse Guards, facing St. James's Park. As the day falls on a Sunday this year, the review will be held on the 23d. The hour for the troops to assemble is 10, A.M.

There are also certain days set apart during the London season, at intervals, say, of two or three weeks, on which the Queen formally receives the wives and daughters of the foreign ambassadors and of the ministers and great officers of state, such ladies of rank as may desire to be presented to her, and others, members of a less pretentious circle of society, who may desire to go to the expense of a very elaborate and costly court dress for the purpose of spending a few moments in the glittering presence of royalty. A foreign lady obtains the right of *entrée* at these "drawing-rooms," as they are called, through the ambassador representing her country at the Court of St. James. All that is required, after having enlisted the good offices of the minister, is to proceed forthwith to a court milliner and dressmaker, and engage her services. Ladies must *de rigueur* wear plumes, lappets, and trains; and *débutantes* are always expected to wear white dresses; jewelry, of course, at discretion. It is proper, also, to be able to drive to the palace in an imposing carriage with imposing coachman and footmen, each of whom should be provided with a huge bouquet stuck imposingly in his waistcoat.

What entitles ladies in England to come before their sovereign is a difficult question to answer. Of course, no one of questionable character would, for a moment, knowingly be permitted to be present; so that the fact of attending these receptions is, with English ladies, a kind of diploma of moral respectability. Moreover, it confers upon them the right of demanding from an English ambassador resident at a foreign court the privilege of presentation to the sovereign to whom he may be accredited, — a matter of some social importance to English ladies travelling on the continent of Europe. The sight opposite Buckingham Palace on these occasions is really worth seeing, and will furnish the visitor with a fair idea of the grandness, not to say gaudiness, of state pageantry as it exists in England. A lady writing in "The Queen," the lady's newspaper of England, has thus described the scene: —

"The sight in the Mall and at St. James's Park was really worth seeing, what with the carriages and the detachment of Scots Fusilier Guards passing to and fro, to say nothing of the mounted band in its gold-bedizened uniform. New liveries are the general rule on these occasions; and the bouquets carried by both coachmen and footmen grow larger and more imposing each season: these, and a very cursory peep of a nodding plume, a pretty face, and a few yards of tulle, seemed to give intense satisfaction to hundreds of people who lined all the routes to the palace.

"Reaching the palace-gates, and passing through the courtyard, you arrived at a second quadrangle, where from beneath a fine portico, the steps covered with crimson cloth, you found yourself in the grand entrance-hall, paved with variegated marble, and surrounded by columns with imposing Corinthian capitals. Here the spectacle was, as it always is, pretty; the uniforms, the court dresses, the scarlet coats of the servants (all of whom wore the black mourning band on their arm), and the brilliant dresses sweeping up the grand staircase, showed to the best possible advantage; the beef-eaters in their quaint old dress, that has descended to them from Bluff Hal's reign, adding not a little to the vista. From the top of this staircase you crossed the picture-gallery, and then, by slow degrees, made your way through a magnificent suite of rooms until you reached the presence-chamber; but in the meanwhile, unless you arrived very late, you were pretty sure to have an hour's waiting before you. There was plenty to see, however. The suite of rooms is very fine (one of the most imposing is the Blue Drawing-Room); for they are all lined with rich silk damask in lieu of paper, and have heavy ornamental ceilings, one mass of gilding, gold panellings, gold candelabra, and heavy, costly decorations everywhere. In this Blue Room hang full-length likenesses of the Prince Consort and the Queen by Winter-halter; and in every room are pictures worth seeing, espe-cially notable among them some specimens of Dutch art in the last room which you enter as you leave the Throne Room.

"The rule is, that, as you arrive, you take up your position in the last apartment open; for, as the rooms fill, the gentle-men-at-arms (very imposing, by the by, in their red uniforms and high helmets, with long waving plumes) cross their hal-berds, and prevent farther progress. For the benefit of those about to be presented, on whose account I give so many minute details, I may as well say, that, in good truth, there is nothing at all formidable in the ceremony, every thing is made so easy. The attendants remove your train, and arrange it properly on the ground: you have only to follow the lady immediately before you, on the edge of whose train you will very probably be treading; and very probably, too, you will have an opportunity of seeing her presented first. When you find yourself immediately in front of the Queen, the lord-chamberlain, who stands next her, will take your card from your hand (you must be sure to have removed your right-hand glove), and read your name, and that of the lady who presents you, to her Majesty. You courtesy low, place your ungloved hand under the sove-reign's extended before you, bend over it and kiss it, rise, and make your reverences to the royal personages beside her. It doesn't take half as long to do as I have taken to describe it; and, before you hardly know where you are, your train has been replaced on your arm by the royal pages.

Others will be in front of the Queen; and the officials will first persuasively, then peremptorily, request you to move on. People are apt to be frightened by the fact that they must walk backwards away from the sovereign, and by no means turn their back upon her: but there is no real difficulty about it; for, by the time you have made a few steps, the crowd has interposed between you and the royal circle, and, *nolens volens*, you betake yourself to the next room, where an occasional glimpse of a feather is about all you can see of what is going on in the apartment you have just left."

THE CLUBS.

Speaking roughly, there is not a single class, profession, or trade, in England, but has its representative club-house. Take the Church: besides a Clerical Club, there is the splendid Senior University, the no less splendid Junior University, and the fine old Oxford and Cambridge, — all on the south side of Pall Mall. The Army: there is probably not a more magnificent building in London, as far as outside appearance and interior splendor go, than the Army and Navy Club, leading into St. James's Square from Pall Mall; add the Senior United Service, the Junior United Service, and the Naval and Military (Lord Palmerston's old house in Piccadilly), and you have four palaces which are supported by the two combatant services in England. Literature is represented by the Athenæum, Pall Mall; the Arts, by the Garrick, near Covent Garden; the Law, by the Law Club; the Civil Service, by the elegant Thatched House Club; the Indian Services, by the Oriental and East-India United Service in St. James's Square: the Diplomatic Service, by the Travellers in Pall Mall. Then, as far as politics are concerned, both sides of the House of Commons are represented, — the Liberals, by the Reform (south side of Pall Mall) and the Junior Reform; the Conservatives, by the Carlton (south side of Pall Mall), the Junior Carlton, and the Conservative in St. James's Street. Trade can boast of two club-houses, — the City *par excellence*, and the Gresham. Medicine is well represented in the Medical Club. Country squires and county magistrates meet at Arthur's in St. James's Street. There is an Engineers' Club, a Farmers' Club, a Cobden Club (free-trade), a Public-Schools Club, a

8

Fox Club (hunting), a Four-in-hand Club, an Alpine Club, and some scores of others, which it would be tedious to mention. "Pooh!" says the reader; "mere trumpery affairs, most of them; a first-floor suite of rooms, perhaps!" Not so, but splendid edifices, — whereof there is not the like, as club-houses, in any country of the world, — in which all the requirements of opulent life, all the comforts, nay, the luxuries, of princely habitations, are combined; where, for a moderate annual subscription, a man of character is admitted into a circle of the very *élite* of his fellows; where he will find well-selected and extensive libraries, containing newspapers and pamphlets from all parts of the world; where, according as his tastes incline, he may amuse himself in saloons devoted to play (billiards and cards), in elegant libraries devoted to reading, or in drawing-rooms of the most splendid description, devoted to conversation; where the man who goes in for good living may drink wine of the best, eat food cooked by the most experienced of *chefs*, and be served by the neatest and most attentive of waiters; and where he will be able to receive and entertain strangers in a manner which it would be impossible for him to do at his own home, unless provided with an income amounting to that possessed by the richest in the land. A walk in Pall Mall will take in most of the clubs. Externally these buildings are amongst the most magnificent in the great English capital; while, as far as internal splendor is concerned, they throw completely into the shade many of the finest residences of leading English noblemen. They afford representations, too, of nearly every species of architecture; and although a few are remarkable for incongruities of taste, and the discordant effects which invariably attend attempts to unite different and naturally inharmonious schools, they are yet among the most imposing buildings in London, and their like cannot be found in any capital whatever.

Though differing considerably in their architectural styles, and somewhat in their internal arrangements also, there is yet much similarity within the walls of London clubs; and certain features are common to all. Most of them have a striking hall, or entrance, access to which is obtained, in some instances, at once from the street; in others through a small and comparatively unadorned vestibule, to heighten the effect of the interior splendor; and nearly all can boast a grand staircase leading to the drawing-rooms and libraries, which, in point of elegance and breadth of way, reminds one, and not unworthily, of the glories of the Louvre. As you enter, in the vestibule, generally, sits installed a porter, in the uniform livery of the club, to take charge of all letters, &c., for the various members, to answer all inquiries of strangers; and who (a most necessary duty) notes the name of each member as he enters or leaves the club-house, in order to be able, without hesitation, to say "Yea" or "Nay" to the oft-repeated question, "Is Mr. So-and-so within the club?" From the interior of the vestibule a small waiting-room, furnished with every convenience for writing notes and so forth, branches off, which is devoted to the reception of visitors.

Each of the London clubs has some little speciality of its own; and each vies with the other in securing some exclusive advantage to its members.

The Senior University Club is said to have the best cellar of wine in London; the Union Club is most celebrated for its cookery; and the Thatched House, late Civil Service, for its general comfort. The Oriental goes in for Indian dishes and Madeira, both of which are to be had there in perfection; and the Naval and Military will send up the most perfect of *late* suppers. The Army and Navy has the grandest smoking-room. Soyer, the great cook, was the presiding genius of the Reform Club kitchen for many years; and it may be mentioned as by no means an unusual thing for London clubs to pay these chief cooks as much as four thousand dollars (gold) a year, — a large sum in England.

The Athenæum Club has between thirty and forty thousand volumes lining the shelves of its library; the Reform can also boast a magnificent and valuable collection; the same with the Carlton and the Senior University. The Senior United Service and Army and Navy Clubs have each valuable shelves of works bearing on naval and military subjects; and the Law Club has the first law library in England. A courteous letter to a member may, perhaps, be the means of getting permission to view one or other of these splendid mansions.

CHRIST'S HOSPITAL.

It would be difficult to select a spot within the city walls of old London possessing more general attractions for the stranger than Newgate Street. The name is at once familiar as the site on which is built the historical and far-famed prison. Overlooking and within stone's-throw of both is that great and grand landmark of London, — St. Paul's Cathedral, the huge dome of which, with its glittering cross and orb of gold, may be seen towering far up into the skies, a tribute of man to his Maker. The curious and somewhat remarkable Church of St. Sepulchre — from the graveyard of which the last earthly exhortation has been read to some hundreds of criminals passing on their way to Tyburn — stands at one end of the venerable thoroughfare; the General Post-Office, and the splendid new Telegraph Office of London, at the other; and within sight of both is the graceful spire of one of Wren's most celebrated churches, — in which lie buried the remains of Baxter, author of " The Saints' Rest," — and the noble hall, and gray, massy towers, of the famous Christ's Hospital.

The school was founded by King Edward the Sixth, June 26, 1553, on the site of the famous Gray-Friars Monastery; and although Edward founded this institution as a part of a general scheme of charity for London, which had for its purpose the providing for the wants of the sick poor, the thriftless poor, the aged poor, the afflicted poor, and the vicious poor, in process of time the qualifications for admission of children to Christ's Hospital have been more and more relaxed, until the one *sine quâ non* of Edward's time, that they should be poor fatherless children, no longer exists. The government of the charity — which, in passing, we may state is the second richest in Great Britain — is vested in a President, the Duke of Cambridge, a Treasurer, Mr. Allcroft, a gentleman well known in the city of London, and a Board of Governors, comprising every class of persons, from the Queen and royal family down to the most humble ex-pupil of the school. To admit of a person's becoming a Life-Governor, it is necessary that his character should be above reproach, and that he should have subscribed four hundred pounds to the school-fund, which entitles him always to have one boy in the institution on his own presentation, and to a vote at general meetings of the governors.

A boy, before he can be admitted, is expected to be above the age of seven, and under nine: he must be of good bodily health, and be able to read and write. This being so, nothing further is required but for the lad to present himself with his parents at one of the quarterly meetings of the Board of Almoners, a sort of sub-committee of the governors, when the question is put to the vote, "Shall A B be admitted on C D's presentation to the benefits of the ancient and noble foundation of Christ's Hospital?" The answer being "Yea," the boy is admitted; and henceforth every social distinction of class, so far as he is concerned, vanishes. He becomes one of this grand little republic, and forthwith adopts the uniform of its members, the same as that worn in 1552, in Edward's time, — a blue-cloth gown with silvered buttons, black velvet knee-breeches, yellow stockings, shoes, a red leather belt, and clerical bands of white linen. Christ's Hospital not only clothes, feeds, boards, and educates her children gratuitously, but, in a measure, provides for them at starting in life; and, what is more, she never once loses sight of them in after-years. In connection with the institution are several charities for assisting "old boys" in distress, and a society possessed of considerable funded property, formed of ex-scholars themselves, called the "Benevolent Society of Blues."

School-work all through the year begins in the morning at 9, and ends at 12; in the afternoon at 2, and ends at 5. The meals are taken in the Great Hall; next to Westminster, the noblest in London: and every thing in the way of diet is clean, ample, and wholesome. Before each of the meals, which consist of breakfast, dinner, and supper, a portion of Scripture is read, and grace said by one of the Grecians from a pulpit of beautiful carved work in the centre of the hall, one only of the many attractions of this really splendid building, which, among other things, contains a magnificent collection of old paintings, and one of the finest organs in London. The boys dine at 1, and strangers are permitted to be present.

ETON "FOURTH OF JUNE."

Eton "Fourth of June" — one of the grand events of the London season — is all that now remains of those masquerading holidays so peculiarly and wholly English, and so interesting to Americans, which, for the most part, were invented in the foundation-schools of England, of which Eton College is the foremost representative.

A· quondam captain of the Eton-College boat-club says, "The Fourth-of-June procession of boats was instituted in commemoration of a visit of George the Third, and is held on his birthday. It is the great trysting-day of Eton, when her sons gather from far and wide, — young and old, great and small, no matter who or what, as long as they are old Etonians; that magic bond binding them all together as brothers, and levelling, for the time, all distinctions of age or rank." The proceedings begin with the "speeches," delivered in the "Upper School," in Greek, Latin, French, Italian, German, and English. The speeches being got through, and what is termed "absence" being called in the old quadrangle of the college, a rush is made for the provost's house, where a grand luncheon is served for distinguished old Etonians, and where you may meet half the cabinet, a fair sprinkling of the "lords," the majority of the bench of bishops, a field-marshal or two, a half-dozen full admirals, a hundred or so of the members of the "Commons," and all who are distinguished in every line of life throughout Great Britain. Entertainments on a smaller scale are going on in the various tutors' houses for the boys themselves. At three o'clock there is full choral service in the chapel, — one of the finest collegiate chapels in England, well worth the journey from London to visit; and after sisters, mothers, and cousins have refreshed themselves with tea, a gay sight awaits them at the Brocas, a large open meadow down by the side of the river, from whence starts the procession of boats to Surly Hall, a public house of that name, on the right bank of the Thames, some three and a half miles from the bridge which separates Eton from Windsor. It is a queer and picturesque gathering, — Grenadier-Guardsmen and Life-Guardsmen, boatmen and fishermen, young folks from behind London counters, with the ordinary admixture of street-minstrels, lollipop-venders, gypsies, fruit-sellers, and policemen greeting the boys and their people. The boats are divided into two classes, — upper and lower. The upper division consists of the Monarch (ten oar), the Victory, and the Prince of Wales; the lower boats being the Britannia, Dreadnought, Thetis, and St. George. All are eight oars, with the one exception we have named. The flotilla is preceded by the Eton racing eight-oar, manned by a picked

crew, who are to contend at Putney or Henley. Each boat
has its distinctive uniform; the crews of the upper division
wearing dark-blue jackets and trousers, and straw hats with
ribbons displaying the name of the boat in gold letters;
those of the lower wearing trousers of white jean, and all
ornaments and embroidery being in silver. The cockswains
of the upper boats are dressed in admiral's uniform, with
gold fittings, sword, and cocked hat; those of the lower, as
midshipmen, in appropriate dress, with huge nosegays as
big as themselves stuck in their breasts. Upon a given
signal from the stroke-oar of the ten-oar, all embark; and
the procession, headed by a quaint, old-fashioned boat rowed
by Thames watermen, containing the band of the Life-
Guards, passes in front of the spectators and carriages on
its way to Surly Hall. The scene, as the boats' crews warm
to their work, is wonderfully striking. Military bands
strike up; the Windsor bells peal out; there are nods, and
wavings of handkerchiefs, from the banks; the silken flags
are dipped so as to trail along in the water; and there
is much cheering and general clapping of hands from the
assembled thousands of sight-seers. After a few toasts, and
as much champagne as can fairly be disposed of in a short
time, the captain of the boats gives the order for all to re-
embark; and the flotilla returns to Eton in the same order.

When the boats have arrived at the Brocas, the last act of
the day is gone through. The very moment the daylight
has departed, a rocket from an island in front of the boat-
houses assures every one that the final scene is set. Off
they go,—squibs, crackers, Roman candles, port-fires, set
pieces, Chinese fire, glittering serpents, and flights of rockets.
The townsfolk on the bridge, and the great people on the
banks, supply the orthodox moan of surprise as the rockets
burst in the still night into stars of blue, green, crimson, and
gold; and round about and in and out the punts, skiffs,
wherries, and miniature barges, you may see the Eton crews
rowing their orthodox " three times " round the eyot in the
middle of the stream. Then the boats toss their oars, and
salute; the fine old bells in the Curfew Tower ring out a
merry peal; the Eton Arms, with the motto *Floreat Etona*,
are written in letters of fire; the boys cheer; the bands play
" God save the Queen; " the last squib splutters in a slow
and agonizing death; and old Farmer George's birthday
will surely have been well and truly kept by the descendants
of his young friends of his Royal College of Eton.

FOUNDLING HOSPITAL.

We would most strongly advise all interested in the care and education of children to look in upon the Foundling Hospital in Guilford Street, Russell Square; and it might be well for the visit to be paid on Sunday. Haydn declared that the most powerful effect he felt from music was from the singing of the London charity children. The girls and boys of the Foundling Hospital are the very pick of these charity children, and are famed for their singing. It is impossible to describe the beautiful effect of the fresh young voices swelling from the pyramid of little ones ranged on each side of the chapel, and towering to the topmost pipes of the grand organ; which, by the way, was the gift of Handel. The chapel of the Foundling Hospital, during divine service on Sunday, is one of the most lovely sights in the world; and if the man or the woman who has listened to the singing of the children there doesn't come away the better for it, then there is no such thing in the world as human sympathy. This children's chapel, which has now become famous, rose at the sound of the glorious music of Handel. It was from the organ, his own gift, that he drew forth, we believe, the sublime notes of the "Messiah." Here he played to entranced thousands, and helped, by those gifts which God had so abundantly bestowed upon him, to alleviate the burdens of his fellow-creatures less abundantly provided for. By one performance of Handel's, it is said, the charity netted over ten thousand dollars; and we are not so sure but what the great composer gave the copyright of the "Messiah" to the governors, by which they netted several thousands more. It is most gratifying to find that the foremost men of those who represented the infancy of painting in England were not behindhand with the sister art in doing good deeds to the asylum. Hogarth, Gainsborough, Hayman, Highmore, and Wilson contributed paintings to decorate the walls of the court-room (to be seen), as Handel contributed his music to the good of the chapel. If the Foundling Hospital is indebted to these men, as she unquestionably is, for what they have done for her, lovers of art are indebted to the Foundling Hospital for giving the first hint for an exhibition of British art, which afterward culminated in that Royal Academy which has given to the world so many glorious paintings. See also "Churches."

HOUSE OF COMMONS.

To the average American citizen, whose idea of delibera-
tive bodies is obtained from the legislatures of the several
States, or, at best, from the Senate and House of Representatives at the national capital, the scenes presented during a
session of the English House of Commons are of never-fail-
ing interest, and, when compared with the more simple ceremonies and methods in vogue at home, bring out into bold
relief the truth of the assertion so often made, that both
countries are — in fact, if not in form — republican in their
essential characteristics.

When the visitor to London has had a surfeit of dinings-
out, of scientific conversaziones, of operas, theatres, and the
like, — the staple attractions during the London season, —
there are few pleasanter ways of spending a quiet evening in
the great English capital than lounging on the comfortable
and somewhat exclusive bench of the Speaker's Gallery of the
House of Commons (admission to be had through the United-
States minister), and watching the proceedings in the British
Legislature. There are many worse ways, too, of whiling
away an hour or so than mingling with the crowd of con-
stituents in the corridors of the House, and listening to the
remarks of a communicative friend on the ways, manners,
and customs of the people of England's anointed. If that
friend should happen to be official, or in any way connected
with the House, so much the better: the time spent in this
way will prove not only amusing, but instructive. Americans
who take London on their tour through Europe rarely have
the time or the inclination, or even the opportunity, for "doing" the Houses of Parliament thoroughly; and, even if
they had, it would doubtless be found that few would care
to avail themselves of the offer of a good friend to shut
themselves up for four or five hours on a hot summer's evening, listening, perhaps, to a dull debate, when pleasanter
things are to be had at the opera. Nevertheless, there is
something entertaining to be found even in the House of
Commons. It is something to see Mr. Speaker enter the
House after the same dignified manner that his predecessors
in the same high office have done for a century or so before
him, and to note the way in which Mr. Superintendent of
the A division of Metropolitan Police demands, " Way for
Mr. Speaker."

Just as the hour-hand of the clock points to four, and the minute-hand to ten, Mr. Superintendent of Police requests passage to the chair freely and becomingly for Mr. Speaker. Then we may see enter from a side-passage, to the right of the corridor containing those magnificent frescoes by Ward, Maclise, and others, a quiet-looking gentleman in a court suit of black ; just such a suit as George Washington may have worn when first President of the United States, — black small-clothes, black silk stockings, and shoes with large steel buckles, a dress-coat (likewise of black) with steel buttons, a very long, square-cut waistcoat of the same, an exquisitely frilled shirt, and a dainty sword in a black sheath, with a wonderful handle of polished steel. This gentleman precedes another in the same costume, who carries upon his shoulder "the Bauble," — a big, heavy, cumbrous-looking gold mace, that may almost be said to be a part of the British Constitution ; for it represents the power of the elected representative of the Commons of England, — the Speaker. At the moment the next personage steps upon the scene, Mr. Superintendent says quietly, "Hats off! — hats off for Mr. Speaker!" All persons must then remove their hats, with the one notable exception of such members of the House as may be present themselves. These merely raise theirs as the Speaker passes them, and only of courtesy; it being the peculiar privilege of the Commons to wear their hats or not in their own place of meeting, as they think fit; and the stranger will notice that they exercise this right pretty generally during the debates, except when speaking.

A flutter of excitement; and Mr. Speaker, in a full-bottomed wig, and robes of black silk, passes through the lobby into the House, followed by his train-bearer, chaplain, and secretary. When all have passed through, a little bell rings : an usher steps forward, and in a loud voice informs the "lobby" that "Mr. Speaker is at prayers." A lull in the conversation ensues for about five minutes; when the same bell rings again, and the same official, in the same voice, informs those present that "Mr. Speaker is in the chair." Whereupon an ugly "rush" is made by honorable members through the doorway into the House itself ; and we can then enter the House, too, by a little Gothic doorway to the right of the members' door.

Without describing the architectural glories of the place, suffice it to say, that on the floor of the House, exactly opposite to where we are sitting, is the Speaker's chair, of carved oak, with a green shade overhead to keep off the glare from the gaslight; the Treasury or Government Benches being to the right, the Opposition or Conservative Benches to the left, of the chair. Immediately in front of, and with their backs to, the Speaker, are the three clerks of the House, in wig and gown, seated at the table, on which stand the scarlet-leather despatch boxes of the ministers, the division glass, and at the foot of which lies, most conspicuous of all, the mace. Exactly above the Speaker's chair is the Reporters' Gallery, of some forty or fifty little pews, each London newspaper having one of its own; and above the Reporters', screened from the gaze of the curious, is the gallery set apart for ladies. Running right round the four sides of the House are the galleries set apart for peers, M. P.'s, and "distinguished strangers;" and immediately over where we are sitting is the "Strangers' Gallery," reserved for the *hoi polloi.* The matters set down for debate are on the notice-board in the lobby, which the Speaker enters from his corridor; but any one of the attendants, or policemen on duty, by a polite request, will furnish the programme of the night's sitting. Ladies can only be admitted through application to the sergeant-at-arms, supported by the minister's recommendation. The House of Commons may be seen on Saturdays. See "Places and Sights."

INNS OF COURT.

Of the many interesting relics of the past to be found in the capital of England, there are few so interesting, or so worthy of note, as those old hostels, or abodes of the practisers and students of the law, called the "Inns of Court." They are the last working institutions in the nature of the old trade-guilds to be met with anywhere throughout the world. The lawyers still guard the entrance to the law in England, and prescribe the rules under which it shall be practised there; and it is a fact somewhat remarkable, that these voluntary societies of barristers should have managed to engross and preserve such a privilege in the midst of the wonderful changes that have taken place even in England in the course of the present century.

These Inns of Court, so called because their inhabitants belonged to the king's court, are four in number, — the

Inner Temple and the Middle Temple in Fleet Street,
Lincoln's Inn in Chancery Lane, and Gray's Inn in Holborn.
At one time, they formed a university almost as powerful
as either Oxford or Cambridge. Students flocked to them
in abundance; and, whereas the students of the two great
universities were drawn from the poorer ranks of society,
the scholars of the law university were invariably the sons
of the wealthy. To be a law-student, was, in the olden time,
to be a stripling of quality; and the Inns of Court of days
gone by enjoyed much the same patrician prestige and *éclat*
as now belong to the aristocratic colleges of Christ Church
at Oxford, and Trinity College, Cambridge. Though the
Inns-of-Court men were for many generations, almost without exception, gentlemen, yet this soon began to wear off;
and in the eighteenth century the bar of England ceased to
comprise among its industrious members a large aristocratic
element; although, even now, after the fashion of four
centuries since, young men are still induced to enter their
names as students for the sake of honorable companionship,
good society, and social prestige. The Inns are teeming
with historic interest; and a stranger would do well to spend
an hour or so in traversing the old squares and cloisters of
those venerable institutions. See " Churches."

DINNER OF THE ROYAL LITERARY FUND.

Generally, in the first or second week in May, the dinner
of the Royal Literary Fund of Great Britain takes place in
London, which usually draws a brilliant array of notable
men together, — ministers of state, ambassadors, great church
dignitaries, and members of all the foremost professions of
the United Kingdom. This Royal Literary Fund of Great
Britain is the only literary charity in the world; and it
deserves the earnest, heartfelt sympathy of those who are
content to recognize the great benefits the world has derived
from the disinterested exertions of literary men. It is not
necessary to go into the question of adequate remuneration
for literary labor in the present day: experience proves, that,
as a general thing, literary men find it equally as hard to
live now by the fruits of their brain-labor as they did in the
days gone by; and the Literary Fund recognizes this fact.
It is one of the characteristics of this noble institution, that

it extends its assistance to the foreign as well as to the English author: its bounty has been experienced by the suffering scholar of every nation, from Iceland to the uttermost bounds of Southern Europe; and it is the boast and pride of the institution, that it allows no national or political distinction to loosen that common bond of brotherhood which ought to unite the literary men of all countries. Another worthy point in connection with the administration of the funds of the Royal Literary Fund is, that the names of those who apply to the institution are never known to any but the Secret Committee, before whom the application comes. No less a sum than five hundred thousand dollars has been secretly voted in this way to thirteen hundred applicants who have been compelled to seek assistance at some period of their lives, — distinguished men whose fame is the proudest inheritance of their countrymen. In a few words, in the language of the distinguished secretary of the institution, Mr. Blewitt, "The historian, the poet, and the divine; the moralist, who has confirmed the interests of virtue; the dramatist, who has beguiled thousands of their tears; the mathematician; the philosopher, who has clothed the truths of science in the graces of literary composition; and the professional writer on law and physic, whose works have become text-books in the schools, — have found the Royal Literary Fund ever ready to minister to their wants, and to shield the knowledge of them from public observation." Tickets to this dinner may be had of the secretary, 10 John Street, Adelphi; price one guinea. All literary men will find themselves interested in the proceedings.

ST. PAUL'S CATHEDRAL,

The masterpiece of Sir Christopher Wren, built on the site of Old St. Paul's, which originated with Maurice, Bishop of London, in 1083. This bishop, to use the expressive words of Dugdale, began in that year "the foundations of a most magnificent pile. So stately and beautiful was it, that it was worthily numbered among the most famous buildings; the vault, or undercroft, being of such extent, and the upper structure so large, that it was sufficient to contain a vast number of people." Nearly six hundred years afterwards, —

viz., in 1666, — Old St. Paul's was destroyed by fire. In Dryden's words, —

"The daring flames peeped in, and saw from far
    The awful beauties of the sacred choir;
    But, since it was profaned by civil war,
    Heaven thought it fit to have it purged by fire."

Futile attempts were made to patch up and restore the cathedral ; but Gothic architecture, after which style Bishop Maurice's structure was built, being looked upon as little short of barbarous in the seventeenth century, no pains were taken to preserve what must have been one of the most exquisite relics of the best periods of the Middle Ages. It is difficult to help regretting this in the case of a cathedral, that, it would almost seem of right, should take precedence over the glorious old Abbey of Westminster ; yet if it had been patched up, as was attempted, the mediæval work would doubtless have been mutilated and Italianized, and Wren's conception of the glorious dome and its noble body, that now delights the eyes of the millions of London, would never have seen the light. The Cathedral, as it now stands, is the noblest building in Great Britain in the classic style. Its first stone was laid June 21, 1675. Divine service was performed for the first time Dec. 2, 1697, on the day of thanksgiving for the peace of Ryswick ; and the last stone laid ———, 1710, thirty-five years after the first. The whole cathedral was begun and completed under one architect, Sir Christopher Wren ; one master-mason, Mr. Thomas Strong ; and while one bishop, Dr. Henry Compton, presided over the diocese ; the whole cost being $3,739,770, which was provided by a tax on coals brought into the port of London.

COST OF ADMISSION.

Whispering, Stone, and Golden Galleries..........0*s*. 6*d*.
Ball 1 6
Library, Great Bell, and Geometrical Staircase 0 6
Clock......... ....0 2
Crypt, — Wellington's and Nelson's Monument....0 6
                                                   ———
                                                   3 2

There are several very fine statues in the body of the church. Sir Christopher Wren, Nelson, and Wellington lie buried here ; several very distinguished English painters, including the late Sir Charles Landseer ; and the engineers who designed Blackfriars and Waterloo Bridges. The monuments are elaborate as works of art, and were erected at great cost. See " Churches."

THE TEMPLE CHURCH.

"On the 10th of February, in the year from the incarnation of our Lord 1185, this church was consecrated in honor of the blessed Mary, by our Lord Heraclius, by the grace of God Patriarch of the Church of the Resurrection, who hath granted an indulgence of fifty days to those yearly seeking it."

This was the inscription formerly on the stone-work over the little door next the cloister, marking the date of the foundation of one of the most remarkable, chaste, and beautiful of the churches of England. The Temple Church was the chief ecclesiastical edifice of the proud and powerful order of the Knights Templars in Britain, and is now the place of worship belonging to the lawyers of the Honorable Societies of the Inner and Middle Temple in London. Heraclius, above mentioned, was Patriarch of Jerusalem, and, at the date the church was consecrated by him, was visiting Britain, endeavoring to obtain succor from Henry the Second, king of England, against the formidable power of the famous Saladin. The church as it now stands is the most beautiful and perfect relic of the order of Knights Templars in existence.

It would be hardly possible to suggest a better means of preventing the imagination of a reader from conceiving the true character and effect of such a wonderful old church as the Temple than by giving a careful and accurate architectural description of the building. Such places must be seen : they cannot be described. The view impressed at once upon the eye is what is desired, and is what systematic description cannot possibly give. Words of the most general, rapid, and suggestive character can very inadequately convey to the general reader the real glories of such a place. To know and appreciate them, you must stand on the very threshold of the solemn structure, — now restored to the simple majesty it possessed near seven hundred years ago, — and look in upon the interior of the church in its most elegant prospective aspect, upon its rich nave, its splendid chaste aisles, its magnificently painted windows. You should rest for a moment in the " Round " chapel, beside the tombs of those who fought in Holy Land in the time of the Crusades, and conjure up visions of the great past, — of the time when the Christian patriarch of the early church exercised his sacred functions within its walls ; of the days

when the mailed knights of the most holy order of the
Temple of Solomon — the sworn champions of the Church
of Christ on earth — unfolded the banner of the red cross
amid " the long-drawn aisles," and offered their swords upon
the altar to be blessed by the ministers of religion. What
a flood of recollections must cross the mind of the student
of history at such a time! If imagination can be stirred by
external influences, it should surely be active here.

In this very spot, under the roof of this little church,
during the holy fervor of the Crusades, the kings of England and the haughty legates of the Pope were wont to
mix with the armed bands of the Templars. Here were
buried, in the twelfth and thirteenth centuries, some of the
most remarkable characters of that age. Around the altar
— the church-doors closed, and at midnight — stood the
stern military friars, while the solemn ceremonies attendant
upon the admission of a novice to the holy vows of the
Temple were being performed. It was the severe religious
exercises, the vigils that were kept up at night in this old
church, together with the reputed terrors of the penitential
cell connected with it, that gave rise to those strange and
horrible tales of impiety and crime, of magic and sorcery,
which led to the unjust and terrible execution at the stake
of the Grand-Master and some hundreds of the Knights
Templars themselves, and finally to the suppression and
annihilation of their powerful order.

The historical recollections and associations of the place
are so powerful as to throw a charm around the venerable
building, ten thousand times more potent than mere architectural beauty would succeed in eliciting. Yet the Temple Church does possess architectural excellence also, and
that, too, of the very highest order. One part of it, indeed,
the chapel proper, as a specimen of the early pointed style
of architecture, stands alone and matchless.

The organ of the church was built in the reign of Charles
the Second, and was selected by competition; Purcell and
Dr. Blow being the organists selected to play at the trial;
the infamous Chief Justice Jeffries, then a member of the
Inner Temple, being the person selected as umpire to decide
on the relative merits of the instruments submitted for trial.
Schmidt was the maker of it; and it is considered to be his
masterpiece.

Not far from the altar is a white marble tomb over the
remains of the learned Selden, who died in 1654. " He

was," says Wood (Athenæ), "a great philologist, antiquary, herald, linguist, statesman, and what not." His funeral-sermon was preached by Archbishop Ussher. And in the little vestry beneath the organ-gallery is a marble tablet to Oliver Goldsmith, buried at the east end of the choir, April 9, 1774. There are memorials in the church erected to Plowden, the jurist; to Howell, writer of "The Familiar Letters;" to Edmund Gibbon, an ancestor of the historian; to Lord-Chancellor Thurlow; and to other eminent English English lawyers. There is also, on the south wall, a tablet to Ann Littleton, 1623, daughter-in-law to Sir Edward Littleton, with the following quaint epitaph:—

> "Keep well this pawn, thou marble chest;
> Till it be called for, let it rest:
> For, while the jewel here is set,
> The grave is but a cabinet."

But, most wonderful of all, in the Round, the oldest part of the present fabric, lie buried men, who, centuries ago, in the defence of the Christian faith, fought against the Saracens in Palestine, and then came back across the seas from the Holy Land to die amongst their brethren, the Templars, in Britain. These famous monuments of the Crusaders, with the cross-legged effigies of the buried knights, in token that they had assumed the "cross," and taken the vow to march to the defence of Christendom, are amongst the most marvellous relics of that age. Here is a monument that takes one's thoughts backward, through long vistas of years, to the time when the proud barons of England desolated their country so fearfully, and in a measure paved the way for that famous meeting at Runnymede, between the nobles of Britain and their sovereign, which ended in the signing of the Great Charter of English liberty. It displays the effigy of Geoffrey de Magnaville, slain by an arrow, and buried here in 1144. Another slab is here erected over the remains of one of the greatest warriors and statesmen who shine in English history,—William Marshall, Earl of Pembroke, a man who, in those days of lawlessness, rescued England from the danger of a foreign yoke, established tranquillity throughout the country, and secured the young Prince Henry, afterwards Henry III., in the peaceable and undisputed possession of the English throne. Shakspeare alludes to him in his grand tragedy of "King John," as the eloquent intercessor with the king on behalf

9

of the unfortunate Prince Arthur. He died in 1219. Next
to those of this great man repose the remains of a youthful
warrior, who, in common with the best and bravest of that
land, raised the standard of rebellion, and was amongst the
foremost of those bold patriots who obtained the sign-manual
of King John to Magna Charta, — Robert, Lord de Ros,
buried in 1227. Next to the tomb of Lord de Ros is the
effigy of a stern warrior, with his arms crossed on his breast,
at one time a Master of the Order of the Knights Templars;
and one of the great name of Plantagenets — William Fifth,
son of Henry the Third — lies next to him. A goodly roll
of the illustrious dead! See also "Churches."

THE TOWER OF LONDON.

"*Prince Edward.* — I do not like the Tower, of any place.
Did Julius Cæsar build that place, my lord?
Buckingham. — He did, my gracious lord, begin that place;
Which, since, succeeding ages have re-edified.
Prince Edward. — Is it upon record, or else reported
Successively from age to age he built it?
Buckingham. — Upon record, my gracious lord."

Ay, upon record! The spot is so old as to date back to
the times of the Romans, the Saxons, and the Normans in
Britain; truly, as to length of days, without rival among
palaces and prisons throughout the world, — a rare old place,
among the rarest of the oldest on the earth. Keep well in
under the shadow of the old walls, and mark well the bul-
warks of the fortress. St. Thomas's Tower, or Traitors'
Gate: here's a wonder to begin with. — an edifice, the work
of Henry the Third, the eldest son of John, — that king who
signed the Great Charter of English liberty. The arched
channel, which gives the secondary appellation of Traitors'
Gate, is one of the purest examples of art, and one of the
noblest arches in the world; and the spot is as sacred as any
that marks the more notable events in English history.
Through the grim old archway once passed Buckingham,
no man's enemy but his own, though the professed enemy of
the ambitious Wolsey, — a man, we are told, "apparently too
vain, and incautious in disposition." Here it was, in this
very place, on one of these very stones perhaps, that Elizabeth stood, refusing to land, until the lords who escorted her

threatened to use force; placing her foot upon the stairs, and saying aloud, with the energy peculiar to her character, "Here landeth as true a subject, being a prisoner, as ever landed at these stairs; and before thee. O God! I speak it, having none other friend than thee." In January of 1640, Strafford came back to the Tower through this gateway, with the axe towards him, — that Strafford. who, with composed and undaunted air, from the scaffold told the furious populace that were ready to tear him in pieces, " He was come there to satisfy them with his head; but that he much feared the Reformation. which was begun in blood, would not prove so fortunate to the kingdom as they expected, and he desired." Fisher the cardinal, and Surrey the elegant poet and distinguished soldier, landed here prisoners; so did Sir Walter Raleigh and Lady Jane Grey, and, tradition says, Wallace and Bruce, "names in which," says Mr. Hepworth Dixon, " the splendor, poetry, and sentiment of England's national story are embalmed."

The curious old tower hard by, of Norman build, with walls of wondrous thickness. has been made familiar to us in the seventh scene of the fifth act of the third part of Shakspeare's Henry VI. " *The Tower of London. Enter King Henry with a book, and Gloucester with the Lieutenant on the Tower walls."* In the upper chamber of this Bowyer Tower, after the total defeat of the Lancastrians at Tewkesbury, during the wars of the Roses, in 1471, Henry VI. was murdered by the Duke of Gloucester, whose after-deeds as Richard III. seemed to authorize the belief of his taking part in any act of blood and cruelty. But a few yards, and the villanous Gloucester is again before us: for in a room of the Bloody Tower were lodged Edward V., and his brother the Duke of York; and here, from behind a stair, were said to have been found the bones of these ill-fated youths in the reign of the second Charles. Every one knows the story of the murder of the infant princes: the hired ruffians of the duke smothered one of the boys with a pillow, and cut the other boy's throat with a knife. But the associations of this same Bloody Tower are, if one may use the expression, far more glorious than infamous; for at one of its grated windows wrote the founder of the State of Virginia. This was where, Mr. Hepworth Dixon tells us, he compounded his famous cordial; and this was where he distilled his essences and spirits, received the visits of Prince Henry, and designed ships; and upon the wall he took his daily walk. " That

villain, Waad," as Raleigh had only too much cause to call
his one-time jailer, played his petty spite off on his eminent
prisoner by curtailing his little liberty in the garden on
which the grated window opened. Nevertheless, here came
his friends to express their sympathy, — the Earl of Northumberland, a man of considerable learning of that day;
Piercy, a great chemist; and Hoskins, a poet and philosopher of his day, who is mentioned by Ben Jonson as "the
man who polished him." Prince Henry too, who was wont
to say to his friends that "his father (James I.) was the
only man who would have shut up such a bird in a cage,"
would come here and help to while away the tedious
hours of Raleigh's captivity.

The great man's confinement here was close, and his
treatment mean. Only two small chambers were allowed
him, two servants; and the charge for diet, coals, and candles for his household, was twenty gold dollars — for those
days, a very extravagant sum — a week. He went out bold-
ly to death from a lodging hard by.

Not far off is the Beauchamp Tower, deriving its name
from the Earl of Warwick imprisoned there in 1397, — a
wonderful museum of inscriptions, devices, and coats-of-
arms, sculptured by sad inmates (Anna Boleyn among the
number) to beguile the hours of imprisonment, many, many
long years ago. The guide will show a sentence rudely
carved, with a nail probably, bearing the superscription,
" Arundell, June 22, 1587. *Quanto plus afflictionis pro Christo
in hoc sœculo, tanto plus gloriæ cum Christo in futuro.*" There
you have (again quoting from the learned author of "Her
Majesty's Tower") in few words the whole character of
Philip Howard, Earl Arundell, an austere man, the tenor
of whose behavior was not unbecoming the primitive ages
of the Christian Church. The two points of his duty were
how to pray and how to fast. He died fasting. And there
is another word, carved on the wall of yonder prison, the
Brick Tower, that tells whole chapters of love, of ambition,
and suffering, — carved by the hand of a foolish but affec-
tionate husband. Here it is: " IANE." Lord Guilford
Dudley dug the word out of the masonry before he went out
of his prison, but a boy, to die like a man, — to be carried, a
bleeding corpse, headless, before the window of the unfortunate nine-days' queen, his bride. A fearfully dismal hole is
the Bowyer Tower. In one of its chambers, the gloomiest
of all, George, Duke of Clarence, brother to Edward IV., was

in the fifteenth century, — the fifteenth century, and yet one may stand in the place now ! — tradition says, drowned in a butt of Malmsey wine. The warder will point out the green plot of grass where the cheery old Latimer met another Tower-warder. " What, my old friend ! " said the prelate : " how do you ? I am come to be your neighbor again." And the old bishop might have added, " Until I go to my glorious but awful death along with my brothers of Canterbury and London."

Harrison Ainsworth writes, —

> " The axe was sharp, and heavy as lead:
> As it touched the neck, off went the head."

There is the axe in a room over yonder, and the block, all notched, by its side ; and the instruments of torture, — the thumb-screws and the maiden.

Guy Fawkes howled with agony down in one of the vaults which we shall see. He thought he could bear it; but " that villain, Waad," called his men, and bound his prisoner to the rack. After thirty minutes of the cord and pulley, the conspirator gasped out faintly, that he would tell them all he knew. While this was going on, Little John, Garnet's faithful servant, lay a-dying on straw not far off. He ripped himself open with a knife, and bled to death deliberately, fearing the rack might make him disclose his master's secrets, and, in his weakness and his agony, he might be tempted to betray the lives of men who had always been his friends. A noble death !

What awful tales of incarcerations, tortures, and murders, the wonderful old fortress tells ! Had the walls tongues, could they discourse, what doleful and appalling events they could unfold of human privations and sufferings ; of the tyranny of power, and the endurance of the oppressed ; of the merciless vindictiveness of one, and the profound fortitude, philosophy, and dignity of another ; of glories that have passed away, and of new grandeurs and new usages that have arisen ; of the once gorgeous halls, in which high revel has been kept by kings, and of the fearful agony, foreshadowing the bitterness of death to come, which has been suffered by miserable beings in the vaults beneath !

The chief points of attraction in the Tower are centred in the Armories and Jewel-House, over which visitors are conducted by the warders, generally old soldiers, dressed in the quaint garb of Henry the Eighth's yeomen of the guard.

The crown-jewels of England, kept here, are said to be worth three million pounds. The state-crown of her present Majesty of England, which stands at the top of the case of jewels, consists of a band or diadem of gold, with four arches rising almost perpendicularly from the circlet, elevated slightly at their intersection, where rests a mound of gold with a cross. A cap of purple and ermine fits the band where it rests on the head; and the gold work is ornamented with flowers and fillets and roses, enriched with jewels of wonderful value. There is a row of one hundred and twenty-nine pearls on the lower part of the band, above the ermine border; and a row of one hundred and twelve pearls on the upper part, between which, in front of the crown, is a large sapphire. At the back are a sapphire of smaller size and six other sapphires, between which are eight emeralds. Above and below the seven sapphires are fourteen diamonds: and around the eight emeralds, one hundred and twenty-eight diamonds. Between the emeralds and the sapphires are sixteen trefoil ornaments, containing one hundred and sixty diamonds. Above the band are eight sapphires, surmounted by eight diamonds, between which are eight festoons, consisting of one hundred and forty-eight diamonds. There is a tradition that the large sapphire in this crown, bought by George the Fourth, came out of a famous ring of Edward the Confessor, long treasured up at his shrine, and the heritage of which was supposed to give to his successors great and miraculous powers of blessing. In the centre of a Maltese cross on this "precious diadem" is a magnificent ruby, said to have been given to Edward, Prince of Wales, son of Edward III., called the Black Prince, by Don Pedro, king of Castile, after the battle of Najera, near Vittoria, in 1367. It was worn by Henry V. of England in his helmet at the battle of Agincourt, in 1415. According to Eastern custom, it is pierced quite through, the upper part of the piercing being filled with a small ruby. The *fleurs-de-lis* between the crosses of the crown contain rose-diamonds, each flower having a ruby in the centre. The four arches are composed of oak-leaves and acorns, with leaves of rose, table, and brilliant diamonds; the arches, &c., containing nearly eight hundred diamonds. Four large pear-shaped pearls are suspended from the upper part of the arches. The gross weight of this crown is thirty-nine ounces, eight pennyweights; and the total value of the stones in it is estimated at six hundred thousand dollars; and they may be summed up as follows : " One large ruby irregularly polished, one large broad-spread sapphire, sixteen sapphires, eleven emeralds, four rubies, thirteen hundred and sixty-three brilliant diamonds, twelve hundred and seventy-three rose-diamonds, one hundred and forty-seven table-diamonds, four drop-shaped pearls, and two hundred and seventy-three pearls."

WESTMINSTER ABBEY.

There is no other church in the world, with the solitary exception, perhaps, of the Kremlin at Moscow, which is so rich in historical associations as Westminster Abbey. In the words of Dr. Stanley, the eloquent and learned dean of this famous cathedral, " Here lies the body of the Confessor, himself like the now decayed seed from which the wonderful pile has grown. Around his shrine are clustered not only the names, but the early relics, of the principal actors in every scene of history. Seventeen kings lie here, from Edward the Confessor to George II.; and ten queens lie buried with them, amid England's greatest statesmen, warriors, divines, poets, and scholars."

Of the Anglo-Saxon line of monarchs, Sebert, king of the East Angles, and his queen Ethelgonda, lie beneath a sarcophagus of Purbeck marble, where, shorn of its gems, stands the marble shrine of the last of the Saxon kings, — St. George's predecessor in the patron-saintship of England, — Edward the Confessor. And, besides the Confessor, nine of the early wielders of England's sceptre lie in Westminster Abbey, the warrior-kings Edward I., Edward III., and Henry V., enshrined in marble altar-tombs; that of the last-named wanting the silver plates and silver head of the hero's effigy, removed by some sacrilegious thieves so long ago as 1546. Weak Henry III., and that degenerate scion of a noble stock, Richard II., have no meaner tombs than better-deserving monarchs. A marble urn, erected by Charles II., suffices to record the interment of the supposed bones of Edward V. and his brother Richard of York. The shrewd founder of the Tudor line rests in one tomb with his consort, the Rose of York; his famous grand-daughter shares her canopied altar-tomb with her sister and predecessor; while not far from the grave of Elizabeth and Mary is that of the former's thorn in life, — Mary of Scotland. You may stand

by the tomb of one of the wives of Henry VIII., and of his
son by Jane Seymour, Edward VI.; and out of seven queen-
consorts, not counting Anne of Cleves, the aforesaid wife of
the eighth Henry, Westminster Abbey shelters the remains
of Eleanor of Castile, the queen of many crosses; Philippa
of Hainault, of Nevill's Cross renown; Anne of Bohemia,
and Elizabeth of York. Charles II. lies here, William III.
and Queen Mary, Queen Anne, George II., and Queen
Caroline. The wealth of exquisitely-designed monuments
resting over the graves of the illustrious dead is prodigious;
and the sublime beauty of the Abbey itself must commend
it to the admiration of all who have heard, or even read, of
this grand and glorious temple of God. It will attract all
those who love to worship their Creator in the "beauty of
holiness;" and it must make a lasting impression on the
thoughtful student as "the only national place of sepulture
in the world, — the only spot whose monuments epitomize a
people's history." It would be entirely unnecessary, and out
of the scope of our purpose, to give a lengthy description of
every thing which is important, and necessary to be seen,
in the Abbey. The visitor must look about him, and judge
for himself, and be content with this simple and cursory
sketch of some of the glories of a church, the whole of
which it would take a man his lifetime to faithfully and
properly chronicle.

The Chapter House of the Abbey should certainly be seen.
It was, during three centuries of English history, the meeting-
place of the House of Commons, and was built in 1250 by
Henry III. When the House of Commons was first con-
vened in the parliament of 1265, called by Earl Simon de
Montfort, after the battle of Lewes, summoning two knights
from every shire, two citizens from every city, and two bur-
gesses from every borough, these began sitting in Westminster Hall, side by side with the earls and barons, the
bishops and abbots, who constituted the House of Lords.
But from and after 1282, with a view to separate acts of
self-taxation, the different estates of the realm were assembled in places apart from each other. The Commons were
then to be provided with temporary accommodation in Westminster Abbey, for the convenience of being near the other
members of the king's parliament in Westminster Palace
and Hall. They sometimes used to sit in the refectory of
the ancient monastery, now destroyed; but at other times in
the Chapter House, as might best suit the occasions of the

abbot and his monks. Upon this tenure of good will and custom, as it appears, did the representatives elect of the Third Estate continue, nearly three hundred years, to occupy the quarters assigned to them, probably at the king's request, in the precincts of the Abbey. But, on the dissolution of the ancient monastery in 1540, the Chapter House passed into the possession of the Crown. From that time the dean and chapter held their meetings in the Jerusalem Chamber, the Chapter House becoming a depository of public records. In 1865, after the removal of the records to the Rolls House, on the eight hundredth anniversary of the foundation of the Chapter and the six hundredth anniversary of the House of Commons, its restoration was undertaken by Sir Gilbert Scott, at the request of the British Society of Antiquaries.

It may not seem wholly out of place here to direct the attention of Americans to the fact, that Dean Stanley, one of the broadest in his views, fervent in his teaching, and eloquent in the pulpit, of the divines of the Church of England, usually preaches, at the afternoon service on Sundays, from May to July inclusive. The Abbey-doors are opened at 2.30, P.M.; and the service begins at 3. There is daily service in the Abbey at 7.45, A.M., 10, A.M., and 3, P.M. See also " Churches."

WESTMINSTER HALL.

Turning away from the Abbey, Westminster Hall faces you, east. Pause for an instant in Palace Yard, and mark the stone moulding, or string-course, that runs round the grand old building, — the largest hall not supported by pillars in the world, with the exception of the Hall of Reason at Padua. The crouching White Hart, cut upon the stones, was done by masons who worked for one Master Henry de Yeveley, foreman of works to three successive kings, but who supervised this little piece of masonic embellishment four hundred and seventy-six years ago. The device was the favorite device of England's Second Richard, of the house of Plantagenet, who ascended the throne 1377. The hall itself is two hundred and ninety feet long by sixty-eight broad; is entirely unsupported by pillars; and the roof is the finest existing example of scientific carpentry extant. The statuary in it must be left to be judged by the visitor for himself.

Now for one or two points of history intimately associated with the building. By a clause in Magna Charta, 15th June, 1215, it is declared that "Common Pleas shall not follow the Court, but shall be held in some certain place." In the year 1224, the ninth of King Henry III., the oldest son of him who signed the Great Charter, the law courts of England, four in number, — Sir Edward Coke observes that no man can tell which of them is most ancient, — were permanently established in Westminster Hall. Here they are still held, on the right hand as you enter, — the Chancery, the Queen's Bench, the Exchequer, the Common Pleas. Here, also, the ancient kings of England held their parliaments: and the very first meeting of the parliament after the White Hart had been carved aloft, and the hall was ready for use, was for deposing the very king who had caused the work to be done.

There will be one scene, of all others, present to the mind as we stand in Westminster Hall, before which every thought upon its Norman founder and its Plantagenet and Tudor associations must fade away. Here a king was tried, and condemned to death, who, by the sovereign people's law, could do no wrong. Here, in this very hall, the world beheld the amazing spectacle of a great nation sitting in judgment on its sovereign, the descendant of a long line of illustrious kings.

At the upper end of the hall, just upon the long flight of stone steps leading to the corridors of the Houses of Parliament, on scarlet-covered benches, — "all of blowdy colors for the tryers," — sat seventy of the king's judges to judge the king. In the centre, upon a raised platform, was a chair of more than ordinary beauty, covered with crimson velvet and gold, for Bradshaw, the president of the people's court. A large table, covered with rich Turkey carpet, upon which lay the mace and sword of justice, was opposite him there. And here, over on the other side of the table, facing Bradshaw, was the chair for Charles. On either side, as we stand, galleries were erected for the convenience of spectators; and behind, on the right and left hand of the king's chair of crimson, were arranged the soldiers and officers of the court. A strong bar ran across the centre of the hall, behind which the populace in a dense mass crowded. Moreover, those leads and windows were filled with soldiers; for the judges were afraid, Bradshaw most of all.

"Oyez!" and silence is made, and the tall man with the longish, handsome face, and the Vandyke beard and mustache, and the long, rich brown hair, and the beautiful languishing eyes, is brought in. He looks sternly at his judges. then at that gallery, then at this,—just as a well-bred actor. between the parts, towards the spectators,—and now sits down. Though a man of highest breeding, he keeps his head covered, becauses he refuses to show the least respect for the court. He sits unmoved, careless, looking up here, and then looking up there, maintaining his usual placidity of countenance, only smiling a bit contemptuously by and by when some of the more absurd and daring allegations in the charge are made. · The several names in the roll of the " tryers " are called over by the clerk at the table. A pause is made for the great Lord-General Fairfax to answer.

" He has more wit than to be here ! " cries a voice from the gallery.

But there is little stir made at the cry, though Bradshaw looks a little frightened, and fingers a little nervously the high-crowned beaver hat, lined with steel, that lies at his elbow.

The charge runs thus, and is read : Charles Stuart, King of England, is accused, " in the name of the people of England "—

" No, not the hundredth part of them ! It is false! Where are they ? Oliver Cromwell is a traitor ! " again cries the voice in the gallery.

A burly, steel-clad colonel of infantry desires some soldiers to fire into the gallery, from where the voice issues.

" Down with her ! " shout the crowd.

" For God's sake " —

But no need to shout ; the Lady Fairfax, womanly woman that she was, is compelled to retire, and goes to her home, happier that she has spoken her protest.

To the charge, " In the name of the people of England, Charles Stuart is accused of treason, tyranny, of all the murders and rapines that had happened in the war ; weightiest charge of all, that he had raised war against the parliament," what will this Charles Stuart answer ?

" Sir," says Bradshaw, rising from his chair, " you have heard your charge, containing such matters as appear in it ; and in the close it is prayed that you answer to your charge, which this Court expects."

" By what authority," asks the king,—for he had been posted upon the law by Sir Matthew Hale,—" by what authority do you bring your most rightful sovereign to trial against the public faith? By what authority?" emphatically he demands. Again he bids them declare by what authority his subjects have arrogated to themselves the power of constituting themselves the king's judges. Nevertheless, whatsoever they did, he, Charles Stuart, was resolved not to betray the charge committed to him by God, and confirmed by ancient descent.

Bradshaw, in his brutal way, will hear nothing. The king is called to account by authority of the people of England, by whose election he was admitted king. "What becomes of your divine right now, Sir King?"

"But," the king replies, "the kingdom descended to me in no wise." He was by no means "elected:" his right as sovereign of England was confirmed by hereditary right, extending over a thousand years. He stood there that day to assert the liberties of the people of England, in fact, by refusing this unlawful and arbitrary authority claimed by the court. What is this assembly? It does not represent the people of England. The authority and power of the people is shown in the parliament; and one element of that parliament is absent, — the lords. Moreover, where is the king? King, lords, and commons constitute the parliament which represents the people. "I desire again that you will produce your authority for trying me."

Bradshaw again and again interrupts: the king's protests are evidently having some weight. See how that man nods his head, and this judge shifts about uneasily in his chair, and the soldier over there looks half ashamed of his treason! If this goes on much longer —

The court must be adjourned; and Charles goes back whence he came, under the inconceivably brutal dismissal of the president.

Then another day comes, when the king stands again in the same place; and Cook, the solicitor for the self-styled people of England, moves that Charles Stuart may make a positive answer to the charges against him. More protests. There were weighty reasons why he could not prosecute his defence before the judges, and acknowledge a new form of judicature. By what law had ever any judges power to erect a judicature against their king? Why, they themselves derived their own power of the king. God's law commanded obedience unto princes: nor by man's laws, nor by the laws of the land, had they any authority.

The Court were abundantly satisfied of their authority; neither would they hear any reasons that would detract from their power.

" Where in all the world is that court," asks Charles, " in which no place is left for reason ? " At least they will permit him to exhibit his objections in writing; which if they can satisfactorily answer, then he will yield himself to their jurisdiction.

Bradshaw becomes angry : he frets, he fumes. The court shall be adjourned again. The soldiers are more brutal than on the first day. They resort to all manner of disgusting and offensive insults : they even, in their rude insolence, mix powder in the palms of their hands, and fire it so that the stench shall offend the smell of the dainty king. What cares he, poor man ? He knows full well their ignorance. He turns about, and lifts his eyes, and smiles upon them, as if to say, " They know not what they do." An officer comes forward to remove Charles Stuart.

" Remember that 'tis your king from whom you turn away your ear," says he. " In vain, certainly, will my subjects expect justice from you who stop your ears to your king, ready to plead his cause."

" God bless you, sir ! " says an honest fellow in steel hard by the king's chair; which provokes a lusty blow from the man's superior.

" Methinks," says Charles, " the punishment exceedeth the offence," and so passes out.

Again the third day comes ; and the rabble shout for justice and execution. The king again protests. The president threatens. On the morning of the fourth and last day a scene occurs in a lodging over yonder, where Bradshaw, in robe of scarlet, awaits the hour for the court's assembling.

Dame Bradshaw fears both God and man : she is dreadfully concerned for the king. She beseeches her husband, by his hopes of happiness here and hereafter, to absent himself from the bench that day, — the 24th of January, 1649. " Do not," she implores, " sentence this earthly king, for fear of the dreadful sentence of the King of heaven. You have no child : why should you do such a monstrous act to favor others ? "

" Tush ! " says the husband. Yet he confesses, musingly, the king has done him no harm. " He shall have none except what the law commands." Intoxicated man !

This great hall is crowded again ; for humanity is brutal

at times. Judgment was to be proclaimed. The judges are all seated; the soldiers cease their scoffing; the spectators look anxious, and wish the land was well rid of the trouble. The king alone is unmoved. Then that infatuated Bradshaw begins a vulgar, tiresome, and absurd tirade, wherein he aggravates the contumacy of the king, and asserts the hatefulness of his crimes. He produces parliamentary authority (especially out of Scotland) for punishing kings. He affirms that the power of the people of England over their king is not less. This man has waged war against the parliament: he is a tyrant, a traitor, a murderer, and a public enemy to the Commonwealth. He (Bradshaw) argues that *rex est, dum bene regit, tyrannus qui populum opprimit,* and by this definition lodges on the king arbitrary government which he sought to put upon the people. The king's treasons are a breach of trust to the kingdom as his superior; and he is therefore called to an account. *Minimus majorem in judicium vocat.* His murders are many too; for is he not wholly responsible for those committed in the wars between him and his people? All this innocent blood cannot be cleansed but by the blood of him that shed the blood. Then judgment is given.

"This Court doth adjudge that he, the said Charles Stuart. as a tyrant. traitor, murderer, and public enemy to the good people of this nation, shall be put to death by severing his head from his body."

Then all the judges rise as a tacit acknowledgment of their acquiescence and consent. "Will you hear me for a few moments?" asks the king. Bradshaw will not hear him. "Sir, you are not to be heard after the sentence."

"No, sir?" inquires Charles.

"No, sir, by your favor. Guards, withdraw your prisoner!" impetuously shouts the president.

And this great hall of England's kings was cleared till it was wanted for another great scene in England's history. That day was not far off. On the 26th of June, 1657, Cromwell was installed here Lord-Protector of the Commonwealth of Great Britain and Ireland.

SUBURBAN RESORTS.

Not the least of the luxuries of visiting London is to know that within half an hour's ride of its miles of crowded streets — to the east, west, north, or south — is country, which for rare beauty cannot be surpassed in any other part of England. Nothing, indeed, can be more lovely than the neighborhood of Richmond, or more delicious than a summer morning's roamings through the avenues of blooming chest-nut-trees in Bushey Park. There is no part of England at all to be compared for luxurious cultivation to Kent. And Middlesex can show something of the quiet beauties of sub-urban London in Hampstead and the neighborhood about the Baroness Burdett-Coutts's charming residence at High-gate Hill. There can't be much difficulty in choosing a place where a day may be spent amid green fields and health-giving air, away from the toil and hubbub and smoke and dirt of great London. You may, should incli-nation serve, go down to the sea for a trifle in a swift lit-tle river steamer, studying " cockney " life aboard, and won-dering by the way at the prodigious extent of mercantile London; at its acres of docks, and miles of shipping, and great granaries, and warehouses and stores full of the rich products from countries in every quarter of the globe. You may see the Union Jack floating from that beautiful pile of solid buildings built by Charles II. at the foot of Green-wich Park, and point out to your friends one of the first arsenals in the world at Woolwich. You may view that marvel of modern London, the pumping station of the Lon-don Main Drainage Works at Crossness; and onward yet to the sea, past the uplands of Kent in the distance on the right, and the lowlands of Middlesex in the left foreground, vividly bringing to the imagination the scenes in " Great Expectations." You shall pass sweet little Rosherville, with its tiny yachts at anchor in the still water under the terrace ; and dart by Gravesend ; and soon be off the Nore, drinking in — the doctors can say how much in an hour — draughts of ozone from the ocean, a fresh lease of life for the morrow.

London gets fatiguing after several days of continuous sight-seeing; and then it would be well for the visitor to plan out for himself a day's outing in the suburbs. There are Mortlake and Twickenham, and Richmond, Kew, and

Windsor, — all places on the outskirts of which a great deal of the quiet life of rural England may be studied. This advertisement appears in the London newspapers during the summer months : " Kew Gardens are open free to the public every day, including Sunday. The Iron and Citizen Steamboats run to Kew daily, calling at Putney and Hammersmith every half-hour; commencing at 11, A.M., from the Cadogan Pier, Chelsea, in conjunction with the ordinary ten-minutes Chelsea boats."

Here is the very opportunity. Take a steamboat from Westminster Bridge to Chelsea, and you will be sure of catching the Kew boat on the half-hours. Kew Gardens are rich in flowers of every hue, and trees and plants of every kind. Not the millionnaires of the metropolis, not the Duke of Devonshire at Chatsworth, not royalty itself at Windsor or Buckingham Palace, can make a more goodly show.

There are two attractions at Kew, — the Botanic Gardens and the Pleasure Grounds, covering seventy-five acres of ground. Money has been wisely and lavishly spent upon the place. An immense conservatory, with accompanying flower-gardens, has been prepared; many new and superior plant-houses have recently been erected; a museum founded; a pinetum planted; and the whole has been thrown open for the benefit of the public. To fill these gardens and conservatories, all the ends of the earth are ransacked for their floral treasures. The Museum of Economic Botany is of great value to the student.

One tree in the open grounds has a peculiar interest. It is a willow, now fifty feet high, which, when planted in 1825, was a small twig cut from one of the trees which overhung the grave of Napoleon at St. Helena. As an accompaniment to the entrance-gates, the large conservatory on the right was brought from Buckingham Palace. The splendor of the palm-house at once attracts the eye. It contains nearly an acre of glass. The total length is 362 ft. 6 inches, the centre portion being 137 ft. 6 inches long, 101 ft. wide, and 69 ft. high to the top of the lantern light: the wings are each 112 ft. 6 inches long, 50 ft. wide, and 33 ft. to the lantern. A gallery runs round the centre portion of the house at a height of 27 ft. above the floor. For plants requiring a heat of eighty degrees, twelve boilers are placed in two vaults under the house; and upwards of 4¼ miles of iron pipes, distributed under the floor and stone tables surrounding the house, give a heating surface of about 28,000 superficial feet. The heated air ascends through a perforated floor of cast-iron plates, supported on iron columns and girders, except where stone-paved paths interfere. The rain-water is conveyed through hollow pillars of support to a tank under a stone shelf round the whole of the interior of the building, where its temperature is raised by its close contiguity to the heating-pipes. The tank is capable of containing 42,000 gallons. Water is also supplied from the River Thames by means of a steam-engine and pumps, from an iron tank fixed at a height of seventy-five feet in the tower, whence pipes distribute the water to the gallery and other parts of the house. The cost was altogether 33,000*l.* The temperate house was erected at a cost of about 10,000*l.* It is money well spent; for the gardens are amongst the finest of their kind in the world.

A very economical trip indeed is to take the rail at King's Cross, and go down to the Alexandra Park at Muswell Hill. We would suggest to all American lovers of English scenery to visit this spot in Northern London; for it recalls many scenes of other times. Time out of mind, the citizens of old London have rejoiced in the green lands of old Hornsey; and in the old time many a stately and royal cavalcade has passed that way. Hornsey Wood was the ground where monarchs would hunt in days gone by; and in the middle of this same wood was a chapel where lived — it is said — a holy saint who cured a Scottish king of a mortal complaint; and ever since that day, some centuries back. Muswell Hill has kept a name among the places in England celebrated for their sanitary virtues. At its foot poets have loved to nestle. " Lalla Rookh " was written in a cottage on one side of it; Sam Rogers sleeps in pretty Hornsey churchyard close by; Leigh Hunt was born in the village of Southgate, but a half-mile off on the other side. Climb the hill on a clear day, and you will have before you one of those panoramas exclusively English in their beauty. At your feet lies Wood Green, not long since a wild common, now a thickly-populated town. Here is Hornsey; there is Highgate, with its rural beauties, not the least of which are the grounds about Holly Lodge, the abode of the lady whose name has become famous everywhere for her munificent, unostentatious Christian charity. Coleridge's Hampstead is not a great way off, — that Hampstead about whose lanes and by-paths Charles Dickens often loved to linger, and which is associated with the great men and statesmen, and poets

10

and painters, of other days. Elia — dear, good Elia — crops up, too, in the memory ; for there in the distance lies Charles Lamb's Enfield. We can see Tottenham and Edmonton, and the vestiges of Epping Forest, and the glimmering in the distance of the Crystal Palace at Sydenham. Muswell Hill is a spot rarely visited by Americans, yet surrounding it are some of the prettiest bits of scenery in the world.

Every one goes to Richmond ; and every one dines at the Star and Garter, when he or she gets there; and every one lolls out of the window, and exclaims, "How superbly lovely!" Or, if every one doesn't, every one ought to ; for it happens to be one of the most fairy-like spots in existence. Sir Walter Scott gives the following description of it in the "Heart of Mid-Lothian." Jeannie Deans accompanies the Duke of Argyll in his carriage from London to seek an interview with Queen Caroline. "After passing through a pleasant village [Richmond], the equipage stopped on a commanding eminence, where the beauty of English landscape was displayed in its utmost luxuriance. Here the duke alighted, and desired Jeannie to follow him. They paused for a moment on the brow of a hill to gaze on the unrivalled landscape which it presented. A huge sea of verdure, with crossing and intersecting promontories of massive and tufted gorses, was tenanted by numberless flocks and herds, which seemed to wander unrestrained and un-bounded through the rich pastures. The Thames, here tur-reted with villas, and there garlanded with forests, moved on slowly and placidly like the mighty monarch of the scene, to whom all its other beauties were but accessories, and bore on its bosom a hundred boats and skiffs, whose white sails and gayly-fluttering pennons gave life to the whole. 'This is a fine scene,' said the duke to his companion : 'we have nothing like it in Scotland.' — 'It's braw rich feeding for the cows, and they have a fine herd of cattle here,' replied Jeannie; 'but I like just as well to look at the crags of Arthur's Seat, and the sea coming in against them, as at a' the muckle trees.'" Richmond should be seen in the month of June. It is a charming drive from London, especially by way of Wandsworth and Wimbledon Common. For those who cannot afford the time or expense, trains leave nearly every hour from Waterloo Bridge.

Another beautiful outskirt of London is Hampton Court, by South-western Railway, three-quarters of an hour distant from Waterloo Station. The state apartments are open gra-

tuitously to the public on every day except Friday (when
they are closed for the purpose of being cleaned), from 10
o'clock, A.M.. until 6 o'clock (*Sundays* from 2 to 6), from the
1st of April to the 1st of October, and the remainder of the
year from 10 until 4. The Vinery in the Private Garden, and
the Maze in the Wilderness, are open every day until sunset:
for these a small fee is required by the gardeners who show
them. Guide-books (price 6*d*. and 3*d*.), containing a complete catalogue of the pictures, may be had in the Palace.

WINDSOR.

Windsor is inexpressibly lovely; and one long summer's
day must be spent in studying its many and varied beauties.
The state apartments at the Castle are open gratuitously on
Mondays, Tuesdays, Thursdays, and Fridays,—from 1st
April to 31st October, between 11 and 4; and from 1st
November to 31st March, between 11 and 3. Tickets may
be procured at Messrs. Colnaghi, printsellers, 14 Pall Mall,
east. The Castle must be seen; St. George's Chapel must
be looked over very carefully; a walk must be taken in the
glorious park; and a point should be made of taking a drive
by the Long Walk (three miles long) to Virginia Water.
Guide-books may be procured of Messrs. Colnaghi, at the
price of a penny.

The scenery in many parts of Windsor Great Park is
especially lovely, and chiefly from the disposition of the
trees. Several of the largest are known by the names of
former royal occupants of the castle: thus there is an oak
in the Broad Walk called William the Conqueror's Oak,
said to be over twelve hundred years old. Jesse, in his
" Scenes and Occupations of Rural Life," says, " It may not
be generally known that some of the queens of England
have been in the habit of choosing an oak or beech tree in
Windsor Forest, to which they have given their names,
which, with the date of the month, and year of selection, is
engraved on a brass plate, and screwed securely to the tree.
In one of the most beautiful and retired parts of the forest
may be seen Queen Anne's Oak, the oak of the amiable
wife of George II., Queen Caroline, the oak of Queen
Charlotte, the oak of the excellent Queen Adelaide, as
well as that of her present Majesty."

But perhaps the greatest attractions at Windsor are to be found in St. George's Chapel, which is one of the most celebrated edifices in the world, being the chapel of the Knights of the Garter. It is rich in historic interest, and is a grand specimen of the florid-Gothic style of architecture in vogue in the days of Edward the Fourth. The interesting archives of the Record Office in London show a patent of Richard II., with the date 1390, describing the chapel as falling into ruins, and appointing a clerk of the works to superintend its repair. The salary of this functionary was to be two shillings a day (somewhere about three thousand dollars per annum of modern American money) ; and the name of the man first appointed to the post was Geoffrey Chaucer!

The greater part of the edifice, as it now stands, may be attributed to Edward the Fourth ; and as a specimen of the elegant style of the architecture of that time, known as the florid-Gothic, it is at once the most beautiful and complete to be found throughout England. Its interior space is formed into a choir, nave, and correspondent aisles ; the choir being divided from the nave by a magnificent screen of artificial stone. The roof is elliptical in form, — composed of stone, — rising from tall, slender pillars, which gives the interior of the chapel a surprisingly light and elegant appearance.

Entering the choir from the nave, beneath the organ gallery, the sight is one of the most impressive that can be imagined. On either side, almost black with age, are the carved stalls of the Knights of the Garter, the canopies being sculptured in the most delicate yet fantastic Gothic. Above, hanging solemnly still, are the rich silken banners of each knight, with his mantle, sword, helmet, and crest on a pedestal below. In front, over the altar, is a splendid example of art by one of the most celebrated painters of the last century, West, — the Last Supper. The wainscoting surrounding the communion-table is rich in wonderful carving. The lofty windows of ancient stained glass throw streams of mellowed light on the marble pavement below ; and the whole forms a picture, which, once seen, is not readily forgotten.

There are whole pages of history written in few words on the backs of some of the stalls of the Knights of the Garter. As the chapel is so entirely associated with that order of chivalry so highly prized in Europe, a few words on its origin may not seem out of place. The most probable cause of its foundation was the strong passion for military glory that reigned within the breast of Edward the Third, its acknowledged founder. With the intent that his knights might have an opportunity of increasing their skill and hardihood by chivalrous exercises, he provoked among them a spirit of emulation and amity by restoring the ancient order of the " Table Ronde," which, according to the testimony of old authors, was soon after the Conquest, and occasionally until the reign of Edward the Confessor, erected in England for the entertainment of knights assembled to exercise themselves in feats of strength and courage, — qualities which then constituted almost the only recommendation to distinction.

The following, translated from Beltz's " History of the Order," explains the whole thing in a few words : —

"King Edwarde made a great feast at Wyndesore at Christmas, where he renewed the Round Table and the name of Arture, and ordered the order of the Garter, making Sainct George the patrone thereof."

The date of this record is anterior to 1344. As regards the adoption of a garter as the symbol of the order, there is a variety of conflicting opinion : the most generally accepted story is, that, at a ball, the garter of the queen, or of some lady of the court, fell off casually as she danced. The monarch, one of the most courteous men of his time, picked it off the ground, and, observing the smiles of the courtiers at what might have been considered an act of gallantry, exclaimed, " *Honi soit qui mal y pense ;*" adding, that a garter should soon be held in such high estimation, that they should account themselves happy to wear it.

On the back of the stalls in the choir, engraved on little plates of copper, are the names, titles, and arms of each knight that has occupied a seat in the chapel from the date of the foundation of the order. On the decease of a knight, his sword, banner, and other insignia, are taken down : but the plate remains as a record ; and very curious records they form. From them we learn that Charles V., Emperor of Germany, and another celebrated man, Francis I. of France, forgot their ancient rivalry in one respect by submitting to be enrolled members of a society whose fundamental charter is unswerving fidelity to the common cause of *brotherhood.* The quaint old heraldic engravings further say, that, in 1418, Sigismund, Emperor of Germany; in 1452, Casimer, King of

Poland; a little later on, the unfortunate Earl of Surrey, of
"Bluff King Hal's" times; nearer our own times still,
Charles I., whose body is buried not far off from the stall he
once occupied; William of Orange: the first gentleman of
Europe; Nicholas, Emperor of Russia; Napoleon III. of
France; William, Emperor of Germany; Leopold, Emperor
of Austria; the Sultan of Turkey: the King of the Belgians,
— all consented to become knights of the order, and to send
their insignia of knighthood, and banners of silk, to pro-
claim in the Temple of Peace their common hatred of war.
By the rules of the order, the sovereign of Great Britain can
command a chapter to be held, and summon all knights to
attend it, under certain penalties. Of course, the foreign
members of the order would be exempt by courtesy; but
what nice little meetings might have been brought about if
the sovereign from time to time had stood on his rights, and
insisted, as essential to the dignity of the order, that every
knight should attend in his stall at a chapter! There had
been no need then for any " Field of the Cloth-of-Gold."

Not far from the altar, on the north side, is a small gallery called the " Queen's Closet." It is a plainly-furnished
room, with sofa and chairs in purple velvet. The wainscot
and canopy are in the Gothic style, painted to imitate Norway oak. The queen uses it on all occasions on which she
attends service in the chapel.

Below this gallery the remains of Edward the Fourth are
deposited. Over his tomb is an exquisite monument in
steel. representing a pair of gates between two Gothic towns,
said to have been wrought by the hand of the celebrated
Quentin Matsys, the blacksmith of Antwerp. On a flat
stone at the base of the monument are the words, "King
Edward IV. and his Queen Elizabeth Widdville." This
vault was entered in 1789 in presence of King George. The
remains were found enclosed in a leaden and wooden coffin,
the latter measuring six feet three inches in length. Near
the bones of the king was another coffin, supposed to have
contained the body of Elizabeth Widdville. When the dis-
covery was communicated. the neighboring inhabitants
pressed with such eagerness to obtain a view and some relic
of the remains, that the skeleton of the king, which upwards
of three centuries had failed to reduce to its native element, would have been frittered away in as many hours if
the doors of the chapel had not been closed against the press
of people.

Henry the Sixth was also buried near the choir-door. In the royal vault, Henry the Eighth, Jane Seymour, and Charles the First, are buried. A manuscript memorandum in the possession of the castle authorities, written by one of the late chapter clerks (a Mr. Sewell), affirms, that "upon opening this vault for the interment of a still-born child of the Princess of Denmark, afterwards Queen Anne, he went into the vault, and there saw the coffins of King Henry VIII. and Queen Jane; also the coffin of King Charles I., covered with velvet, with a label on the cover, whereon was marked, 'King Charles, 1648;' that the velvet of the coffin and pall was sound, and in no ways rent; that the pall laid over the coffin was as first flung on at the burial; that the vault was small; and that the new-born child was laid upon the coffin of the king."

In a small chapel off one of the aisles, Lincoln, Queen Elizabeth's Lord High Admiral, is buried. The figure of the earl in armor, with his feet resting on a greyhound, is on the top of his tomb. One of the most exquisitely beautiful monuments in St. George's Chapel is the cenotaph of the Princess Charlotte of Wales. It represents the princess entirely covered with a cloth with the exception of one of the hands, watched by female attendants. Her apotheosis takes place above; while the spirit, which is a good likeness of its earthly tenement, is seen rising from a mausoleum in the background. A wonderful light shines upon the face of the figure from a painted window on the opposite side, producing an effect of surpassing loveliness.

The stained glass windows are splendid examples of ancient art: one of them, the west window, fills the entire width of the nave; whilst another, over the altar, in the choir, is considered a *chef d'œuvre*, and cost some thousands of pounds. The whole of the ceiling of the chapel proper is decorated with the arms of many sovereigns and knights of the Order of the Garter, beautifully emblazoned; and all the decorations in the choir and around the wainscoting of the altar are in accordance with the same designs. The services of the Church of England are read daily in the chapel, morning and afternoon. On Sundays the seats are free to visitors, even when the royal family is present; and, if a person be fond of fine music and singing, he will hear both at St. George's Chapel. Dr. Elvey of Oxford presides at the organ; and the members of the choir are selected from the best male singers in England.

COOK'S TOURS

TO

IRELAND AND SCOTLAND.

ISSUED SINGLY, OR IN COMBINATION WITH OCEAN
STEAMER AND CONTINENTAL TOURIST
TICKETS,

BY

COOK, SON, & JENKINS,

Tourist and Excursion Managers, 262 Broadway, New York;
and 104 Washington St., Boston.

The routes in the following pages, covering all the points of tourist interest in Ireland, Scotland, or England, are specially arranged for the benefit
of those who may wish to visit these countries alone, or who may wish to take
them *en route* to the Continent, as they can be worked in combination with all
the tickets in our programmes, either *going* or *returning*. These tickets are
good in either direction, and will suit equally well those landing at QUEENS-
TOWN, CORK, LONDONDERRY, BELFAST, or GLASGOW, on their outward voyage, or those who may wish to embark at those places on their return voyage.

SPECIAL NOTICE. — These tickets embrace
the line of every railway company in Ireland, and
are issued at a reduction of twenty per cent
below ordinary fares, for the benefit of Cook's
American Tourists only. Passengers who desire
to visit Ireland or Scotland, en route to London
and the Continent, must procure such tickets pre-
vious to sailing, or otherwise pay ordinary fares.
They are available for either first or second class.

154

IRISH TOURS,

FOR PASSENGERS LANDING AT QUEENSTOWN.

Fares Quoted in Gold.

Tours combining the Mountains of Kerry and Killarney Lake District.

ROUTE 1.—Queenstown to London, *via* rail to Cork, Macroom, thence across the mountains of Kerry by jaunting-car, passing Inchigeela, Glengariffe, Kenmare, to Killarney, rail to Mallow, Limerick Junction, Kildare, Dublin, thence steamer to Liverpool, and rail to Burton, Matlock, through the Derbyshire Peak District, Bakewell (for Chatsworth), Rowsely (for Haddon Hall), Derby, Leicester, London, or *vice versa*.

First class..$25 80
Second class... 20 75

ROUTE 2.—Queenstown to London, *via* Cork, Macroom, and car to Inchigeela, Glengariffe, Kenmare, and Killarney, thence rail to Mallow, Limerick Junction, Kildare, Dublin, Balbriggan, Drogheda, Dundalk, Enniskillen (Loch Erne), Omagh, Strabane, Londonderry, Portrush (Giant's Causeway), Coleraine, Belfast, thence across Irish Channel by steamer around the Isle of Man to Barrow, Lancaster (Windermere and Cumberland Lake district), Leeds, Ambergate (for Haddon Hall and Chatsworth), Derby, Leicester, Bedford, London, or *vice versa*.

First class.................................... $35 95
Second class................................... 28 75

ROUTE 3.—Queenstown to London, *via* Cork, Macroom, Inchigeela, Kenmare, Killarney, Mallow, Dublin, Drogheda, Dundalk, Belfast, by steamer to Barrow, thence rail *via* Lancaster, Leeds, Sheffield, Ambergate Junction (for Derbyshire), Derby, Leicester, London, or *vice versa*.

First class..$29 75
Second class... 24 00

ROUTE 4.—Queenstown to London, *via* Cork, Macroom, Inchigeela, Glengariffe, Kenmare, Killarney, Mallow, Kildare, Dublin, Balbriggan, Drogheda, Dundalk, Portadown, Belfast, thence across Channel, *via* Royal Mail Line of steamers, to Greenock, and up the Clyde, passing Dunbarton Castle, to Glasgow, thence rail to Edinburgh, Melrose (for Abbotsford), Carlisle, Leeds, Sheffield, Derby, Leicester, Bedford, London, or *vice versa*.

First class..$39 00
Second class... 31 25

ROUTE 5. — Queenstown to London, *viâ* same as Route No. 4, to Glasgow, thence by rail to Ayr (the home of Burns), and Carlisle, Leeds, Sheffield, Derby, Bedford, London, or *vice versâ.*

First class...$39 25
Second class.. 31 25

ROUTE 6. — Queenstown to London, *viâ* Cork, Macroom, Inchigeela, Kenmare, Killarney, Mallow, Dublin, Drogheda, Dundalk, Enniskillen (Loch Erne), Londonderry, Portrush (Giant's Causeway), Belfast, Greenock, River Clyde, Glasgow, Ayr (or Edinburgh, or Melrose), to Carlisle, Leeds, Derby, Leicester, London, or *vice versâ.*

First class...$45 75
Second class.. 36 00

ROUTE 7. — Queenstown to London, *viâ* Cork, Macroom, Inchigeela, Kenmare, Killarney, Mallow, Dublin, Drogheda, Dundalk, Enniskillen (Loch Erne), Londonderry, Portrush (Giant's Causeway), Belfast, Greenock, Glasgow, thence to Loch Lomond, Loch Katrine, Trossachs, Callander, Stirling, Edinburgh, Melrose, London, or *vice versâ.*

First class...$51 40
Second class.. 41 00

ROUTE 8. — Queenstown to London, *viâ* Cork, Macroom, Inchigeela, Glengariffe, Kenmare, Killarney, Mallow, Limerick Junction, Clonmel, Waterford, over Channel to New Milford, through South Wales, to London, or *vice versâ.*

First class...$24 00
Second class.. 19 25

---◆---

Tours combining the Mountains of Kerry, Lakes of Killarney, and the Connemara District.

ROUTE 9. — Queenstown to London, *viâ* rail to Cork, Macroom, jaunting-car to Inchigeela, Glengariffe, Kenmare, Killarney, rail to Mallow, Limerick, Ennis, Athenry, Galway, Athlone, Mullingar, Dublin, thence steamer, over Irish Channel, to Liverpool, Woodley (for Manchester), Buxton, Matlock, Bakewell (for Chatsworth), Rowsely (for Haddon Hall), Derby, Leicester, Bedford, London, or *vice versâ.*

First class...$34 80
Second class.. 29 45

ROUTE 10. — Queenstown to London, *viâ* rail to Cork and Macroom, car to Glengariffe, Kenmare, and Killarney, rail to Mallow, Limerick, Ennis, Athenry, and Galway, coach, through the Western Highlands and Connemara, to Westport, passing the finest scenery in the counties Galway and Mayo, thence rail to Castlebar, Roscommon, Athlone, Mullingar, Dublin, across Irish Channel to Liverpool, rail to Woodley (for Manchester), Matlock Baths, Buxton, Bakewell (for Chatsworth), Rowsely (for Haddon Hall), Derby, Bedford, London, or *vice versâ.*

First class...$34 80
Second class.. 29 45

ROUTE 11. — Queenstown to London, *viâ* rail to Cork, Macroom, car to Inchigeela, Glengariffe, Kenmare, and Killarney, rail to Mallow, Limerick, Ennis, Athenry, Galway, Dublin, Drogheda, Dundalk, Enniskillen, Londonderry, Portrush, Belfast, thence over Channel, around the Isle of Man to Morecambe, Barrow, and rail to Lancaster (for Cumberland Lake District), Leeds, Sheffield, Ambergate (for Haddon Hall, Chatsworth, and Derbyshire Peak District), Derby, Leicester, Bedford, London, or *vice versa.*

First class..$39 45
Second class... 31 65

ROUTE 12. — Queenstown to London, *viâ* rail to Carlisle and Macroom, jaunting-car to Inchigeela, Glengariffe, Kenmare, and Killarney, rail to Mallow, Limerick, Ennis, Athenry, Galway, thence by car through the Western Highlands to Westport, rail to Castlebar, Roscommon, Athlone, Mullingar, Dublin, steamer, over Irish Channel, to Liverpool, Woodley (for Manchester), Matlock Baths, Buxton, Bakewell (for Chatsworth), Rowsely (for Haddon Hall), Derby, Leicester, Bedford, London, or *vice versa.*

First class..$34 80
Second class 30 45

ROUTE 13. — Queenstown to London, *viâ* rail to Cork and Macroom, car to Inchigeela, Glengariffe, Kenmare, Killarney, rail to Mallow, Limerick, Ennis, Athenry, Galway, Athlone, Dublin, Dundalk, Enniskillen (Loch Erne), Londonderry, Portrush (Giant's Causeway), Belfast, steamer to Greenock and Glasgow, rail either *viâ* Ayr or Edinburgh and Melrose to Carlisle, Leeds, Sheffield, Ambergate Junction (for Derbyshire), Derby, Leicester, London, or *vice versa.*

First class..$48 75
Second class... 38 90

ROUTE 14. — Queenstown to London, *viâ* rail to Cork and Macroom, jaunting-car to Inchigeela, Glengariffe, Kenmare, Killarney, rail to Mallow Junction, Limerick, Ennis, Athenry, Galway, car through Western Highlands to Westport, rail to Castlebar, Roscommon, Athlone, Mullingar, Dublin, Balbriggan, Drogheda, Dundalk, Enniskillen (Loch Erne), Omagh, Strabane, Londonderry, Portrush (Giant's Causeway), Belfast, steamer of Royal Mail Line to Greenock, the Clyde, and Glasgow, rail to Edinburgh, Melrose for Abbotsford, Carlisle (or rail to Ayr and Carlisle), Leeds, Sheffield, Ambergate Junction (for Haddon Hall, Chatsworth, and Derbyshire Peak District), Derby, Leicester, Bedford, London, or *vice versa.*

First class $54 45
Second class... 43 65

ROUTE 15. — Queenstown to London, *viâ* rail to Cork and Macroom, car to Inchigeela, Glengariffe, Kenmare, Killarney, rail to Mallow, Limerick, Ennis, Athenry, Galway, Dublin, Dundalk, Enniskillen (Loch Erne), Londonderry, Portrush (Giant's Causeway), Belfast, steamer to Glasgow, then *viâ* Loch Lomond, Loch Katrine, Trossachs, Callander, Stirling, Edinburgh, Melrose, to London, or *vice versa.*

First class..$53 25
Second class......... .... 43 90

ROUTE 16. — Queenstown to London, *viâ* rail to Cork and Macroom, jaunting-car to Inchigeela, Glengariffe, Kenmare, and Killarney, thence rail to Mallow, Limerick, Ennis, Athenry, and Galway, car through Western Highlands to Westport, Castlebar, Roscommon, Athlone, Dublin, Balbriggan, Drogheda, Dundalk, Enniskillen (Loch Erne), Omagh, Strabane, Londonderry, Coleraine, Portrush (Giant's Causeway), Belfast, Royal Mail Line of steamers across the Channel to Greenock, up the Clyde to Glasgow, thence by steamer, coach, and rail, to Loch Lomond, Loch Katrine, Trossachs, Callander, Stirling, Edinburgh, Melrose (Abbotsford), Carlisle, Leeds, Sheffield, Ambergate Junction (for Derbyshire Peak District, Haddon Hall, and Chatsworth), Derby, Leicester, Bedford, London, or *vice versa.*

First class..$60 65
Second class.. 49 65

ROUTE 17. — Queenstown to London, *viâ* rail to Cork and Macroom, thence by car to Inchigeela, Glengariffe, Kenmare, Killarney, rail to Mallow, Limerick, Ennis, Athenry, Galway, thence to Waterford, and by steamer across the Channel to New Milford, *viâ* Cardiff to London, or *vice versa.*

First class..$30 35
Second class.. 24 25

ROUTE 18. — Queenstown to London, *viâ* rail to Cork, thence by car to Inchigeela, Glengariffe, Kenmare, Killarney, rail to Mallow Junction, Limerick, Ennis, Athenry, Galway, car through Western Highlands to Westport, rail to Castlebar, Roscommon, Athlone, Mullingar, Dublin, Balbriggan, Drogheda, Dundalk, Portadown, Belfast, Portrush (Giant's Causeway), and rail to Belfast, thence across Channel by Royal Mail Line Steamer to Greenock, Dumbarton, and Glasgow, thence steamer, coach, and rail, to Loch Lomond, Loch Katrine, the Trossachs, Stirling, Edinburgh, Melrose (Abbotsford and Dryburgh), Carlisle, Leeds, Sheffield, Ambergate Junction (for Haddon Hall, Chatsworth, and Derbyshire Peak District), Derby, Leicester, Bedford, London, or *vice versa.*

First class..$60 70
Second class.. 50 65

ROUTE 19. — Queenstown to London, *viâ* same route as No. 18, to Glasgow, thence by rail to Ayr (the birthplace of Burns), Carlisle (for Cumberland Lakes), Leeds, Sheffield, Ambergate Junction (for Haddon Hall, Chatsworth, and the Derbyshire Peak District), Derby, Leicester, London, or *vice versa.*

First class..$54 45
Second class.. 44 65

ROUTE 20. — Queenstown to London, *viâ* rail to Cork and Macroom, car to Inchigeela, Glengariffe, Kenmare, and Killarney, car to Mallow, Limerick, Ennis, Athenry, and Galway, car through Western Highlands to Westport, rail to Castlebar, Roscommon, Athlone, Mullingar, Dublin, Balbriggan, Drogheda, Dundalk, Enniskillen (Loch Erne), Omagh, Strabane, Londonderry, Coleraine, Portrush (Giant's Causeway), Belfast, steamer over Channel, around Isle of Man, to Morecambe and Barrow, rail to Lancaster (for Cumberland Lakes), Leeds, Sheffield, Ambergate Junction (for Haddon Hall, Chatsworth, and Derbyshire Peak District), Derby, Leicester, Bedford, London, or *vice versa.*

First class..$44 95
Second class.. 36 90

Direct All-Rail Tours, including Killarney.

ROUTE 21. — Queenstown to London, *viâ* Cork, Mallow, Killarney, and back to Mallow, Kildare, Dublin, thence by steamer over Channel to Liverpool, Woodley (for Manchester), Buxton, Matlock Baths, Bakewell (for Chatsworth), Rowsely (for Haddon Hall), Derby, Leicester, Bedford, London, or *vice versa.*

First class..$25 80
Second class.. 20 75

ROUTE 22. — Queenstown to London, *viâ* Cork, Mallow, Killarney, and back to Mallow, Kildare, Dublin, Balbriggan, Drogheda, Dundalk. Portadown, Belfast, thence by steamer over Channel to Morecambe and Barrow, and rail to Lancaster (for Cumberland Lakes), Leeds, Sheffield. Ambergate (for Haddon Hall, Chatsworth, and Derbyshire Peak District), Derby, Leicester, Bedford, London, or *rice versa.*

First class...**$25 25**
Second class... 20 00

ROUTE 23. — Queenstown to London, *viâ* Cork, Mallow, Killarney, and back to Mallow, Kildare, Dublin, Balbriggan, Drogheda, Dundalk. Enniskillen (Loch Erne), Omagh, Strabane, Londonderry, Coleraine, Portrush (Giant's Causeway), thence steamer over Channel, around Isle of Man, to Barrow, rail to Lancaster (for Cumberland Lakes), Leeds. Sheffield, Ambergate (for Haddon Hall, Chatsworth, and Derbyshire Peak District), Derby, Leicester, Bedford, London, or *rice versa.*

First class...**$32 45**
Second class... 24 80

ROUTE 24. — Queenstown to London, *viâ* Cork. Mallow. Killarney, and back to Mallow. Kildare, Dublin, Balbriggan. Drogheda. Dundalk, Portadown. Belfast, thence by Royal Mail Steamer across Channel to Greenock, the Clyde, and Glasgow, thence rail to Edinburgh, Melrose (Abbotsford), Carlisle, Leeds, Normanton (for York), Ambergate Junction (for Haddon Hall, Chatsworth, and Derbyshire Peak District), Derby, Leicester, Bedford, London, or *rice versa.*

First class...**$35 75**
Second class... 27 25

ROUTE 25. — Queenstown to London, *riâ* Cork, Mallow. Killarney, Mallow, Kildare. Dublin, Balbriggan, Drogheda, Dundalk, Portadown. Belfast, Royal Mail Steamer across Channel to Greenock, the Clyde, and Glasgow, thence by rail, coach, steamer, and rail, to Loch Lomond, Loch Katrine, the Trossachs, Callander. Stirling, Edinburgh, Melrose (Abbotsford and Dryburgh Abbey), Carlisle, Leeds, Sheffield, Normanton (for York), Ambergate (for Haddon Hall, Chatsworth, &c.), Derby, Leicester, Bedford, London, or *rice versa.*

First class..................................**$42 00**
Second class 32 35

ROUTE 26. — Queenstown to London, *viâ* Cork, Mallow, Killarney, Mallow, Dublin, Drogheda, Dundalk, Enniskillen (Loch Erne), Londonderry, Portrush (for Giant's Causeway), Belfast, Glasgow by steamer and rail to Balloch, Loch Lomond, Loch Katrine, Trossachs, Callander, Stirling, Edinburgh, Melrose, Leeds, Derby, London, or *vice versa.*

First class...**$48 25**
Second class... 37 00

ROUTE 27. — Queenstown to London, *riâ* Cork, Mallow, Killarney, Mallow, Limerick Junction, Tipperary. Waterford, across Channel to New Milford, and through Wales *viâ* Cardiff to London, or *rice versa.*

First class **$20 50**
Second class... 15 35

ROUTE 28. — Queenstown to London, *viâ* Cork, Mallow, Killarney, Mallow, Kildare, Dublin. Mullingar. Longford, Sligo, and back to Dublin, Balbriggan, Drogheda, Dundalk, Portadown, Belfast, steamer across Channel to Greenock and Glasgow, thence rail *viâ* Ayr (or *viâ* Edinburgh and Melrose), Carlisle, Leeds, Sheffield, Derby, or *vice versa.*

First class **$35 75**
Second class... 27 30

ROUTE 29. — Queenstown to London, via Cork, Mallow, Killarney, Mallow, Kildare, Dublin, Mullingar, Athlone, Galway, thence by car through Western Highlands to Westport, rail to Castlebar, Roscommon, Dublin, Balbriggan, Drogheda, Dundalk, Portadown, Belfast, Portrush (Giant's Causeway), and back to Belfast, Royal Mail Steamer over Channel to Greenock, the Clyde, and Glasgow, rail to Edinburgh, Melrose (Abbotsford), Carlisle, Leeds, Normanton (for York), Ambergate (for Haddon Hall, Chatsworth, &c.), Derby, Leicester, Bedford, London, vice versa.

First class $57 45
Second class....................................... 45 80

ROUTE 30. — Queenstown to London, via Cork, Mallow, Killarney, Mallow, Limerick, Ennis, Athenry, Galway, Athlone, Mullingar, Dublin, Balbriggan, Drogheda, Dundalk, Portadown, Belfast, Royal Mail Steamer to Greenock, the Clyde, and Glasgow, thence rail to Edinburgh, Melrose, Carlisle, Leeds, Sheffield, Ambergate (for Haddon Hall and Chatsworth), Derby, Leicester, Bedford, London, or vice versa.

First class..$39 25
Second class 30 25

ROUTE 31. — Queenstown to London, via Cork, Mallow, Killarney, Mallow, Limerick, Ennis, Athenry, Galway, Athlone, Mullingar, Dublin, Balbriggan, Drogheda, Dundalk, Portadown, Belfast, thence by steamer across Irish Channel, around Isle of Man, to Barrow, and rail to Lancaster (for Cumberland Lakes), Leeds, Normanton (for York), Sheffield, Ambergate (for Haddon Hall and Chatsworth), Derby, Leicester, Bedford, London, or vice versa.

First class..$29 75
Second class....................................... 23 00

ROUTE 32. — Queenstown to London, via Cork. Mallow, Killarney, Mallow, Limerick, Ennis, Athenry, Galway, Athlone, Mullingar, Dublin, Balbriggan, Drogheda, Dundalk, Enniskillen (Loch Erne), Omagh, Strabane, Londonderry, Coleraine, Portrush (Giant's Causeway), Belfast, steamer across the Irish Channel to Barrow, thence by rail to Lancaster (for Cumberland Lakes), Leeds, Normanton (for York), Sheffield, Ambergate (for Haddon Hall and Chatsworth), Derby, Bedford, London, or vice versa.

First class..$35 95
Second class....................................... 27 70

ROUTE 33. — Queenstown to London, via Cork, Mallow, Killarney, Mallow, Limerick, Ennis, Athenry, Galway, Athlone, Mullingar, Dublin, thence by steamer over Channel to Liverpool, and rail to Woodley (for Manchester), Buxton, Matlock, Bakewell (for Chatsworth), Rowsely (for Haddon Hall), Derby, Leicester, Bedford, London, or vice versa.

First class..$25 80
Second class 19 70

ROUTE 34. — Queenstown to London, via rail to Cork, Mallow, Killarney, Mallow, Limerick, Ennis, Athenry, Galway, thence by car through the Western Highlands to Westport, and rail to Castlebar, Roscommon, Athlone, Mullingar, Dublin, and steamer across the Channel to Liverpool, rail to Woodley (for Manchester), Buxton, Matlock, Bakewell (for Chatsworth), Rowsely (for Haddon Hall), Derby, Leicester, Bedford, London, or vice versa.

First class..$31 30
Second class....................................... 23 45

ROUTE 35. — Queenstown to London, *viâ* rail to Cork, Mallow, Killarney, Mallow, Limerick, Ennis, Athenry, Galway, thence by car through the Western Highlands and Connemara District to Westport, rail to Castlebar, Roscommon, Athlone, Dublin, Balbriggan, Drogheda, Dundalk, Enniskillen (Loch Erne), Omagh, Strabane, Londonderry, Coleraine, Portrush ((Giant's Causeway), Belfast, thence by Royal Mail Steamer to Greenock, the Clyde, Glasgow, thence by rail (*viâ* Ayr or Edinburgh), Melrose, Carlisle, Leeds, Sheffield, Ambergate (for Haddon Hall and Chatsworth), Derby, Bedford, London, or *vice versa.*

> First class...$50 95
> Second class.. 40 70

ROUTE 36. — Queenstown to London, *viâ* rail to Cork, Mallow, Killarney, Mallow, Kildare, Dublin, Mullingar, Athlone, Galway, Athenry, Ennis, Limerick, Waterford, and across the Channel to Milford Haven, thence by rail through Wales to London, or *vice versa.*

> First class................. ....$33 30
> Second class.. 23 45

ROUTE 37. — Queenstown to London, *viâ* rail to Cork, Mallow, Killarney, Mallow, Kildare, Dublin, Mullingar, Athlone, Roscommon, Castlebar, Westport, thence by car through the Western Highlands to Galway, and rail to Athenry, Ennis, Limerick, Waterford, across the Channel to Milford Haven, and through Wales to London, or *vice versa.*

> First class...$38 80
> Second class.. 31 25

ROUTE 38. — Queenstown to London, *viâ* Cork, Killarney, Limerick, Athenry, Galway, thence to Dublin, Drogheda, Dundalk, Enniskillen (Loch Erne), Londonderry, Portrush (Giant's Causeway), Belfast, steamer to Glasgow, Loch Lomond, Loch Katrine, Trossachs, Callander, Stirling, Edinburgh, Melrose, to London, or *vice versa.*

> First class................................:............$51 70
> Second class.. 39 95

ROUTE 39. — Queenstown to London, *viâ* rail to Cork, Mallow, Killarney, Mallow, Limerick, Ennis, Athenry, Galway, then car through the Connemara Highlands to Westport, and rail to Castlebar, Roscommon, Athlone, Mullingar, Dublin, Balbriggan, Drogheda, Dundalk, Portadown, Belfast, Portrush (Giant's Causeway), and back to Belfast, thence by Royal Mail Steamer across Irish Channel to Greenock and Glasgow, thence by rail, boat, and coach, to Loch Lomond, Loch Katrine, the Trossachs, Callender, Stirling, Edinburgh, Melrose, Carlisle, Leeds, Sheffield, Ambergate, Derby, Bedford, London, or *vice versa.*

> First class...$56 30
> Second class.. 44 75

---◆---

Direct Tour, omitting Killarney.

ROUTE 40. — Queenstown to London, *viâ* Cork, Limerick, Athenry, Galway, Dublin, Drogheda, Portadown, Belfast, Portrush (Giant's Causeway), back to Belfast, steamer to Barrow, rail *viâ* Leeds, Derby, Leicester, London, or *vice versa.*

> First class...$32 70
> Second class 27 20

11

ROUTE 41.—Queenstown to London, viâ Cork, Limerick, Athenry, Galway, Dublin, Drogheda, Portadown, Belfast, Portrush (Giant's Causeway), back to Belfast, steamer to Glasgow, Loch Lomond, Loch Katrine, Trossachs, Glasgow, Edinburgh, Melrose, Waverley route, to London, or vice versa.

First class........ ....$46 55
Second class..................................... 36 50

ROUTE 42.—Queenstown to London, viâ Cork, Limerick, Athenry, Galway, Dublin, Drogheda, Dundalk, Enniskillen (Loch Erne), Londonderry, Portrush (Giant's Causeway), Belfast, steamer to Barrow, rail viâ Leeds, Derby, Leicester, London, or vice versa.

First class...$33 70
Second class...................................... 25 25

ROUTE 43.—Queenstown to London, viâ Cork, Limerick, Athenry, Galway, Dublin, Drogheda, Dundalk, Enniskillen (Loch Erne), Londonderry, Portrush (Giant's Causeway), Belfast, steamer to Glasgow, rail viâ Ayr or Edinburgh, and Melrose to Carlisle, Leeds, London, or vice versa.

First class $42 25
Second class.................................... 32 45

ROUTE 44.—Queenstown to London, viâ same as above to Glasgow, thence to Loch Lomond, Loch Katrine, Trossachs, Glasgow, Edinburgh, Melrose (Waverley route), to London, or vice versa.

First class..............................$48 45
Second class............................... 37 45

ROUTE 45.—Queenstown to London, viâ Cork, Limerick, Ennis, Athenry, Galway, Athlone, Mullingar, Dublin, then by steamer over Irish Channel to Liverpool, and rail viâ Woodley (for Manchester), Buxton, Matlock, Bakewell (for Chatsworth), Rowsely (for Haddon Hall), Derby, Leicester, Bedford, London, or vice versa.

First class......:................................$22 55
Second class................................... 17 25

ROUTE 46.—Queenstown to London, viâ rail to Cork, Limerick, Ennis, Athenry, Galway, thence car through the Western Highlands to Westport, rail to Castlebar, Roscommon, Athlone, Mullingar, and Dublin, steamer over Channel to Liverpool, rail to Woodley, Buxton, Matlock, Derby, Leicester, Bedford, London, or vice versa.

First class..$28 00
Second class.................................... 22 95

ROUTE 47.—Queenstown to London, viâ Cork, Limerick, Athenry, Galway, Dublin, Drogheda, Portadown, Belfast, Portrush (Giant's Causeway), back to Carlisle, Leeds, Sheffield, London, or vice versa.

First class.......................................$36 25
Second class.................................... 27 70

ROUTE 48.—Queenstown to London, viâ Cork, Mallow, Kildare, Dublin, steamer to Liverpool, and rail to London.

First class.......................................$19 00
Second class.................................... 14 25

ROUTE 49.—Queenstown to London, viâ Cork, Dublin, Drogheda, Portadown, Belfast, steamer across Channel to Glasgow, Loch Lomond, Loch Katrine, Trossachs, Callander, Stirling, Edinburgh, Glasgow, Waverley route, to London, or vice versa.

First class.......................................$38 75
Second class.................................... 29 75

ROUTE 50.—Queenstown to London, *via* Cork, Limerick, Athenry, Galway, Dublin, Drogheda, Dundalk, Enniskillen (Loch Erne), Londonderry, Portrush (for Giant's Causeway), Belfast, across the Channel to Barrow, rail to Leeds, Derby, Leicester, London, or *vice versa.*

First class...$32 70
Second class 25 25

For Passengers landing at Londonderry.

ROUTE 51.—Londonderry to London, *via* rail to Strabane, Omagh, Enniskillen (Loch Erne), Dundalk, Drogheda, Balbriggan, Dublin, Mullingar, Athlone, Galway, Athenry, Limerick, Waterford, and across the Channel to Milford Haven, thence through Wales to London, or *vice versa.*

First class.......................................$29 75
Second class........................... .... 22 85

ROUTE 52.—Londonderry to London, *via* rail to Strabane, Omagh, Enniskillen (Loch Erne), Dundalk, Drogheda, Balbriggan, Dublin, Mullingar, Athlone, Roscommon, Castlebar, Westport, thence by car through the Connemara Western Highlands to Galway, and rail to Athenry, Ennis, Limerick, Waterford, steamer, over Channel, to Milford Haven, and rail through Wales, *via* Cardiff, to London, or *vice versa.*

First class $35 25
Second class.................................... 28 60

ROUTE 53.—Londonderry to London, *via* rail to Coleraine, Portrush (Giant's Causeway), Belfast, Portadown, Dundalk, Drogheda, Balbriggan, Dublin, Mullingar, Athlone, Galway, Athenry, Ennis, Limerick, Waterford, steamer, over Channel, to Milford Haven, rail through Wales to London, or *vice versa.*

First class......................................$31 85
Second class.................................... 24 25

ROUTE 54.—Londonderry to London, *via* rail to Coleraine, Portrush (Giant's Causeway), Belfast, Portadown, Dundalk, Drogheda, Balbriggan, Dublin, Mullingar, Athlone, Roscommon, Castlebar, Westport, car across the Connemara District and Western Highlands to Galway, thence rail to Athenry, Ennis, Limerick, and Waterford, steamer over Channel to Milford Haven, and through South Wales by rail to London, or *vice versa.*

First class.......................................$37 25
Second class.................................... 30 00

ROUTE 55.—Londonderry to London, *via* rail to Strabane, Omagh, Enniskillen (Loch Erne), Dundalk, Drogheda, Balbriggan, Dublin, thence by steamer, over Channel, to Liverpool, and rail to Woodley (for Manchester), Buxton, Matlock Baths, Bakewell (for Chatsworth, the Palace of the Peak), Rowsley (for Haddon Hall), Derby, Leicester, Bedford, London, or *vice versa.*

First class..$18 75
Second class.................................... 14 25

ROUTE 56.—Londonderry to London, *via* rail to Coleraine, Portrush (Giant's Causeway), Belfast, thence steamer, over Channel, around to Isle of Man, to Barrow, thence rail to Lancaster (for Cumberland Lakes), Normanton (for York), Sheffield, Ambergate (for Chatsworth and Haddon Hall), Derby, Leicester, Bedford, London, or *vice versa.*

First class...................... ....$16 40
Second class.................................... 11 70

ROUTE 57. — Londonderry to London, *via* rail to Coleraine, Portrush (Giant's Causeway), Belfast, Portadown, Dundalk, Drogheda, Balbriggan, Dublin, and steamer, over Channel, to Liverpool, thence by rail to Woodley (for Manchester, 7 miles distant), Buxton, Matlock Baths, Bakewell (for Chatsworth, the Palace of the Peak), Rowsely (for Haddon Hall), Derby, Leicester, Bedford, London, or *vice versa*.

First class..$20 85
Second class... 15 55

ROUTE 58. — Londonderry to London, *via* rail to Strabane, Omagh, Enniskillen (Loch Erne), Dundalk, Drogheda, Balbriggan, Dublin, Kildare, Mallow, Killarney, Limerick Junction, Waterford, over Channel to Milford Haven, and through Wales to London, or *vice versa*.

First class..$32 00
Second class... 24 15

ROUTE 59. — Londonderry to London, *via* rail to Coleraine, Portrush (Giant's Causeway), Belfast, Portadown, Dundalk, Drogheda, Balbriggan, Dublin, Kildare, Mallow, Killarney, Limerick Junction, Waterford, and steamer, over Irish Channel, to Milford Haven, thence rail through Wales, *via* Cardiff, to London, or *vice versa*.

First class..$34 10
Second class... 25 50

ROUTE 60. — Londonderry to London, *via* rail to Strabane, Omagh, Enniskillen (Loch Erne), Dundalk, Drogheda, Balbriggan, Dublin, Mullingar, Athlone, Galway, Athenry, Ennis, Limerick, Killarney, Limerick Junction, Clonmel, Waterford, steamer, over Channel, to Milford Haven, thence through Wales to London, or *vice versa*.

First class.............. ....$35 50
Second class... 27 15

ROUTE 61. — Londonderry to London, *via* rail to Coleraine, Portrush (Giant's Causeway), Belfast, Portadown, Dundalk, Drogheda, Balbriggan, Mullingar, Athlone, Galway, Athenry, Ennis, Limerick, Killarney, Limerick Junction, Clonmel, Waterford, and steamer, over Channel, to Milford Haven, thence rail through Wales to London, or *vice versa*.

First class..$37 60
Second class... 28 45

ROUTE 62. — Londonderry to London, *via* rail to Strabane, Omagh, Enniskillen (Loch Erne), Dundalk, Drogheda, Balbriggan, Dublin, Mullingar, Athlone, Roscommon, Castlebar, Westport, thence by car across the Western Highlands of Connemara to Galway, and rail to Athenry, Ennis, Limerick, Killarney, Limerick Junction, Clonmel, and Waterford, thence steamer, over Channel, to Milford Haven, and rail to London through Wales, or *vice versa*.

First class..$41 00
Second class 32 85

ROUTE 63. — Londonderry to London, *via* rail to Coleraine, Portrush (Giant's Causeway), Belfast, Portadown, Dundalk, Drogheda, Balbriggan, Dublin, Mullingar, Athlone, Roscommon, Castlebar, and Westport, thence by car, through the Western Highlands of Connemara, to Galway, thence rail to Athenry, Ennis, Limerick, Killarney, Limerick Junction, Clonmel, and Waterford, thence steamer, over Channel, to Milford Haven, and rail to London through Wales, or *vice versa*.

First class..$43 15
Second class... 35 25

Route 64. — Londonderry to London, *riâ* rail to Strabane, Omagh. Enniskillen (Loch Erne), Dundalk, Drogheda, Balbriggan, Dublin, Mullingar, Athlone, Roscommon, Castlebar, Westport, thence by car. through the Western Highlands of Connemara, to Galway, thence rail to Athenry, Ennis, Limerick, and Killarney. thence by car to Kenmare, Glengariffe and mountains of Kerry to Macroom, rail to Cork, Limerick Junction, Clonmel, and Waterford, and steamer, over the Channel, to Milford Haven, and rail to London *viâ* Wales, or *rice versa.*

First class...$46 25
Second class.................... .... 37 85

Route 65. — Londonderry to London, *viâ* rail to Coleraine, Portrush (Giant's Causeway), Belfast, Portadown, Dundalk, Drogheda, Balbriggan. Dublin, Mullingar. Athlone, Roscommon, Castlebar, Westport, and same as route above to London, or *vice versa.*

First class...$47 35
Second class.................................... 39 15

Route 66. — Londonderry to London, *riâ* rail to Strabane, Omagh Enniskillen (Loch Erne), Dundalk, Drogheda, Dublin, Mullingar, Athlone, Galway, Athenry, Limerick, Killarney. Mallow. Kildare, Dublin, across Channel to Liverpool, thence rail to Woodley (for Manchester, seven miles distant), Buxton, Matlock Baths, Bakewell (for Chatsworth, the Palace of the Peak), Rowsely (Haddon Hall), Derby, Leicester, Bedford, London, or *vice versa.*

First class...$37 25
Second class...................................... 28 60

Route 67. — Londonderry to London, *riâ* rail to Coleraine, Portrush (Giant's Causeway). Belfast, Portadown, Dundalk, Drogheda. Balbriggan, Dublin, Mullingar, Athlone, Galway, and same as above to London, or *vice versa.*

First class...$42 85
Second class...................................... 35 45

Route 68. — Londonderry to London, *viâ* rail to Coleraine, Portrush (Giant's Causeway). Belfast, Portadown, Dundalk, Drogheda, Balbriggan, Dublin, Mullingar Athlone, Roscommon, Castlebar, Westport, thence by car, through the Western Highlands of Connemara, to Galway, and rail to Athenry, Ennis, Limerick. Killarney. Mallow, Kildare, Dublin, and steamer, over Channel, to Liverpool, thence rail to Woodley (for Manchester), Buxton, Matlock, Bakewell (for Chatsworth), Rowsely (for Haddon Hall), Derby, Leicester, Bedford, London, or *vice versa.*

First class...$48 85
Second class...................................... 35 75

Route 69. — Londonderry to London, *riâ* rail to Strabane, Omagh, Enniskillen (Loch Erne), Dundalk, Drogheda, Balbriggan, Dublin, Mullingar, Athlone, Roscommon, Castlebar, and Westport, thence by car, through the Western Highlands of Connemara, to Galway, thence rail to Athenry, Ennis, Limerick, and Killarney, thence by car, across the mountains of Kerry, to Kenmare, Glengariffe, Inchigeela, and Macroom, rail to Cork, Mallow, Kildare, Dublin, and steamer, over Channel, to Liverpool, rail to Woodley (for Manchester), Buxton, Matlock, Bakewell (for Chatsworth, the Palace of the Peak), Rowsely (for Haddon Hall), Derby, Leicester, Bedford, London, or *vice versa.*

First class...$48 00
Second class...................................... 39 35

ROUTE 70. — Londonderry to London, *viâ* rail to Coleraine. Portrush (Giant's Causeway), Belfast, Portadown, Dundalk, Drogheda, Balbriggan, Dublin, Mullingar, Athlone, Roscommon, Castlebar, Westport, and same as above to London.

First class.. $50 40
Second class....................................... 42 70

ROUTE 71. — Londonderry to London, *viâ* rail to Strabane, Omagh, Enniskillen (Loch Erne), Dundalk, Drogheda, Balbriggan, Dublin, Portadown, Belfast, steamer across Channel to Greenock, the Clyde, and Glasgow, thence rail to Edinburgh, Melrose (Abbotsford and Dryburgh), Carlisle, Ingleton, (for Cumberland Lake), Leeds, Sheffield, Ambergate (for Chatsworth, Haddon Hall, and the "Peak" District), Derby, Leicester, Bedford, London, or *vice versa.*

First class...................................... $32 25
Second class..................................... 24 70

ROUTE 72. — Londonderry to London, *viâ* rail to Coleraine, Portrush (Giant's Causeway), Belfast, steamer over Channel to Greenock, the Clyde, and Glasgow, then rail *viâ* Ayr (the home of Burns), or to Edinburgh, Melrose (Abbotsford), Carlisle, Ingleton (for Cumberland Lake), Leeds, Sheffield, Ambergate (for Chatsworth, Haddon Hall, and the "Peak" District), Derby, Leicester, Bedford, London, or *vice versa.*

First class................................... $24 90
Second class..................................... 19 00

ROUTE 73. — Londonderry to London, *viâ* rail to Coleraine, Portrush (Giant's Causeway), Belfast, thence by steamer across the Channel to Greenock, the Clyde, and Glasgow, thence by rail, boat, and coach to Loch Lomond, Loch Katrine, the Trossachs, Callander, Stirling, Edinburgh, Melrose (Abbotsford, Dryburgh), Carlisle, Leeds, Sheffield, Ambergate (for Chatsworth, Haddon Hall, and the "Peak" District), Derby, Leicester, Bedford, London, or *vice versa.*

First class.. $31 15
Second class..................................... 24 00

ROUTE 74. — Londonderry to London, *viâ* rail to Coleraine, Portrush (Giant's Causeway), Belfast, steamer across Channel to Greenock, the Clyde, and Glasgow, thence by rail, boat, and coach to Helensburg, Loch Long, Loch Lomond, Loch Katrine, the Trossachs, Callander, Stirling, Edinburgh, Melrose (Abbotsford), Carlisle, Leeds, Sheffield, Ambergate (for Haddon Hall and Chatsworth), Derby, Leicester, London, or *vice versa.*

First class $31 65
Second class 24 80

ROUTE 75. — Londonderry to London, *viâ* rail to Coleraine, Portrush (Giant's Causeway), Belfast, steamer over Channel to Greenock and Glasgow, thence by boat down the Clyde to Ardrishaig and the Crinan Canal to Oban (for Staffa and Iona), Ballachulish (for Glencoe and Banavie), Banavie to Inverness *viâ* Caledonian Canal, railway from Inverness *viâ* Kingussie, Blair-Athol, Pass of Killicrankie to Dunkeld, Perth, and Edinburgh, thence to Melrose, Carlisle, Leeds, Sheffield, Ambergate, Derby, Leicester, London, or *vice versa.*

First class $41 15
Second class .... 32 55·

ROUTE 76. — Londonderry to London, *viâ* rail to Coleraine, Portrush (Giant's Causeway), Belfast, steamer over Channel to Greenock, the Clyde,

Glasgow, rail, coach, and steamer to Balloch, Lóch Lomond, Glenfalloch, Killin, Kenmare, Aberfeldy, Dunkeld, Perth, Edinburgh, thence rail to London, *riả* Melrose (Abbotsford), Carlisle, Leeds, Sheffield, Ambergate, Derby, Bedford, or *vice versa.*

> First class $31 05
> Second class 24 80

ROUTE 77. — Londonderry to London, *riả* rail to Coleraine, Portrush (Giant's Causeway), and Belfast, thence steamer to Greenock and Glasgow, thence by boat down the Clyde to Ardrishaig, then through the Crinan Canal to Criman and Oban (for Staffa and Iona), Oban to Ballachulish (for Glencoe and Banavie), Banavie, *viả* Caledonian Canal, to Inverness, thence by rail to Blair-Athol Pass of Killicrankie, Dunkeld, Perth, Edinburgh, Melrose, Carlisle, Leeds, Sheffield, Ambergate, Derby, Leicester, London, or *vice versa.*

> First class..$41 15
> Second class 32 55

ROUTE 78.— Londonderry to London, *viả* rail to Coleraine, Portrush (Giant's Causeway), and Belfast, steamer over Channel to Greenock and Glasgow, thence down the Clyde to Ardrishaig, through the Crinan Canal to Oban (for Staffa and Iona), thence to Ballachulish (for Glencoe), Banavie, and through the Caledonian Canal to Inverness, thence by rail to Keith, Aberdeen, Perth, Stirling, Edinburgh, Melrose, Carlisle, Leeds, Sheffield, Ambergate, Derby, Leicester, Bedford, London, or *vice versa.*

> First class..$41 45
> Second class...................................... 32 55

ROUTE 79. — Londonderry to London, *viả* rail to Coleraine, Portrush (Giant's Causeway), and Belfast, thence by steamer across the Channel to Greenock and Glasgow, thence by boat to Oban through the Kyle of Bute and the Crinan Canal, thence by steamer to Portree and Strome Ferry, and by Skye Railway to Inverness, thence rail to Blair-Athol, Dunkeld, Perth, Fife, Edinburgh, Melrose, Carlisle, Leeds, Sheffield, Ambergate, Derby. Leicester, Bedford, London, or *vi·e versa.*

> First class..$43 90
> Second class 35 55

ROUTE 80.— Londonderry to London, *viả* rail to Coleraine, Portrush (Giant's Causeway), and Belfast, thence steamer across the Channel to Greenock and Glasgow, thence steamer down the Clyde, through the Kyles of Bute to Oban, *viả* Ardrishaig and Crinan, thence by steamer to Portree and Strome Ferry, Skye Railway to Inverness, thence rail to Kingussie, Blair-Athol, Killicrankie, Dunkeld, Stirling, Edinburgh, Melrose, Carlisle, Leeds, Sheffield, Ambergate, Derby, Leicester, Bedford, London, or *vice versa.*

> First class $43 90
> Second class...................................... 35 55

Specimens of Extended Tours in Ireland, combining the Highlands of Scotland.

ROUTE 147. — Queenstown to London, *viả* Cork, Mallow, Killarney, Limerick Junction, Kildare, Dublin, Balbriggan, Drogheda, Dundalk. Newry, Portadown, Belfast, steamer to Glasgow, Ardrishaig, Crinan Canal, Oban (for Staffa and Iona), Ballachulish (for Glencoe), Banavie, Caledonian Canal, Inverness, rail to Dunkeld, Perth, Edinburgh, Melrose (for Abbotsford), Carlisle, Ingleton (for English Lakes), Leeds, Sheffield, Derby, Leicester, Bedford, London, or *vice versa.*

> First class..$52 00
> Second class 40 80

ROUTE 148. — Queenstown to London, *riâ* Cork, Macroom, car over the Mountains of Kerry to Inchigeela, Glengariffe, Kenmare, Killarney, Mallow, Limerick Junction, Kildare, Dublin, Balbriggan, Drogheda, Dundalk, Newry, Portadown, Belfast, steamer to Glasgow, Ardrishaig, Crinan Canal, Oban (for Staffa and Iona), Ballachulish (for Glencoe), Banavie, Caledonian Canal, Inverness, rail to Dunkeld, Perth, Edinburgh, Melrose (for Abbotsford), Carlisle, Ingleton (for English Lakes), Leeds, Sheffield, Derby, Leicester, Bedford, London, or *vice versa.*

First class **$55 45**
Second class **34 80**

ROUTE 149. — Queenstown to London, *riâ* Cork, Mallow, Killarney, Limerick, Ennis, Athenry, Galway, car through the Western Highlands of Connemara to Westport, rail to Castlebar, Roscommon, Mullingar, Dublin, Balbriggan, Drogheda, Dundalk, Newry, Portadown, Belfast, steamer to Glasgow, Ardrishaig, Crinan Canal, Oban (for Staffa and Iona), Ballachulish (for Glencoe), Banavie, Caledonian Canal, Inverness, rail to Dunkeld, Perth, Edinburgh, Melrose (for Abbotsford), Carlisle, Ingleton (for English Lakes), Leeds, Sheffield, Derby, Leicester, Bedford, London, or *vice versa.*

First class **$61 00**
Second class **49 45**

ROUTE 150. — Queenstown to London, *riâ* Cork, Macroom, car over the Kerry Mountains to Inchigeela, Glengariffe, Kenmare, Killarney, rail to Limerick, Ennis, Athenry, Galway, car through the Western Highlands of Connemara to Westport, rail to Castlebar, Roscommon, Athlone, Mullingar, Dublin, Balbriggan, Drogheda, Dundalk, Newry, Portadown, Belfast, steamer to Glasgow, Ardrishaig, Oban (for Staffa and Iona), Ballachulish (for Glencoe), Banavie, Caledonian Canal, Inverness, rail to Dunkeld, Perth, Edinburgh, Melrose (for Abbotsford), Carlisle, Ingleton (for English Lakes), Leeds, Sheffield, Derby, Leicester, Bedford, London, or *rice versa.*

First class **$64 50**
Second class **53 40**

ROUTE 151. — Queenstown to London, *riâ* Cork, Mallow, Killarney, Mallow, Kildare, Dublin, Balbriggan, Drogheda, Dundalk, Enniskillen (Loch Erne), Omagh, Strabane, Londonderry, Coleraine, Portrush (Giant's Causeway), Antrim, Belfast, steamer to Glasgow, Ardrishaig, Oban (for Staffa and Iona), Ballachulish (for Glencoe), Caledonian Canal, Inverness, rail to Dunkeld, Perth, Edinburgh, Melrose (for Abbotsford), Carlisle, Ingleton (for English Lakes), Leeds, Sheffield, Derby, Leicester, Bedford, London, or *vice versa.*

First class **$58 20**
Second class **45 00**

ROUTE 152. — Queenstown to London, *riâ* Cork, Macroom, car over the Kerry Mountains to Inchigeela. Glengariffe, Kenmare. Killarney, rail to Mallow, Kildare, Dublin. Balbriggan, Drogheda, Dundalk, Enniskillen (Loch Erne), Omagh, Strabane, Londonderry, Coleraine, Portrush (Giant's Causeway), Antrim, Belfast, steamer to Glasgow, Ardrishaig, Oban (for Staffa and Iona), Ballachulish (for Glencoe), Banavie, Caledonian Canal, Inverness, rail to Dunkeld, Perth, Edinburgh Melrose (for Abbotsford), Carlisle, Ingleton (for English Lakes), Leeds, Sheffield, Derby, Leicester, Bedford, London, or *vice versa.*

First class **$61 70**
Second class **49 50**

ROUTE 153. — Queenstown to London, *riâ* Cork. Mallow, Killarney, Limerick, Ennis, Athenry, Galway, car through the Western Highlands of Connemara to Westport, rail to Castlebar, Roscommon, Athlone, Mullingar,

Dublin, Balbriggan, Drogheda, Dundalk, Enniskillen (Loch Erne), Omagh, Strabane, Londonderry Coleraine. Portrush (Giant's Causeway), Antrim, Belfast, steamer to Glasgow, Ardrishaig, Oban (for Staffa and Iona), Ballachulish (for Glencoe), Banavie, Caledonian Canal. Inverness, rail to Dunkeld, Perth, Edinburgh, Melrose (for Abbotsford). Carlisle, Ingleton (for English Lakes), Leeds, Sheffield, Derby, Leicester, Bedford, London, or *vice versa.*

> First class $68 20
> Second class. 54 20

ROUTE 154. — Queenstown to London, *via* Cork, Macroom, car over the Kerry Mountains to Inchigeela, Glengariffe, Kenmare, Killarney, rail to Limerick, Ennis, Athenry, Galway, car through the Western Highlands of Connemara to Westport, rail to Castlebar, Roscommon. Mullingar, Dublin, Balbriggan, Drogheda, Dundalk, Enniskillen (Loch Erne), Omagh, Strabane, Londonderry, Portrush (Giant's Causeway), Coleraine, Antrim, Belfast, steamer to Glasgow, Ardrishaig, Oban (for Staffa and Iona), Ballachulish (for Glencoe), Banavie, Caledonian Canal, Inverness, rail to Dunkeld, Perth, Edinburgh, Melrose (for Abbotsford) Carlisle, Ingleton (for English Lakes), Leeds, Sheffield, Derby, Leicester, Bedford, London, or *vice versa.*

> First class $70 70
> Second class 58 15

ROUTE 155. —Queenstown to London, *via* Cork, Mallow, Killarney, Mallow, Kildare, Dublin, Balbriggan, Drogheda, Dundalk, Newry, Portadown, Belfast, steamer to Glasgow, Ardrishaig, Crinan Canal, Oban, Portree, Strome Ferry, rail to Inverness, Dunkeld, Perth, Edinburgh, Melrose (for Abbotsford), Carlisle, Ingleton (for English Lakes), Leeds, Sheffield, Derby, Leicester, Bedford, London, or *vice versa.*

> First class $54 50
> Second class 46 85

ROUTE 156. — Queenstown to London, *via* Cork, Macroom, car over the Kerry Mountains to Inchigeela, Glengariffe, Kenmare, Killarney, rail to Mallow, Kildare, Dublin, Balbriggan, Drogheda, Dundalk, Newry, Portadown, Belfast, steamer to Glasgow, Ardrishaig, Crinan Canal, Oban, Portree, Strome Ferry, rail to Inverness, Dunkeld, Perth, Edinburgh, Melrose (for Abbotsford), Carlisle, Ingleton (for English Lakes), Leeds, Sheffield, Derby, Leicester, Bedford, London, or *vice versa.*

> First class $58 20
> Second class 47 80

ROUTE 157. — Queenstown to London, *via* Cork, Mallow, Killarney, Limerick, Ennis, Athenry, Galway, car through the Western Highlands of Connemara to Westport, rail to Castlebar, Roscommon, Athlone, Mullingar, Dublin, Balbriggan, Drogheda, Dundalk, Newry, Portadown, Belfast, steamer to Glasgow, Ardrishaig, Crinan Canal, Oban, Portree, Strome Ferry, rail to Inverness, Dunkeld, Perth, Edinburgh, Melrose (for Abbotsford), Carlisle, Ingleton (for English Lakes), Leeds, Sheffield, Derby, Leicester, Bedford, London, or *vice versa.*

> First class.... ....$63 70
> Second class....................................... 52 45

ROUTE 158. —Queenstown to London, *via* Cork, Macroom, car over the Kerry Mountains to Inchigeela, Glengariffe, Kenmare, Killarney, rail to Limerick, Ennis, Athenry, Galway, car through the Western Highlands of Connemara to Westport, rail to Castlebar, Roscommon, Athlone, Mullingar, Dublin, Balbriggan, Drogheda, Dundalk, Newry, Portadown, Belfast, steamer to Glasgow, Ardrishaig, Crinan Canal, Oban, Portree, Strome

Ferry, rail to Inverness, Dunkeld, Perth, Edinburgh, Melrose (for Abbots-ford), Carlisle, Ingleton (for English Lakes), Leeds, Sheffield, Derby, Leices-ter, Bedford, London, or *vice versa*.

First class...$66 25
Second class................................... 56 40

ROUTE 159. — Queenstown to London, *via* Cork, Mallow, Killarney, Mal-low, Kildare, Dublin, Balbriggan, Drogheda, Dundalk, Enniskillen (Loch Erne), Omagh, Strabane, Londonderry, Coleraine, Portrush (Giant's Cause-way), Antrim, Belfast, steamer to Glasgow, Ardrishaig, Crinan Canal, Oban, Portree, Strome Ferry, rail to Inverness, Dunkeld, Perth, Edinburgh, Mel-rose (for Abbotsford), Carlisle, Ingleton (for English Lakes), Leeds, Shef-field, Derby, Leicester, Bedford, London, or *vice versa*.

First class....... ....$58 20
Second class................................... 45 55

THE WINDSOR.

FIFTH AVENUE, ... NEW YORK.

HAWK & WETHERBEE,

Proprietors.

The New York Tribune,

THE LEADING AMERICAN NEWSPAPER.

UNITED STATES

GOVERNMENT

PASSPORTS

OF GREAT IMPORTANCE

To persons travelling in Europe as a means of introduction, and identification at Banks, and
in the event of trouble between
adjacent countries,

FURNISHED BY

JAMES G. FREEMAN,

Passport Agent and Notary Public,

FIRM OF

Wm. C. Codman & J. G. Freeman,

40 Kilby Street,

BOSTON, MASS.

𝔓arker 𝔥ouse,

𝔖chool 𝔖treet,

HARVEY D. PARKER.
JOHN F. MILLS.

BOSTON, MASS.

ON THE EUROPEAN PLAN.

WILLIAM ROLLISSON & SONS,

THE NURSERIES,

TOOTING, LONDON.

BULBS, SEEDS, TELEGRAPH CUCUMBER, FRUIT TREES, PALMS,
ORNAMENTAL FOLIAGE PLANTS, HARDY HERBACEOUS,
AND ALPINE PLANTS, ORCHIDS, STOVE PLANTS.

Messrs. ROLLISSON & SONS respectfully call attention to their splendid
Horticultural Collection, at the Nurseries, Tooting, near London.

Messrs. ROLLISSON will furnish Catalogues and Estimates on application.
Experienced Gardeners to wait on visitors.

OMNIBUSES. — The Omnibuses from Gracechurch Street and Charing
Cross, calling at the " Elephant and Castle," pass the Nurseries frequently
during the day.

W. & A. GILBEY,
Wine Merchants.

Messrs. W. & A. GILBEY respectfully solicit the attention of American connoisseurs and the trade of the United States generally to the great facilities they offer to buyers to select their Wines from a stock from which a twentieth part of the foreign wines consumed in the United Kingdom is supplied. The wines, spirits and liquors sold by their firm are guaranteed to be imported from the place of production as specified in their price-lists, and can be relied upon as being of uniform good quality and value at the prices charged.

Messrs. GILBEY during the year 1872, paid duty to the British Government on the enormous quantity of **1,483,913** gallons of wines and spirits.

[OVER.]

SPECIAL ATTENTION

SMALPAGE & SON,

TAILORS,

41 AND 43

Maddox Street, Bond Street,

LONDON, W.

ALSO

AGENTS IN WEST END

FOR

Cunard and White Star Steamers.

PASSAGES SECURED,

LUGGAGE WAREHOUSED,

Inward Letters Received and Forwarded,

AND GENERAL INFORMATION GIVEN.

Paine's New Pattern
SEA CHAIR.

MANUFACTURED expressly for the Voyage across the Ocean. Knowing that you value comfort as well as pleasure, permit me to recommend from experience my NEW PATTERN SEA CHAIR, *with Foot Rest*. You will find it the most highly prized place on the boat.

Paine's Furniture Manufactory,
141 Frïend and 48 Canal Street,
BOSTON, MASS.

☞ The largest stock of Fashionable Furniture to be found in New England may be seen at this establishment.

JOHNSON & SADLER,

TAILORS

AND

HABIT MAKERS,

6ᵃ Vigo Street, Regent Street,

LONDON.

AND AT

22 MARKET PLACE

CAMBRIDGE.

IMPORTANT TO AMERICANS RETURNING HOME.

NEW REGULATION OF TREASURY DEPARTMENT. — PASSEN-
GERS REQUIRED TO DECLARE CONTENTS OF THEIR TRUNKS.

Every passenger arriving at any port of the United States
from a foreign port is required to make a brief but comprehensive and truthful statement of the number of his or
her trunks, bags, and other pieces of baggage, of the contents of each, and of the articles upon his or her person.
For convenience and uniformity, such statement must be
made on blank forms, designated "Passengers' Baggage
Declaration," which may be had from the captain.

To avoid detention in landing, such statement should be
carefully prepared before arrival, so as to be promptly delivered to the revenue-officer upon demand. The following information will aid in the preparation of the declaration : —

The numbers of the several pieces of baggage will be
given in the proper place, and their contents entered under
two heads : —

1. Baggages not dutiable, which comprise the following
classes : —

A. "Wearing apparel in actual use;" that is, clothing
made up for the passenger's own wear, in reasonable quanti-
ties, may be declared as "wearing apparel."

B. "Other personal effects" (not merchandise), which are
such as are usually carried with or about the person of a
traveller, — as trunks, articles of the toilet, stationery, a
few books, one watch, jewelry, &c., in actual use, and in
reasonable amount, — may be declared "personal effects."

C. "Professional books," "tools of trade," and "household effects," all of which have been used by the passenger
abroad (the last named at least one year), may be declared
as such.

2. Dutiable merchandise. Under this head must be entered all articles not included in "baggage not dutiable," as

above set forth. Among these may be specially mentioned *new* wearing apparel in excess of that in general use, excessive amounts of jewelry, extra watches, articles of *vertu*, *all presents*, piece goods, *and all articles purchased for other persons;* in short, all articles not essential to the personal comfort and convenience of the traveller.

Great care should be taken to make a full and accurate return, and to examine the certificate which the passenger is required to sign.

The columns headed "Appraisement" are not to be filled by the passenger, but left blank.

Upon arrival, the declaration will be delivered to the revenue-officer. The baggage will be examined on board the vessel or wharf, and duties assessed, which are payable in gold coin.

Any piece of baggage containing over five hundred dollars' worth of dutiable merchandise will not be delivered on board, but sent to the public store for examination and appraisement.

Packages containing merchandise exclusively will not be considered as baggage, but must be regularly entered at the custom-house.

All baggage is subject to actual and thorough examination ; and the *persons* of all passengers are liable to search.

Any fraud on the part of passengers, any concealment of the fact, or secreting of articles in the trunks, &c., or on the person, or attempt to bribe a revenue-officer, will render the baggage liable to detention or confiscation, and subject the owner to other legal penalties.

Any complaints against revenue-officers in the discharge of their duties must be made to the collector of the port, who will promptly investigate all charges made.

By order of the Secretary of the Treasury of the United States.

CALENDAR FOR 1874.

JANUARY.	MAY.	SEPTEMBER.

S	M	T	W	T	F	S	S	M	T	W	T	F	S	S	M	T	W	T	F	S
..	..	..	..	..	1	2	3	..	..	..	..	..	..	1	2	..	..	1	2	3	4	5
4	5	6	7	8	9	10	3	4	5	6	7	8	9	6	7	8	9	10	11	12
11	12	13	14	15	16	17	10	11	12	13	14	15	16	13	14	15	16	17	18	19
18	19	20	21	22	23	24	17	18	19	20	21	22	23	20	21	22	23	24	25	26
25	26	27	28	29	30	31	24	25	26	27	28	29	30	27	28	29	30	..	..	..
..	..	..	..	..	..	..	31	..	..	..	..	..	..	..	..	..	..	..	..	..

FEBRUARY.	JUNE.	OCTOBER.

S	M	T	W	T	F	S	S	M	T	W	T	F	S	S	M	T	W	T	F	S
1	2	3	4	5	6	7	..	1	2	3	4	5	6	..	..	..	..	1	2	3
8	9	10	11	12	13	14	7	8	9	10	11	12	13	4	5	6	7	8	9	10
15	16	17	18	19	20	21	14	15	16	17	18	19	20	11	12	13	14	15	16	17
22	23	24	25	26	27	28	21	22	23	24	25	26	27	18	19	20	21	22	23	24
..	..	..	..	..	..	..	28	29	30	..	..	..	..	25	26	27	28	29	30	31

MARCH.	JULY.	NOVEMBER.

S	M	T	W	T	F	S	S	M	T	W	T	F	S	S	M	T	W	T	F	S
1	2	3	4	5	6	7	..	..	..	1	2	3	4	1	2	3	4	5	6	7
8	9	10	11	12	13	14	5	6	7	8	9	10	11	8	9	10	11	12	13	14
15	16	17	18	19	20	21	12	13	14	15	16	17	18	15	16	17	18	19	20	21
22	23	24	25	26	27	28	19	20	21	22	23	24	25	22	23	24	25	26	27	28
29	30	31	..	..	..	..	26	27	28	29	30	31	..	29	30	..	..	..	..	..

APRIL.	AUGUST.	DECEMBER.

S	M	T	W	T	F	S	S	M	T	W	T	F	S	S	M	T	W	T	F	S
..	..	..	1	2	3	4	..	..	..	..	..	..	1	..	..	1	2	3	4	5
5	6	7	8	9	10	11	2	3	4	5	6	7	8	6	7	8	9	10	11	12
12	13	14	15	16	17	18	9	10	11	12	13	14	15	13	14	15	16	17	18	19
19	20	21	22	23	24	25	16	17	18	19	20	21	22	20	21	22	23	24	25	26
26	27	28	29	30	..	..	23	24	25	26	27	28	29	27	28	29	30	31	..	..
..	..	..	..	..	..	..	30	31	..	..	..	..	..	..	..	..	..	..	..	..